Countdown

A Time of Testing

ISBN: 978-1-950791-50-7
Cover and text layout design: Kristi Yoder
Cover art: Peter Balholm

Published by:
TGS International
P.O. Box 355
Berlin, Ohio 44610 USA
Phone: 330.893.4828
Fax: 330.893.2305
www.tgsinternational.com

CENTURY IN CRISIS

1

A.D. 284

Countdown

A Time of Testing

Lester Bauman

Timeline

Historical Timeline	Story Timeline
Birth of Diocletian –245	
	275– Birth of Mark
Emperor Carus dies in Persia –283	
Emperor Numerian dies –284	
Diocletian proclaimed emperor –November 284	
Battle of the Margus River –July 285	
Maximian appointed as junior emperor –August 285	
Maximian promoted to Augustus –286	
Two caesars appointed to assist the Augusti –293	293– Mark marries Lydia
Lactantius moves to Nicomedia as rhetorician –295	
Divination ceremony fails in Antioch –299	299– Christians are forced out of the army
Edict against the Manicheans –March 302	302– Lactantius leaves Nicomedia
Diocletian returns to Nicomedia –January 303	303 February– Cathedral razed; Scriptures burned
Edict published against Christians –February 303	303 February– Severe persecution begins
Fires destroy most of the palace –February 303	
Diocletian abdicates –305	
Emperor Galerius revokes the 303 edict –311	
Both Diocletian and Galerius die –311	

⁹And when he had opened the fifth seal, I saw under the altar the souls of them that were slain for the word of God, and for the testimony which they held: ¹⁰And they cried with a loud voice, saying, How long, O Lord, holy and true, dost thou not judge and avenge our blood on them that dwell on the earth? ¹¹And white robes were given unto every one of them; and it was said unto them, that they should rest yet for a little season, until their fellowservants also and their brethren, that should be killed as they were, should be fulfilled.

—Revelation 6:9-11

Table of Contents

Historical Characters

The following characters were real people. In most cases little is known about them other than their names and positions.

Diocletian. Born a commoner in A.D. 244, Diocletian rose through the ranks of the Roman army to become a cavalry commander under Carus (emperor 282–283). He was proclaimed emperor in 284 after the death of Carus. He was in many ways an excellent emperor, with the success of the empire as his goal. However, his strong emphasis on securing the approval of the Roman gods led him into direct conflict with the Christians, who of course refused to worship the Roman gods. Despite this, he was reluctant to shed blood even during persecution. He was powerless to prevent it, however, when local officials followed Galerius' advice to use capital punishment.

Galerius. He was Caesar during Diocletian's reign but subordinate to Diocletian. His mother was a pagan priestess who pressured Galerius to persuade Diocletian to persecute the Christians. According to Christian writers at the time, he probably set Diocletian's palace on fire so he could blame Christians for setting it. He was married to Diocletian's daughter, Valeria.

Maximian. Emperor of the western half of the Roman Empire (286–305). Promoted to Augustus, but still under Diocletian's direction.

Prisca. Diocletian's wife. As a Christian sympathizer, she may even have been a secret Christian. She was forced to sacrifice to the gods to prove her loyalty after a second fire was set in Diocletian's palace in Nicomedia.

Valeria. Diocletian's daughter. She was married to Galerius and is also thought to have been a Christian sympathizer. Like her mother, she was forced to sacrifice to the gods to prove her loyalty.

Afranius. He was the praetorian prefect during much of Diocletian's reign.

Bishop Anthimus. Anthimus was the chief bishop in Nicomedia and was martyred during the persecution. There is some disagreement among historians whether he died at the time mentioned in this book, or about eight years later, just before the persecution ended completely.

Lactantius. He was a Latin teacher of rhetoric and wrote extensively about Christian apologetics. He lived in Nicomedia until driven out by the persecution. Many basic facts in the last part of the book come from his writing. He viewed the persecution of Diocletian from an apocalyptic perspective, though he changed some of his teaching after Constantine became emperor. Lactantius knew Diocletian before becoming a Christian. Some historians feel his writing is exaggerated, but his is our main eyewitness account.

Fictional Characters

Melinias. General of the army during the first part of Diocletian's reign.

Hiram. Diocletian's secretary.

Mark. Young man born in Nicomedia to a Christian family in A.D. 275. He was ordained a presbyter with the expectation of someday replacing his older mentor, Bishop Anthimus.

Lydia. Mark's wife.

Andrew. Mark's father. A deacon in the church.

Irene. Mark's mother. Her aristocratic family was slaughtered by the Romans for wrong politics when she was a teenager. She was taken in by a local Christian family. Well educated, she passed her love of knowledge on to her son Mark and planted in him the seeds of genuine Christianity.

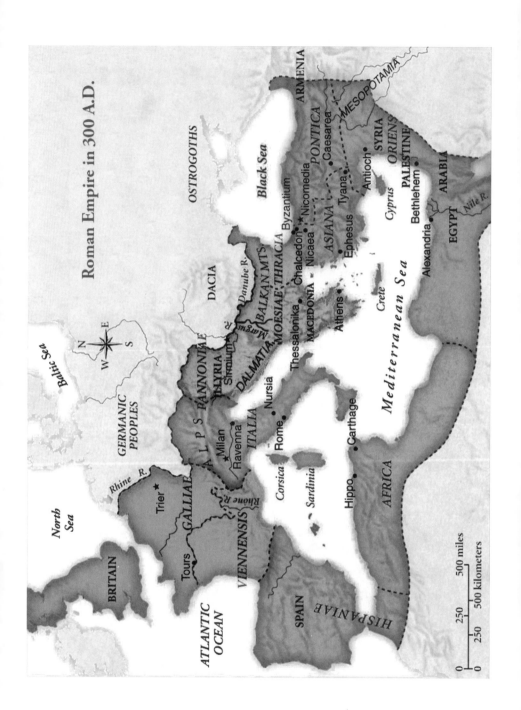

Roman Empire in 300 A.D.

History Is as History Does

The timeline of Diocletian's life forms the historical backbone of this book. In a few places, historical sources or scholars differ, and I was forced to choose which date to use, but the basic facts about Diocletian's life are well known. Of course, to tell this story, I have "interpreted" these facts to show human emotions and motives. I've done the same for the church and various Christians who lived in that setting.

In my research, I encountered a Christian writer who refuted a generally accepted fact about a historic practice of the church in the second and third centuries A.D. He disagreed strongly with the practice in question and stated that it could not have been true "because they were Christians and Christians wouldn't do that."

Writers of historical novels and storybooks occasionally face the pressure to tell the story "as it should have been" instead of telling it as it was. However, doing so seems dishonest, and I have tried to resist that temptation. We live in today's setting and our way seems right to us. The people in this book lived in their setting and their way seemed right to them. That's how life works.

I was also tempted during this writing to focus on the differences between then and now. But in retrospect, I decided that doing so would defeat the purpose of this book. My purpose is to tell the story of Diocletian as sympathetically as I can and show what it would have been like to live as a Christian in those times. To achieve this, I have tried to be realistic about the church of that time and to stay focused on the challenge of persecution.

Would you and I be ready if we had to choose between death or denouncing Christ? We live in unusual times in North America—times of peace and prosperity for Christians.[1] So did the Christians living in 284 A.D. Persecution seemed to be a thing of the past. The church was growing in numbers and prosperity. Life was good. But all this changed quickly.

Life could change quickly for us as well. There are indications that life will change for us. I hope reading this book will help you think seriously about such possibilities.

---

[1] Note that this is not true of all parts of the world. Persecution is a fact of life for many Christians today.

PART I

A.D. 284

A New Emperor

Of the end of those men [who persecuted the Church] I have thought good to publish a narrative, that all who are afar off, and all who shall arise hereafter, may learn how the Almighty manifested His power and sovereign greatness in rooting out and utterly destroying the enemies of His name. And this will become evident, when I relate who were the persecutors of the Church from the time of its first constitution, and what were the punishments by which the divine Judge, in His severity, took vengeance on them.

—Lactantius, *Of the Manner in Which the Persecutors Died,* Chap. 1

1

November 284

Rome had a new emperor—again. With at least ten emperors in the last twenty years, this was nothing unusual. But for some people, especially Christians, it was always unsettling when a new one came along. The questions were always the same: *What kind of man is he? How will he view the followers of Christos?*

It was the proudest day of Diocletian's life—a day he had dreamed about but never really expected to come. But sometimes dreams come true, and now he stood on a hill-side three miles from Nicomedia[1] with his sword held high, acknowledging the cheering soldiers. He had just donned the royal purple, the last step in attaining his new office. Born

---

[1] Nicomedia was chosen as the capital city of the eastern part of the Roman Empire, located in what is now Turkey. It was closer to the frontier than the traditional capital at Rome.

a commoner, Diocletian had worked his way up through the ranks until now, at forty years of age, he was emperor of the Roman Empire. He had reached the top of the ladder.

But there was one detail he needed to take care of before life could go on. Standing beside him, glowering, was the praetorian prefect, a man who had hoped to become emperor. He had been accused of killing the last emperor—and would certainly also kill Diocletian if he had half a chance.

The prefect was the former emperor's father-in-law and the commander of the Praetorian Guard. Ironically, this made him responsible for the new emperor's safety.

Diocletian lowered his sword. He had always been a decisive person; he did now what he knew needed to be done.

"You are guilty of the murder of an emperor," he told the prefect evenly but loudly enough for the crowd to hear. "For this, you must die."

Before the stunned man could react, Diocletian plunged his sword into his former colleague's breast. The soldiers cheered wildly. But they took note as well. Diocletian was not a man to be trifled with.

——— MARK ———

It was a proud day for Mark too. He had bested Lydia in a race to the market and back. Almost ten years old, it had always bothered him that Lydia could run faster than he could. It didn't matter that she could also beat all the other boys in a race, even those a year or two older than he was. He was determined that no girl would come out ahead of him if he could help it. And today he had finally beaten her. True, she had stubbed her toe at the beginning, which might have slowed her down a bit.

He contemplated that for a moment. No, he decided, it was a fair race, and he had won fair and square. He swaggered a little as he walked up the cobblestone street to his home, situated on the bottom floor of an apartment building in the poorer section of Nicomedia.

Irene looked up and smiled as her son entered the house. She was squatting beside a small charcoal brazier that served as her cookstove.

"You look pleased with yourself," she said. She straightened to stretch her back. "What have you been doing?"

"I beat Lydia in a race to the market and back," Mark said smugly. "Maybe now she'll invite me to her next party."

His mother patted him on his shoulder before leaning over her charcoal fire and blowing on it gently. "Don't be surprised if she doesn't," she replied, a hint of a smile flickering across her face. "If you really want to become good friends with Lydia, you should let her beat you sometimes."

Mark looked baffled. "But if I win, she'll like me for being strong," he protested.

His mother squatted beside the little container of hot coals and blew on it again. Little flames flickered through the coals as the fire burned hotter. She shook her head. "That's not how a girl thinks. Boys may think that way, but not girls. Girls admire people who give them a chance to win occasionally."

By now Mark really looked puzzled. "But she laughs at me when she beats me," he insisted. "Why would she do that?"

His mother brushed back a few strands of hair from her forehead. "You'll understand someday," she promised. "Now, go back to the market and get me some bread. Your father will soon be home for supper."

Mark was almost at the market when he met Lydia again. She lifted her nose a little higher and would have slipped past him, but he stopped. "Did you hurt your toe much?" he asked shyly. "I'm sure you would have beat me if you hadn't stubbed your toe."

The barrier in her eyes vanished at his words, and she smiled. "Naw," she scoffed. "It wasn't anything. I just didn't feel like running today."

He laughed. "I have to get some bread for my mother. Want to come along?"

——— DIOCLETIAN ———

Diocletian changed his royal clothing as soon as he got back to his tent. Then he called together the generals and commanders who had chosen him as leader. He had no time for a victory party—he had work to do. The Roman Empire was in dire shape. It hadn't had a strong ruler for over twenty years, and much of the economic and defense infrastructure was on the verge of crumbling.

The men who gathered in the large tent he had set up as a temporary office didn't come for a party either. They knew Diocletian and didn't expect one. The last several emperors hadn't done anything to change the empire for the better. Carus had reigned for only two years and was suspected of having engineered the death of Probus, who had been emperor for six years before him.

Carus had taken the Roman army east across the Tigris River to teach the Persians a lesson. He died there, supposedly struck by lightning due to the wrath of the gods. His son Numerian then led the army back into Roman territory. He too died a mysterious death on the way back to Nicomedia, but the praetorian prefect hid his death until the smell issuing from his coach revealed it to his guards.[2] This mistake on his part led to him being blamed for Emperor Numerian's death.[3]

Diocletian had a whole list of problems to face. Standing beside the rough table that doubled as a desk and podium, he listed them to his "war council" that evening.

He started with the most important one. "First of all, Numerian's brother Carinus was co-emperor with him," he said. "He headed straight for Rome when he heard of his father's death and had the Senate acclaim him emperor in the west."

Most of the men in the meeting were aware of this, so Diocletian continued. "Once Carinus hears about Numerian's death, he will be on his way to avenge him."

Diocletian fastened his gaze on the men seated around the edges of the tent. "We need to be ready for him. I have no intention of being co-emperor with him, and I doubt that he intends to allow me to be one."

The members of the war council knew the volatility of third-century Roman politics as well as Diocletian did. The

---

[2] Some historians discredit this, but most feel it is probably true.

[3] Numerian may have died of natural causes, but the suspicion gave Diocletian a convenient reason to remove a possible competitor.

oldest of them could remember perhaps twenty emperors, only one of which had ruled longer than eight years. Nine or ten emperors had reigned less than a year. The majority had been assassinated or killed in battle fighting against their own people.[4] Roman emperors seldom died a natural death. Diocletian, however, did not intend to join the casualties.

The room grew quiet as he continued. "I will do whatever it takes to succeed. I need your cooperation, but if any of you do not want to work with me, I will give you one chance to leave. I will not punish anyone who wants out now. But if you fail me later, it might be different."

The men in the room exchanged glances, but no one got up. Diocletian nodded his acceptance of their loyalty and sat down behind his desk. "Is there anything that you feel is important to look at right now? We will meet like this at least every week, so you can be thinking about this for the next time."

He paused. Melinias, one of his most experienced generals, spoke up. "We need to think about Carinus. He has a competent army, larger than ours, and it will take everything we have to overpower him. It would be best if we took the initiative. That way we can choose the battleground and the time of year. Those advantages can tip a close battle in one direction."

The men around the circle nodded, and one spoke up. "We need to start planning logistics. We will need food and equipment."

The group nodded in agreement, and Melinias spoke again. "Carinus will need all those things too. If we can force the

---

[4] Only four of the twenty-two emperors of the Gordinian dynasty (A.D. 235-285) are known for certain to have died a natural death or to have been killed in battle against a foreign enemy.

issue before he is ready, it will help us. And if we can cut off his supplies, it will help as well."

"And there may be others who try to take advantage of this situation," a younger man volunteered. "Carinus may have more than one army to fight off. That would also be an advantage."

The talk became more general now, but Diocletian was pleased at their eagerness to face the upcoming challenge. He finally raised his hand to stop the conversation. "This is good. I'm glad for your ideas."

He looked around the room again. "Melinias, I appoint you as our lead general. I will leave logistics and planning in your hands. Choose the people you need and get everyone working on preparations. We will meet again in a few days."

——— MARK ———

Mark returned with the bread a few minutes before his father came home for supper. Andrew was a big man with bushy black hair, a dark complexion, and a ready smile. He came from a long line of believers and enjoyed telling stories of an ancestor about twelve generations earlier who had been converted to Christianity by Timothy in Ephesus. But Andrew wasn't in a story-telling mood tonight.

As Irene put a steaming bowl of lentil porridge on the little table, she wiped beads of perspiration from her forehead and brushed aside a few strands of curly dark hair. She came from a proud lineage of Roman senators, but she seldom spoke of it, since her family and relatives had been killed after being accused of plotting against the government. Only a girl at the time, Irene had been taken in by a Christian family who had found her hiding in an alley after the massacre.

"How was your day?" she asked Andrew.

Andrew's smile vanished. "Everyone in the city was out watching Diocletian's inauguration," he replied after a short pause. "Since there weren't any customers to look after, I went too." He sat on a nearby stool and watched his wife put the finishing touches on their meal.

Irene tensed. "What did you think of Diocletian?"

Andrew stretched and yawned. "It's hard to say. He started out with a bang though. He executed the praetorian prefect himself right in front of the crowd. Apparently the prefect was accused of murdering the last emperor."

Irene looked worried. "Why would the prefect have done that? He's in charge of the emperor's safety."

Andrew shrugged. "I don't know. But new emperors are pretty common in Rome these days. Diocletian may last a month, or he may last twenty years." He glanced at Mark and lowered his voice. "The rumor is that the prefect was hoping to become emperor himself."

Irene grimaced. "Why do these powerful men always think they need more power?" She shook her head.

Andrew pulled his stool closer to the table. "Let's eat while the porridge is still hot," he suggested. "Mark, grab a stool for your mother."

The family bowed their heads and recited a simple prayer of thanks before each dipping out a bowlful of steaming porridge.

Irene watched Andrew and Mark eating their porridge

for a moment, then posed the question upmost in her mind. "Does Diocletian seem like the kind of person who would start another persecution?"

Mark stared at her. "What do you mean?" He looked as puzzled as he sounded. "You mean . . . you mean throw Christians to the lions?"

His father smiled at him. "I don't think we need to worry about that," he assured Mark. "It's been a while since the last persecution."

Irene didn't look so sure. "You said he executed the prefect himself—and right in front of a crowd," she said. "That sounds pretty barbaric to me."

"I think he was just making an impression," Andrew said as he scraped his bowl clean. "He was just showing everyone, especially the soldiers, that he is not one to be trifled with."

Andrew stood up, then added, "At least I hope so. But I guess we can never be sure." He smiled at Irene. "Don't be afraid," he said gently. "God is in control. Diocletian is going to be far too busy strengthening his power over Rome to even think about Christians."

He walked to the door, then paused. "I need to go to a deacons' meeting tonight. We're still talking about building a larger church building. With so many Christians in Nicomedia, we need to think about a bigger building that allows all the Christians in Nicomedia to worship together. Some of the converts are part of the upper class and would like nicer accommodations—maybe even a cathedral."

"I was part of the upper class too at one time, and I don't mind meeting in homes—or even in the fields if necessary,"

Irene said softly. "I sometimes wonder what some of today's Christians would do if they faced real persecution."

Mark had a lot to think about after his father left for the meeting. But suddenly he remembered that he had promised to ask his mother a question for Lydia. It was clearly something Lydia had given a lot of thought.

"Mother, would you teach Lydia to read, as you did me?" Mark asked.

Irene looked pleased, but dubious. "Has she asked her parents about this? They have some pretty strong ideas about girls and what they should be allowed to do."

Mark nodded. "She's been begging them for months to let her get some schooling. She wants to learn to read. They finally decided last night they would allow it, but they don't have enough money to pay for her to go to school. I told her I'm sure you'd teach her without being paid."

"I'd be glad to help her," his mother replied. "Let's walk over to their house and talk to them about it before they change their minds."

Lydia was the youngest child in her family, and all her brothers and sisters had already left home. As a result, she did a lot of work at home, so Irene knew this would be a sacrifice for her parents. Mark, of course, didn't understand all this, but he liked Lydia and was happy that they could help her.

Lydia's parents, Hamas and Maria, lived in an old apartment building that looked as if it could crumble around them at any moment. They were part of the local network of believers, but neither Mark nor his mother had ever been inside their dwelling.

Lydia met them at the door. "Come on in," she invited shyly.

Lydia's father sat on a stool by the fire, carving a tool from a piece of wood. He nodded to them noncommittally, motioning to several more stools. "Maria will be out in a minute. She's cleaning up a bit."

Lydia's mother came bustling into the room a moment later. "Pleased you came over," she greeted them. "Would you like some *calda?*"[5]

Irene sat down on one of the stools. "That would be nice," she replied, smiling. "Mark told me Lydia wants to learn to read, and I thought I'd come over to talk about it."

Lydia's father shifted uneasily on his stool. "Yah, she has this notion that it would make her better. Can't say that I see it that way. But if you want to help her and it doesn't interfere with her work, I suppose it won't matter. We can't afford to pay you though."

Irene took the cup of calda Maria offered her before answering. "That's fine," she assured him. "I'm happy to help Lydia. You won't have to pay me. It is good for children to learn to read and do some figuring. It makes them feel more useful."

"I know what you mean," Maria said, glancing sideways at her husband. "I've often felt so ignorant while listening to someone read the Scriptures in our gatherings. None of our family can read, and it's the only time we get to learn from God's Word."

---

[5] *Calda* was a hot drink consisting of warm water mixed with wine or spices, or often both. Romans seldom drank water or milk, preferring either calda or mulled wine. This included Christians.

"You mean it makes you feel you're married to an ignorant man," Hamas interrupted harshly. "I have more than enough to do just feeding everybody around here, without wasting time reading. I'm fine with what we hear when the elders read to us."

"I know, it's hard," Irene said tactfully. "Maybe once Lydia learns to read, she can read to you sometimes."

"Can't afford to buy any books," Lydia's father muttered. "So that won't happen either."

Irene finished her cup of calda and rose to leave. "When would be a good time for Lydia to come over? Would after supper work, on the evenings when we don't have gatherings?"

Lydia's father just scowled, but Maria nodded. "That should work," she agreed. "And if you need help with anything, don't be afraid to get her to help you. I wish we could pay you for your time, but . . ." She glanced at her husband again.

"That's fine," Irene said. "We'll see how it works." She turned to Lydia. "We have a prayer meeting tomorrow evening, so let's start the next evening."

Mark hadn't said anything during the whole visit, but he had some questions after they left. "Mother, are Lydia's parents poor?"

Irene quickened her step before replying. She knew how dangerous the streets became after dark. "I suppose they are," she said. "But as far as I know they have always had enough to eat."

"But why did her father sound so upset?" Mark asked. "He didn't talk nicely to us at all."

Irene put her hand gently on his shoulder and stepped out

into the middle of the street as they passed an alleyway. "He works very hard and was probably tired," she explained. "And I suppose he feels inferior to us because your father has a good job as a shopkeeper."

"But it isn't our fault he has to work hard," Mark protested. "Even Lydia's mother seemed a bit scared of him."

"She is, I think," Irene replied. She opened the door to their dwelling with a look of relief. The streets were nearly deserted, and it wasn't a good night to be out. She pulled the door shut behind them and lit their lamp from the charcoal fire still burning in the little brazier. "I'm glad he is going to let Lydia come to learn to read. None of his other children ever learned how."

Mark still looked puzzled. "Are we different from other people? Most of the girls who come to the market don't know how to read. And I'm sure their mothers can't either."

"I think the time will come when most people will learn to read, both boys and girls," Irene answered. "But many people don't realize how important it is."

She switched the subject. "Better get ready for bed. It's hard to get up when you get to bed too late."

——— DIOCLETIAN ———

Diocletian met with his war council again a week later.

"Do we move out now, or do we wait until spring to head west toward Carinus?" He glanced around the circle. "It's costing us a lot just to feed the army while we sit here."

Melinias, Diocletian's war general, spoke up. "It's winter,

and marching across Europe to Italy now is going to be difficult. The weather will be poor, and marching day after day in the rain breaks down morale quickly."

Melinias' chief lieutenant agreed. "We've got a good spot right here to winter in, and we can spend the winter in training and sprucing up our equipment."

Diocletian's brow furrowed. "I suppose you're right. I just don't want to give Carinus much time to get ready."

He looked at the others. "How do the rest of you feel? Shall we spend the winter preparing and then pull out in early spring?"

Most of the group nodded their agreement, and Melinias clinched the discussion. "Carinus is facing the same situation. Hopefully he'll come to meet us and save us from going the whole way. In the meantime, maybe someone in the west will challenge him and keep his army busy."

Melinias got to his feet, but sat down abruptly as Diocletian spoke again. "Keep the soldiers busy," he ordered. "If they have nothing to do, they will start to grumble and complain or get into trouble. I expect you to put together a rigorous training schedule. I don't want the men getting soft."

The emperor's eyes narrowed. "And that includes all of you." His voice hardened as he continued. "Too much drinking and carousing have been going on. Several people from Nicomedia have complained of drunken soldiers molesting women after dark. That will stop, and it will stop now. I will hold you accountable if it doesn't."

It was no idle threat.

"Melinias, I want you to stay," he said in closing. "The rest of you are dismissed."

The guard stationed at the tent entrance pulled back the flap for the council to exit, while Diocletian moved over to the simple table that served as a field desk. He motioned to Melinias to join him.

Diocletian picked up a large scroll and unrolled it to reveal a simple map of the central part of the Roman Empire. "We are here," he said, pointing to Nicomedia on the map. "Carinus is here." He pointed to Rome. "Have you thought of the route we should follow, and where we might meet Carinus' army?"

The change of subject took Melinias off guard, but he recovered quickly. "I have," he replied, bending over the map. He pointed to the north end of the Adriatic Sea. "Carinus will need to cross here with his army. There is a Roman road here that runs almost straight east to the Danube River."

Diocletian nodded. "That's right, and the road will make easier travel for his army."

"We can do the same," Melinias replied, pointing to Nicomedia at the other edge of the map. "We can take this road here." He traced the route with his finger. "Then we can follow the Roman road north to the Danube."

He traced the route again with his finger. "Somewhere up here we will probably meet up with Carinus." He straightened up and looked at Diocletian. "The flat plains around the Margus River area would make an excellent battleground, if we can arrange to meet there."

"That coincides closely with my thoughts," Diocletian agreed, looking pleased. "Now if the gods will cooperate and send a strong army for Carinus to fight off before we meet him, we should be able to pull this off."

He let the map spring shut on its own. "How long do you estimate it will take to get to the Margus River? It looks like Carinus has about the same distance we do. But the weather should give us a head start."

Melinias pursed his lips as he thought about this question. "Well, I've traveled that road several times," he finally replied. "With an army, it will probably take about two months, maybe a little less. If we leave after the spring rains let up in April, we should be there by July."

"That sounds about right," said Diocletian. He turned away from the table. "It's bedtime. We have lots to do between now and then." He glanced at Melinias. "You have a lot of responsibility on your hands. Don't let me down. I'll make it worth your while."

MARK

Lydia had been coming for reading lessons for several weeks before they ran into the first hitch. She was an eager student and had already made good progress. But this evening she seemed nervous and distracted.

Lydia had just started an oral reading exercise when someone pounded on the door. Andrew and Irene looked at each other, then Andrew laid aside the leather boot he was repairing and walked to the door.

He undid the latch just as the person on the outside renewed his pounding. Suddenly the door burst open from the force and the man almost fell into the room. Startled, Andrew stepped back to give Lydia's father more room. But Hamas didn't pay any attention to Andrew. He had seen Lydia at the other side of the room.

"You come home with me right now," he barked. "Your mother needs your help this evening, and you don't have time to be sitting over here acting as if you were better than your parents."

He started across the room, but Andrew reached out and took him by the shoulder. "Hold on, my friend," he said calmly. "Maybe we should talk about this before you do something rash."

Lydia's father spun around to face him. "She agreed that she would still do her work as usual if we let her come over here," he replied stiffly. "Tonight there was cleaning to do and she left without finishing it."

His eyes sparked dangerously. "She's been acting uppity all week," he continued. "I should have known better than to let her come over here."

He turned back to Lydia. "You come with me right now and finish your work," he ordered. "You need to learn to obey."

Lydia's face turned pale and her hands trembled as she laid down the scroll she had been holding. "But Mother told me I should go," she said, almost stuttering. "She said I could finish the work tomorrow . . ." Her voice trailed off at the look on her father's face.

Before Hamas could do anything more, the door opened again and Maria staggered in. Her nose was bleeding and one eye was turning black. Her torn dress gave further evidence that someone had knocked her around.

Lydia's father was furious at her interruption. "What do you think you're doing here?" he snarled. "You've made enough trouble for one evening. Lydia is going to learn right now to listen to me and not go telling you her sob stories. If you try to stop me, you'll need to learn along with her."

Mark was trembling with fear by now. He had never seen anything like this. His parents sometimes had little disagreements, but he had never heard his father yell at his mother. And he knew his father had never hit her. He shrank farther back into the dark corner and desperately hoped Hamas wouldn't notice him sitting there.

Irene made the first move. She stepped in front of Lydia and faced the angry man. She showed no sign of fear—even her voice was calm and controlled as she spoke. "Hamas, I think you had better leave Lydia and Maria here with us until you calm down. This kind of outburst is totally out of place. Especially since Maria had given Lydia permission to come here. Lydia didn't do anything wrong."

Andrew saw the look on Hamas's face and stepped to his wife's side before Hamas could react again. "I think you and I need to go for a walk. Irene can bathe Maria's face and get her fixed up a bit while we have a chat."

Hamas glared at Andrew but drew back when he noted the look in his eyes. Andrew was a muscular man, despite his work, and at least six inches taller than Hamas. He was also at least fifteen years younger. Hamas knew he was treading on unhealthy ground. But even so, he had a hard time backing down.

"Just because you're a deacon in the church doesn't mean

you can tell me what to do with my own wife and daughter," he blustered. "All I did was teach Maria her place. There's no law against that."

Andrew stepped forward and took Hamas by the arm. "Let's go on a walk," he repeated. "We follow a higher law than Roman law. Christ's way is not to knock people around."

Mark discovered that he had been holding his breath, and he let it out as his father guided Hamas out the door. Lydia burst into tears and ran to her mother. Maria wrapped her arms around Lydia and cried with her.

Irene didn't hesitate. She put her arms around both of them. "Let's pray together," she said gently. "God can take care of this."

It was almost an hour later when Andrew returned, alone. Lydia and Mark were sitting at the table drinking calda and talking about Lydia's reading lessons. Irene had washed Maria's bruises, and Maria was holding a piece of raw meat over her black eye with one hand while she drank her calda with the other. A second pot of calda was heating on the charcoal stove.

Irene glanced at her husband, a question in her eyes. But he only said, "I'd take some calda if you have any left." He pulled another stool up to the table with Mark and Lydia and smiled at their anxious faces.

"Your father has gone to bed," he told Lydia. "I think he's sorry for how he acted. He said both of you can stay here until morning, then he'll join us for breakfast."

Maria sighed with relief. "Thank you so much for talking to him. He's usually a good man, but he has a terrible temper. I haven't seen him this angry for a long time though."

Andrew nodded and took a sip of calda before answering. "He told me he lost his job today. Apparently his boss also has a bad temper and got angry when he accidentally smashed a clay pot."

Maria's jaw dropped. "He never told us about that. Why didn't he tell us instead of getting so upset?"

"Well, you know how men are," Andrew replied, smiling. "We hate to admit to our wives that we've failed. I think Hamas feels inferior to begin with; he feels like a failure. And this was just another failure."

He put down his mug before adding, "That isn't a good reason for acting as he did, of course, but it does explain why. Then when Lydia left for her reading lessons, it just intensified his feelings."

Maria nodded. "I know. I understand him better than he realizes. But what are we going to do now? We have very little food in the house and no money."

Irene put her arm around Maria's shoulders. "We won't let you starve," she assured her. "The church also has a fund to help people. I'm sure Andrew will work something out for you."

"Yes, the church has a fund," said Andrew, "but I don't think we'll need it. We are shorthanded at the warehouse right now, and Hamas can start working for us tomorrow morning. The work is easier and the pay better than what he was getting."

"Oh, I'm so glad!" Maria exclaimed. "Did you tell him?"

"Yes, I did," Andrew said. "He agreed to give it a try."

Andrew stood up and stretched. "It's been a hard evening for all of us. It's time to get some sleep."

Mark and Lydia both ran errands at the market the next morning. But instead of racing each other, they walked. They had gradually developed a friendship, so they felt comfortable walking together and talking about the happenings of the day before.

"Your father seemed a lot happier this morning," Mark said. "He even apologized to you and your mother."

Lydia jumped over a rock in the roadway before answering. "He usually apologizes after he gets angry. But I have never seen him hit my mother before. That scared me."

"I don't really understand parents, I guess," Mark replied. "Mine get worried sometimes, and sometimes they disagree, especially about church things. But they never fight."

Lydia looked puzzled. "My parents never talk about church things. They mostly talk about not having any money."

Mark tried to explain. "My father thinks the church is doing well, but my mother feels people are forgetting what it means to be a Christian."

They joined a small group of spectators watching a man trying to persuade his donkey to move faster. Instead of speeding up, the donkey stopped stubbornly in his tracks and refused to move. Lydia giggled as the man tried to pull the donkey, but the donkey just dug in its heels.

The lead rope was frayed and finally broke, with the driver landing flat on his back. The crowd applauded while the donkey brayed derisively and ambled off at the same pace as before. The driver, red-faced, scrambled to his feet and brushed himself off. He hurried after the donkey, and they vanished around the street corner.

Mark and Lydia were still laughing when they arrived at the market.

"I'm going to beat you in our next race to the market," Lydia said. "You just watch me."

Mark laughed. "You remind me of the man chasing his donkey."

"Well, then you're the donkey!" Lydia grinned at him and vanished down an alleyway between two rows of vendors.

PART II
A.D. 285
New Ideas

[Nero] first persecuted the servants of God; he crucified Peter, and slew Paul: nor did he escape with impunity; for God looked on the affliction of His people; and therefore the tyrant, bereaved of authority, and precipitated from the height of empire, suddenly disappeared, and even the burial place of that noxious wild beast was nowhere to be seen. This has led some persons of extravagant imagination to suppose that, having been conveyed to a distant region, he is still reserved alive; and to him they apply the Sibylline verses concerning "The fugitive, who slew his own mother, being to come from the uttermost boundaries of the earth"; as if he who was the first should also be the last persecutor, and thus prove the forerunner of Antichrist!

But we ought not to believe those who, affirming that the two prophets Enoch and Elias have been translated into some remote place that they might attend our Lord when He shall come to judgment, also fancy that Nero is to appear hereafter as the forerunner of the devil, when he shall come to lay waste the earth and overthrow mankind.

Lactantius, *Of the Manner in Which the Persecutors Died,* Chap. 2

April 285

The townspeople gave a sigh of relief when spring came and Diocletian's army pulled out. Not only had the army swelled the population of Nicomedia and created a food shortage, but several soldiers had been executed for molesting people. Now maybe things would quiet down.

Diocletian and his guards stood on the hillside, the same spot where his soldiers had proclaimed him emperor, and watched the army pull out. Moving an army of 40,000 men across the country was an art. Melinias had mastered that art, however, and breaking camp went smoothly.

Diocletian smiled as the Roman soldiers marched past in perfect order, four abreast. The sight thrilled him, as always. And this time it was *his* army, under *his* control, to use as *he* wanted to. This was the beginning—the real beginning—of his reign as emperor.

Each soldier carried a large knapsack as well as his weapons. Larger items such as tents were packed on mules coming behind the soldiers, but each soldier was self-sufficient with several days' worth of food and water.

A regiment of cavalry on horseback led the way. The rest of the cavalry brought up the rear, ensuring against any surprise attack from either direction. Not that there was any likelihood of this, but the discipline of maintaining a formal structure was good practice.

It would take hours for the entire camp to go past, but Diocletian had seen what he wanted to see. He turned to the praetorian prefect, Afranius, who stood at his side. "Is my carriage loaded and ready to go?"

When Afranius nodded, Diocletian continued, "Get my horse saddled. I'm not going to travel in a litter or carriage like some wealthy old woman with weak knees."

The prefect risked a grin, which Diocletian ignored, and they started down the hill. Half a dozen members of Diocletian's personal guard followed them. "Will you want your tent set up this evening, sir?" Afranius asked.

"No, I won't use it," Diocletian said shortly. "The weather is good, and I've ordered Melinias to have the men sleep in their bedrolls. It will save time in both the evening and the morning. I'll do likewise."

Then he added, "I want the secretary to ride with me so that I can work while we ride. Hiram will need his equipment to take notes."

Afranius raised his eyebrows. He knew Diocletian had a

reputation for using every minute productively, but he wondered how the secretary would react. Hiram was a hard worker and known for his accuracy, but he didn't enjoy riding horseback. He would undoubtedly have preferred riding in a litter with Diocletian.

However, the emperor's determined look did not welcome discussion.

——— MARK ———

Andrew took Mark with him early that morning to watch the army pull out. The soldiers had broken camp before sunup. They ate breakfast in the faint morning light and pulled on their knapsacks as the sun crept from its bed in the east.

Mark was almost bouncing with excitement. He had not been allowed to go close to the camp during the winter, but now he was finally going to see the soldiers in action. Other townspeople had also gathered to watch, and Mark stood beside his father to watch the spectacle.

The cavalry came first, led by its commander astride a fiery white stallion. Mark was sure the mighty charger was blowing gusts of smoke from his nostrils, but when he pointed it out to his father, Andrew chuckled. "That's just his breath turning to steam in the chill morning air." Mark wasn't so sure. He thought he caught a few flashes of fire behind the stallion's snorts.

On the commander's left rode the trumpeter, ready to convey his leader's commands to the men following them. He rode a gleaming black mare, the opposite of the commander's steed in both appearance and temperament. On the far side of the commander rode the Standard bearer. He held aloft on a pole the proud Roman eagle that led every Roman army into battle.

The eagle was a worthy representation of Rome, and Mark's backbone tingled as he admired the eagle's arrogant glare and the outstretched wings. Jews and Christians despised the Roman eagle as a mere idol cast from bronze. But Mark was young enough to ignore this and catch a glimpse of the unconquered spirit of the king of the skies, representing the matchless spirit of Rome. He cheered along with the crowd as the eagle was carried by.

Wave after wave of cavalry followed the Standard, each four horses abreast, in perfect sequence. The riders were in full battle dress, carrying lances and shields, with the short Roman sword hanging at their sides. It seemed that the horses, like the riders, were aware of the thousands of eyes watching them. Hundreds of riders, followed by thousands of foot soldiers, all marching in absolute order, eyes straight ahead and seemingly oblivious to any distraction—the sight was one Mark never forgot.

Andrew needed to get to work, so they had to leave long before the procession was over. Mark would have liked to stay, and he reluctantly followed his father through the unruly crowd. Most people were pushing to get closer, and Andrew had to almost carve a path for them. This led to several unpleasant encounters, but most people eyed Andrew's muscular arms and shoulders and let them through.

DIOCLETIAN

Diocletian had always loved being on the march. Now that the army was under his complete control and ready to do his bidding, the feeling intensified. He and his entourage of guards and his secretary rode in a slot between two units of foot soldiers.

The morning passed quickly. Diocletian settled easily into the groove of being on horseback again. The movements of his horse quickly became an extension of his own. He had long ago learned that the key to avoiding fatigue and sore muscles on a long ride was relaxing and not allowing his muscles to resist the movement of his horse. It was a lesson that Hiram, his secretary, hadn't learned yet, and Diocletian was first amused, then irritated, at the secretary's attempts to find a comfortable position in the saddle. Finally he pulled to the side of the column of soldiers and motioned Afranius to follow him out of earshot.

Diocletian nodded at the group of horsemen. "Hiram is going to kill himself on this trip if he keeps this up," he growled. "Get one of your men to take him aside and give him some riding lessons."

The prefect looked dubious. "It's going to take more than one lesson to make him comfortable on horseback," he told Diocletian. "He's going to be quite stiff and sore by tonight."

"If he weren't the best secretary in the army, he'd just be driving a mule cart hauling luggage," Diocletian replied in disgust. "But I need him. Take whatever time is needed. He can spend the rest of the day riding in a cart."

Hiram wasn't the only man with sore muscles by the end of the day. Despite the training efforts, many of the soldiers had become a little soft during the winter. Most were happy when the trumpet sounded the end of the day's march and they could set up camp in a large grassy field close to the road.

Despite the early halt, it had been a good day and Diocletian was pleased.

MARK

Mark could hardly stop talking about what he had seen that morning. Irene was amused, but finally decided that he needed to be put to work.

"Why don't you think about your rhetoric assignment for a while," she suggested. "Practice it so that you can read it to Lydia when she comes to do her lessons."

Mark frowned. "Homer's writing is so difficult," he complained. "I wish he had written in Latin, like Virgil. I don't like Greek."

Irene smiled. "Homer's poem, the *Iliad,* is where Virgil got his original ideas," she explained. "We are going to look at his version of the story too. But I want you to learn to read the classic Greek authors."[1]

Mark reluctantly picked up his scroll of Homer's writing. Then he looked at his mother again. "What good will Greek

---

[1] The Iliad is set during the Trojan War, the ten-year siege of the city of Troy by a coalition of Greek kingdoms. Most people have heard of the Trojan horse, which is taken from Homer's writings. Homer wrote in Greek, but Virgil wrote in Latin.

do me anyway? Father usually reads Latin if he reads."

Irene pulled up a stool across the table from Mark. "Latin literature is very shallow compared to Greek. The Greek writers examined the world and the people around them and wrote about them. It's good for you to learn how to think.

"Also, the apostles wrote in Greek," she added. "Most of their writings have been translated into Latin, but Latin doesn't portray the depth of feeling and understanding that Greek does. You will be glad when you are older that you took the time to learn Greek properly."

Mark twisted his lips woefully as she spoke. "How long will it take me to learn all this?"

"Learning takes a lifetime," Irene chuckled. "It was my interest in learning that kept me from going insane after my family was killed." She wiped a tear from the corner of her eye. "I want you to love learning as well. It opens such a door for the human mind."

She rose from her stool and walked over to their little library of scrolls. She picked out one that Mark had never looked at. "After you have gotten a little further with your rhetoric studies, I want to give you some training in logic.[2] That will help you to sort out what you learn in your rhetoric studies."

Mark groaned as he picked up his scroll of Homer and started to read.

---

[2] Ancient logic was a form of philosophy, and Irene would have used the writings of Aristotle to teach it to Mark.

DIOCLETIAN

While Nicomedia was sinking back into its normal sleepy existence, Diocletian's army settled into a daily routine that was far from sleepy. The first trumpet sounded an hour before sunup. This gave the men time to pack their bedrolls, cook their breakfast, and get ready to march. At midday they stopped for a half-hour break, during which they ate a cold meal from their knapsacks. The cavalry watered the horses and checked their hooves. The march continued until about a half hour before sundown, giving the soldiers enough time to gather firewood, lay out their bedrolls, and hopefully renew their water supply.

The daily marches also gave Diocletian a lot of time to think and plan his strategy. If he wasn't dealing with Hiram, that is. His idea of having Hiram riding beside him to take notes was proving quite cumbersome. Not only did Hiram keep dropping his pen and spilling his ink, he was seemingly unable to learn how to ride efficiently. The first time Hiram fell off his horse while trying to catch his falling ink jar, Diocletian just rolled his eyes and looked the other way while the guards picked him up bodily and put him back on his horse. The second time it happened, Diocletian gritted his teeth. The third time was too much.

"Tie him on his horse!" Diocletian barked at Afranius. "And do a good job of it."

But that was only a temporary fix. The guards still needed to pick up parchment sheets or quill pens several times an hour, and in between, the poor man didn't get much accomplished.

Hiram was beyond a doubt the most miserable man on the march.

Diocletian was a stubborn man, but even he finally threw up his hands in defeat. "Get a chariot or a carriage of some sort for Hiram to ride in," he said to Afranius. "This nonsense is driving me insane."

"Yes, sir," Afranius replied. "Do you want him to be part of our group here so he can continue taking notes for you?"

Diocletian was tempted to banish the hapless secretary to the rear of the march and let him breathe the dust stirred up by the army, but he needed someone to compile his ideas.

"Give him a driver, and let him be part of our group," he answered. "Make sure the chariot is big enough to carry three people and Hiram's equipment. And tell him if he falls off the chariot, I'm going to feed him to the jackals."

Afranius noted the look on Diocletian's face and didn't ask any more questions. But as he rode off, he made a mental note to warn Hiram to be careful. He wouldn't put it past Diocletian to do exactly what he said. Hiram was a likeable person and a friend of his, though extremely clumsy. He was, however, a very capable secretary. But would that be enough to keep him from becoming jackal food?

Things went better after that, to the relief of all involved.

This arrangement gave Diocletian time to think about some other problems. The big one, of course, was the upcoming battle with Carinus. He had carefully laid out the battle plans with his general, Melinias, and he really couldn't do anything more on that until he knew where the battle would take place. They had drawn up their plans assuming the fight would occur at the Margus River, an area Melinias was acquainted with.

Diocletian tensed as he mentally worked his way through those plans once more, looking for any loopholes or hidden traps. *I've got to relax. There'll be lots of time to worry once we meet Carinus and his army and get a closer look at the battleground. Hopefully the scouts will give us advance warning.*

His thoughts wandered as he settled back into his saddle again. Going into battle was nothing new for Diocletian. It had been his life for twenty-five years. However, this was his first battle as an emperor, and his entire future depended on winning it. If his army lost, he was a dead man, either at the hands of Carinus' men, or perhaps his own. The odds were high, but that was true of his life as a whole. He shrugged and took a drink from his water bag. He would go down fighting if he had to. But he wasn't going to worry about it now.

The main threat for the empire right now is the barbarians raiding across the Danube River, he thought. *How can we defeat them once and for all? After Carinus is out of the way, I can use his army to help mop them up. A good hard blow will show them who is in charge and set them back a few years. That's something to discuss with my war council when we have a chance.*

But even the barbarian threat wasn't the biggest issue he faced. Stretching from Spain to Persia, and from Britain to northern Africa, Rome was much too big for one man to govern. And every time an emperor died, the fight started all over again. *I need a plan that will take care of both of those problems. Most emperors prepare their oldest son to take control at their death. But that often doesn't work very well. If an emperor has two or three sons, they spend their energy fighting each other instead of establishing the empire.*

He pondered this for a while, turning over the ideas in his mind. He wouldn't be able to put anything in place until the battle with Carinus was over and they had dealt with the barbarians. He had a daughter, but no son, so that made those plans a little harder unless he could find a competent son-in-law to fill in. *I'll have to watch for someone who might fit that bill. My daughter might not care for the idea, but she'll just have to put up with it.*

Diocletian was so deep in thought that he didn't notice it was almost suppertime until a trumpet blast signaled the end of the day's march. It seemed early and he looked up, irritated at the waste of daylight hours.

He turned to Afranius, who was riding close beside him. "Why are we stopping early?"

The prefect glanced at the sky. "Looks like a storm is coming. Melinias is giving us time to get camp set up before the rain starts."

Diocletian frowned but let it pass. They were ahead of schedule and it didn't really matter. Anyway, this might give Hiram time to jot down a few names that had been rolling through his mind.

Afranius hesitated, but when Diocletian didn't comment, he continued. "Do you want us to set up your tent? It could get pretty miserable out here."

Diocletian glanced at the sky. "Yes, set it up," he agreed. "Spread the word to my council that I want a meeting in my tent right after supper. We need to talk about a few things."

New Ideas: April 285

The group had hardly gathered in Diocletian's tent when the storm broke. The men jumped when a deafening crack of thunder split the air. Almost immediately they heard a sizzling sound and smelled brimstone. Afranius yanked open the tent flap to see what was happening, only to face a cloudburst of water. He blinked and backed up, pulling the tent flap shut again.

Then the wind hit. The tent bucked and the canvas crackled under the combined pressure of the rain and the wind. Hiram scrambled to put his writing materials and notes back into his leather satchel.

Afranius recovered first. "Lean against the canvas," he ordered. "It might keep the tent from blowing away."

As the storm roared and the tent flapped wildly in the wind, even Diocletian wondered if this was the end of all his hopes.

Imagine what the history books would say. "Killed in a thunderstorm on his way to overthrow Carinus."

He straightened abruptly. He was *not* going to die crouched in a corner because he was afraid of a thunderstorm. He raised his voice and took control. "All right. Everyone but the guards come over to the entrance so we can get out if the tent blows over."

He had to shout to be heard, but by the time everyone got the message, the rain started to abate and the wind gradually moderated. Everyone started to breathe normally again.

"Well, what brought that on?" asked Melinias. "Never saw

a storm come up that fast before. I think I should go check how everyone is doing."

Diocletian nodded and looked at Afranius. "You'd better go with him. Bring me a report as soon as you can." He looked around at the rest of the group. "We might as well call off the meeting. All of you have other responsibilities right now."

He turned to Hiram. "Where are you sleeping?"

Hiram grimaced. "My driver and I threw a sheet of canvas over the chariot. We were going to sleep under the chariot, but if it's too wet there's enough room for both of us on the chariot floor." He didn't look very happy at the prospect, but Diocletian had other things to worry about besides Hiram's comfort.

"Leave your paper and writing materials here," he told Hiram. "That way they won't get wet." He stepped to the tent door and looked out. The rain had almost stopped, but the ground was soaked and water lay everywhere. Fortunately, the praetorians had pitched Diocletian's tent on high ground and no water was running into it. The rest of the camp had turned into a sea of mud, however. He looked around distastefully in the deepening twilight.

"Well, it looks like you'll be sleeping on the floor of your chariot," he remarked to Hiram. "Either that or in several inches of mud."

Diocletian stepped outside and sniffed. The strong smell of brimstone still hung in the air and told him that lightning had struck close by. *Now that would really have made the historians cackle,* he thought grimly. *Emperor Carus was killed by a lightning bolt last year. Then his son Numerian died this year. No one would have believed that three emperors in a row*

New Ideas: April 285

could have died from natural causes in such a short time. They would have blamed Hiram for taking advantage of the storm to stage my "accidental" death.

The idea of the luckless Hiram being blamed for his death struck him as funny, and he smiled for the first time that day. But the grin faded as quickly as it had come. *I must be getting senile. Such stupid thoughts.*

He shook his head angrily to clear it, then turned as he heard footsteps. Afranius came around the corner of the tent carrying a sputtering torch to light his way.

"Well, it could have been worse," the prefect reported. "Everyone is soaked to the skin, and some of the horses were spooked by the thunder. But no one was hurt, and the guards are rounding up the horses."

Diocletian looked at the sky as the rain started again and pulled his cloak around him. It was a gentle drizzle, but the temperature had dropped substantially. "Come inside," he told the prefect. He chuckled cynically. "Poor Hiram is going to have a miserable night."

Afranius looked at him curiously, but Diocletian ignored his reaction. "I'm going to retire," he said. "No use wasting the whole night." He listened to the raindrops pelting the tent. "It's going to be a miserable night for everyone, actually. And probably a bad day for traveling tomorrow."

──────── **MARK** ────────

Church had been a major part of Mark's life as far back as he could remember. His mother was an ardent follower of Christ, and his father was a deacon in the church. That meant they went to services regularly. This included a four-hour service on Sunday, as well as several prayer meetings during the week.

Since it was Easter weekend, special services began on Thursday evening. A special service, as Mark had learned long ago, meant it would be a long service.[3] Still, some of the excitement of Easter rubbed off on him.

On Saturday evening Mark had a long nap. Andrew woke him just before the ten o'clock service. Mark shivered as they walked through the darkness. "Why do we need to go to services during the night?" he asked, puzzled.

His father glanced around to make sure no one was within hearing distance before replying. "As Christians, we believe the death and resurrection of Jesus are the two most important events that have ever occurred. We try to closely replicate in our services what took place."

Irene noticed that Mark still looked puzzled. "Jesus rose very early on Sunday morning," she explained. "But until then, everything was darkness for those who followed Him." She glanced up at the stars before continuing. "That is why we fast for forty hours before having the Easter morning meal together."

Like any growing boy who hadn't eaten anything for almost two days, Mark was sure he was almost dying of starvation. He glanced hungrily at the basket of food his mother was

---

[3] Preparations for the weekend started forty days before Easter. During Lent, as this period was called, Christians fasted and prayed and gave money for the poor. Any entertainment and unnecessary worldly activities were gradually cut out of the daily routine until Good Friday—a day when no one ate or drank. Since this was the celebration of the death of Christ, even the Eucharist was not practiced on this day. Instead, the Christians gathered on Thursday evening and throughout the day on Friday to listen to public readings from the Gospels and Psalms.

carrying and his stomach growled.

Irene smiled at the sound. "Just focus on the singing and the reading," she suggested. "Try to put yourself into the story of what happened. Then you won't feel as hungry."

The service went faster than Mark expected. As he tried to follow his mother's advice, he was able to grasp the solemnity and beauty of the Gospel story. The time went by quickly as the congregation sang and the priests and deacons read aloud the familiar selections from the Gospels.

At the end of the first service, they sat quietly in the darkness for about fifteen minutes. Then, at the stroke of midnight, they lit the candles again and began the Easter service. Joyful songs filled the old building—even the Scripture readings were sung from memory. Mark was getting sleepy, but his mother was drinking it all in. This was the part of the weekend she enjoyed the most. As she told Mark later, the thought of the Resurrection always thrilled her. Her Lord and Master had conquered death so she could live. It was such a contrast to the darkness and fear of the paganism she remembered from her childhood.

At the end of the service, the presiding priest blessed the baskets of food heaped on the tables at the front of the building. The congregation gathered around and helped themselves. Then they scattered throughout the building, eating and fellowshipping together. Again, it was a joyous time of enjoying each other's friendship.

Mark found Lydia close by and sat beside her to eat. "Did you sleep during the service?" he asked cautiously. "I think this was the first time I stayed awake through the whole service."

"You looked pretty sleepy part of the time," Lydia retorted, avoiding his question. But her conscience caught up with her a moment later and she admitted, "I slept through most of the singing. I just couldn't stay awake any longer." She lifted her nose as if anticipating a smart remark. But Mark just grinned.

Mark and his parents walked home through the early morning, along with other families who had taken part in the celebration. Everyone headed straight for bed. On Easter the regular morning service was canceled, but they gathered again in the afternoon.

3

July 285

For Roman emperors, total control was everything. Getting rid of all dissent was the only way to stay in power. The message was clear—be loyal, or else.

Diocletian's army had arrived at the Margus River. They settled into a permanent camp in the plain bordering the Roman road. The camp sprang up like a well-oiled machine. The regular soldiers set up their tents along the perimeter, leaving room for the supplies and cattle and horses within the large circle. Several cavalry outposts set up camp at strategic spots around the main camp to guard against any surprise attacks. While this took place, Diocletian and his war council rode to an overhanging spur of rock overlooking the area where they planned to do battle with Carinus.

Melinias pointed out the various aspects of his battle plan. He had done his homework well. "Several of our scouts returned yesterday," he announced. "Carinus and his army are a few days from here. This gives us a chance to prepare for the battle. We will try to push ahead as soon as he gets here. We'd like to catch him off guard."

He paused and took a long drink from his water bag. "I'm sure Carinus has scouts out looking for us as well. They have probably told him where we are, so we will have to be alert for any sign of an ambush or other tricks. However, he is leading a Roman army, so we can guess his strategy. He isn't a particularly experienced leader, so hopefully he will just try to hit us headlong and use brute force to defeat us."

Diocletian nodded. "His army is larger than ours, isn't it? But he will know that too if he's done his homework."

Melinias glanced over the plain, trying to envision the coming battle. "If our scouts are correct, Carinus isn't getting along too well with his officers. One of the scouts slipped into their camp and overheard a meeting he was having with his generals." He glanced sideways at Diocletian, then continued. "He was overruling almost every suggestion they made. They weren't very happy. So hopefully their morale is low."

"I've heard whispers of Carinus trying to seduce the wives and daughters of his officers," Afranius spoke up. "Some of the officers are pretty bitter about it."

Melinias nodded. "I've heard about that too. Many a battle has been lost due to bad feelings between the troops and their leader."

Diocletian sat on his horse, looking out over the plains. Now that the defining moment was almost here, he wasn't quite so sure of himself anymore. He had more battle experience than Carinus, but this was the first time he was the man in charge. Once more he went over the battle plan, looking for any weak spot. But he had caught what Melinias had said about Carinus, and he knew his own men wouldn't be happy either if he started to second guess their plans this late in the game. The time for planning was over. For better or worse, they would stick to their strategy.

He squared his shoulders as they walked their horses down the hillside toward the camp. This was the moment of make or break. If they lost this battle, history would forget he ever existed. But there was no use worrying about history. He intended to win. The gods had a plan in mind for him, and he was going to make it happen.

He pushed aside his doubts and forced his mind onto safer ground. "I want to talk with your scouts," he told Melinias. "I'd like a firsthand report of everything they saw."

"I'll bring them over," Melinias replied. "They are pretty optimistic about the whole thing."

Diocletian was a religious man, as far as emperors went. He liked to have the gods on his side, and a sacrifice should help. Early the next morning, the soldiers gathered in their normal ranks to watch the ritual of sacrificing a bull to the god Jupiter.

A group of officers brought the sacred bull to the sacrificial circle. The ritual climaxed when Melinias, who oversaw the

New Ideas: July 285

ceremony, plunged his sword into the bull's throat. The bull bellowed in mortal agony as his lifeblood gushed out. As the beast sank to the ground, the soldiers dropped to their knees as well, worshipping the god they hoped would deliver them in the upcoming battle.

Diocletian knelt with the rest, but frowned as he noticed a scattering of soldiers who didn't kneel. *I need to check into this. These men could lose the battle for us. What are they thinking—risking the wrath of Jupiter on us?*

He stopped Afranius on their way back to his tent. "Did you see that a few of the soldiers refused to kneel when Melinias killed the sacred bull?"

The prefect glanced at him warily. "Yes, I think there were a few," he admitted. "But only a few, not that many."

Diocletian's eyebrows drew together, a reflex action that the prefect had learned to recognize as a danger sign. "What were they doing? And why?" he demanded. "Don't they know they could be executed for disloyalty because of their actions?"

Afranius took his time answering. "Yes, I'm sure they know that. They are Christians and don't worship the Roman gods. They believe in Christos, a Jewish Messiah—"

"I know who the Christians are," Diocletian snapped. "But what are they doing in the army?"

Afranius thought his words through carefully, knowing he was treading on thin ice. "It's true; at one time Christians did not allow their people to join the army. Even now, some do not believe in fighting. But over the last century, more and more of their young men have joined the army. However, they don't worship our gods."[1] He paused for a moment. "Sacrifices like this don't happen very often, and they can usually find a way to avoid them. But today's sacrifice came up too quickly for them to avoid it, so they had to decide whether to be true to their God and risk their lives, or be a hypocrite."

When Diocletian didn't answer, the prefect continued. "They are very good soldiers as a whole, and their commanders tend to overlook their indiscretion at such times."

Diocletian was thinking this through. "Well," he finally replied, "I might let it go this time. The question isn't whether the officers are ready to overlook their indiscretion—it's whether Jupiter will. It's a pretty big risk."

"I suppose the officers tend to think that having another god on our side is worth the risk," Afranius replied. "Though the Christian God is pretty independent by the sounds of it. It's hard to say whether He would join forces with Jupiter to help us or not."

Diocletian frowned. "I doubt it. I'll leave it for now, but I might need to take a closer look at this down the road. Serving gods other than Roman gods sounds almost like treason to me."

The next afternoon Carinus' army set up camp several hours' march away. It was too late to attack that evening, but Diocletian's army was on the march by sunup the next

---

[1] While there were certainly variations from area to area, it is clear that at one point the church rejected members who joined the army. If a soldier already in the army became converted, he was expected to refuse to kill. This gradually changed over the years, but according to Hippolytus (170-235), this was the expected position during his lifetime. (See Bercot, David, *A Dictionary of Early Christian Beliefs*, p. 681.)

morning. Tensions were high, but most of the soldiers were used to fighting and were itching to get their hands on the enemy, even though the enemy consisted of fellow Romans.

Diocletian and Melinias had guessed right. Carinus tried to force his way right through Diocletian's army. Expecting this, Melinias had placed his greatest strength, his cavalry, at the edges. This had a pincer effect, putting pressure on the front and side of Carinus' army. Both sides were clearly well-matched, and at times the battle seemed to go one way and then the other.

Diocletian was watching the battle from the ridge where they had met several days ago. His guards were with him, and he could feel the tension in all of them. But the dust kicked up by the battle made it difficult to see what was going on.

Warfare was rough business, and a soldier's survival hinged on his strength and endurance. Mercy was neither given nor asked for. Every man knew that his chances of coming out unscathed were slender at best. But they had a method behind their madness, and soldiers kept swapping with fresh fighters from the rear as they tired.

By midafternoon, Diocletian was almost at the point of calling out to any god that would listen to him. But suddenly the battle slowed. Something was going on in the ranks of Carinus' army, but he couldn't quite see what it was. He turned to Afranius. "What's happening?"

The prefect looked puzzled. "It seems as if they are backing up and asking for a truce." He shielded his eyes with his hand, trying to figure out what was going on. "Listen, someone is signaling a retreat."

They could clearly hear the trumpet sounding on the far side of battlefield. Afranius turned to one of his men. "Go find out what is happening."

The guard wheeled his horse and set off at a full gallop. It took him almost an hour to return. "Carinus is dead," he said grimly. "It's unclear what happened, but Melinias suspects he was assassinated by his officers. They are requesting a meeting."

The Battle of the Margus left Diocletian the sole ruler of the Roman Empire. The circumstances of Carinus' death were vague, but Diocletian decided to leave well enough alone.[2] He simply had Carinus' army swear an oath of allegiance and then turned his attention to other things. Several groups of barbarians had crossed the Danube River with the intent of pillaging and looting. Right now that was the most important item on his to-do list.

He reappointed most of Carinus' officers and officials, placed Melinias in charge of the now combined armies and headed north to meet the barbarians.

---

[2] They are still vague, but historians believe Carinus was assassinated by someone in his own army.

4

August 285

It turned out to be a short battle. As the barbarians crossed the Danube River, they expected easy pickings. If things went well, they planned to go even farther south. But things didn't go well. They found themselves face to face with a well-trained, well-disciplined, and highly motivated Roman army. Instead of filling their pockets with loot, they dropped everything and fled for their lives.

For Diocletian, it was a good feeling to watch the barbarian armies fleeing like scared rabbits, with the mighty Roman army hot on their heels. He hoped it was a sign of things to come: a united government, a united army, and finally, a united empire. And he was the man in control.

But would it work? That was the question Diocletian had been struggling with, even during the battles of the past several months. Could one man do justice to ruling an empire as large and complex as the Roman Empire?

This question was on his mind again as he sat in his tent that afternoon with Hiram and Afranius. Despite Diocletian's disdain for some of Hiram's weaknesses, his sharp mind made him indispensable. Afranius doubled as Diocletian's chief personal bodyguard, and his regular presence in discussions and planning gradually drew him in as a trusted advisor.

"I want to do something about Rome's money system and taxation," Diocletian told them. "But even more important is to sort out its governing structure."

He glanced at Hiram and Afranius, but neither commented. "Every province from Syria to Britain is boiling with unrest of some sort," he said, grimacing. "I can't be everywhere at once, nor do I want to be."

He got to his feet and started pacing the confines of the tent. "Here's an idea I have. Tell me what you think of it."

As Diocletian rolled out a crude map of the Roman Empire, the three gathered around it. "Presently we have about fifty provinces in the empire. Not all of these are powerful enough to cause major problems or attempt to set up their own government, but a number of them are." He took a deep breath. "I'm thinking of breaking most of them in half and realigning some borders so we have about a hundred provinces. That would take care of the danger of revolts unless several provinces worked together."

Diocletian straightened to his full height and looked at Hiram and Afranius keenly. "But that still doesn't take care of the complexity of administrating an empire as large as the Roman

Empire. So I'm thinking of going several steps further."[1]

He took a drink from a water flask on the table. "After breaking most of the provinces in half, I'd like to appoint an assistant emperor to look after the western part of the empire. For now, I would still be in control, but that could change if necessary.

"Then there is the problem of choosing a new emperor to succeed a deceased emperor. Usually the emperor will appoint a son or two to run the empire in his stead, but that doesn't always work out so well.

"What I'm suggesting is a tetrarchy.[2] We would appoint junior emperors, or Caesars—one to be under me, and one to be under my assistant emperor. They could each oversee smaller groups of provinces. That would keep me from being run off my feet.

"It would also help with the succession problem. The junior emperor could succeed the senior emperor and appoint a new junior emperor to take his place. This would make for a more smoothly operating empire."

Diocletian sat down and took another drink. "So what do you think? I know it would take a few years to put it all in place. Or maybe even a decade or so."

Hiram and Afranius looked at each other, each silently inviting the other to speak first. Afranius finally spoke. "That would

---

[1] Lactantius considered these ideas as being money grabs or power grabs, or both. His view of Diocletian was quite negative. But it seems to me from reading the history of those times that Diocletian did have a genuine concern for the Empire.

[2] *Tetra* means *four*, so the tetrarchy was a rule of four. In Diocletian's time, there were two Augusti (senior emperors): Diocletian in the east and Maximian in the west. They each had a Caesar (junior emperor) under them: Galerius and Constantius. In theory, the Caesars were supposed to take the position of the Augusti when the senior emperors retired, but in reality it didn't hold out that way.

also solve your problem of not having a son to succeed you. Have you given any thought to who will fill these positions?"

Hiram looked up from the notes he had been taking. "If word gets around, there won't be any shortage of applicants," he said dryly. "Most people think an emperor lives a life of ease and luxury."

Diocletian snorted. "That's a large part of the problem. People aren't concerned about the good of the empire. They just want to line their own pockets with money."

"As far as my not having a son . . ." He looked sharply at Afranius and Hiram. "I do have a daughter. I can marry her to the man I choose to be my junior."

Afranius pursed his lips. "But what if he's married already?" he asked dubiously.

"That's no problem. He can divorce his wife and then marry Valeria," Diocletian replied, brushing aside the question. "That's what emperors' daughters are for."

Hiram and Afranius didn't comment, but later they discussed it in private. "I thought Diocletian had more respect for his family than that," Afranius said. "I'm guessing his wife might have more to say about it than he realizes."

Hiram made a face. "Probably," he replied, "but knowing Diocletian, that won't make any difference. By the way, is there any truth to the rumor that his wife is a Christian?"

Afranius looked at Hiram sharply. "Whatever you do, don't suggest anything like that to Diocletian. Prisca is a very kind woman. You don't want to get her into trouble.

"Anyway," he added, "it's only a rumor. She's never been baptized as far as I know, but she has befriended Christians at times. Diocletian isn't that much against Christianity himself, but the empire will always come first. If the Christians threaten the empire, he won't have any mercy."

MARK

A few months later Irene was just finishing a reading lesson with Mark and Lydia when Andrew arrived home from work.

"Why are you early?" she asked. "Is something wrong?"

Andrew pulled a three-legged stool over to the table and sat down before replying. "Not really. We're having a deacons' meeting tonight with the bishops. And it's bound to get late if we don't get an early start."

"Are you still talking about building a cathedral?" Irene asked. "Or has something else come up?"

"Well, both, I guess," Andrew replied. "Several of the local meetings are getting really crowded, so we plan to discuss realigning some of the bishoprics here in Nicomedia. That would mean appointing several new bishops, and a few deacons and presbyters. It's a big proposition, but even if we decided to build a cathedral, we'd need to do it anyway.

"Some of the bishops of the smaller groups are afraid the larger groups are going to become too important if we don't do something to even out the sizes of the bishoprics."

He watched Irene stir the charcoal on the brazier and blow it into flame. "Of course, the bishops of the larger groups are fine with things the way they are. I suppose that in itself is a danger sign."

"How many bishoprics do we have?" Irene asked. "Each of

them has only one bishop, right?"

Andrew nodded. "We have eight bishops and each of them has his own bishopric. We really should have a dozen, so this will take some major overhauling of bishopric boundaries.

"If we aren't careful," he continued, "we will end up with bishops ruling other bishops. We feel that a bishop with a large bishopric shouldn't be more important than a bishop with a smaller one. Nor should it give him more power in the church."[3]

As he expected, it was late when Andrew returned from his meeting. Mark slept in a corner of the main living area. He woke up enough to see that his mother had lit a candle and was making some calda for his father. But he went back to sleep long before his parents went to bed.

"So how was your meeting?" Irene asked quietly as she sat at the table across from Andrew.

Andrew yawned before replying. "Well, it had its ups and its downs. Bishop Dorotheus tried hard to shoot down the whole idea of restructuring the bishoprics, but most of the group took that as proof for the need of it. He backed down eventually. I suppose he will push to build a cathedral in hopes he can be the lead bishop there."

"Do you think the plan to build a cathedral will go through?"

---

[3] At this time, no bishop was known as the Pope. The Roman church, however, was considered by at least some to have a "more powerful pre-eminence [than any] other church." (Iranaeus, *Against All Heresies,* 180 A.D.) This made the bishop in Rome the most powerful in the church from a practical perspective.

COUNTDOWN

Irene asked dubiously. "That will take a lot of money. Shouldn't we be using that money to help the poor?"

Andrew shrugged. "It looks like it's going to go ahead. Bishop Anthimus feels as you do, but he's too humble to fight for his opinions."

"He's my favorite bishop in Nicomedia," Irene said as she refilled their mugs with hot calda. "If we do build a cathedral, I hope he is the bishop placed in charge."

Andrew took a drink of calda. "I think I'd agree with you," he conceded. "But several of the other bishops won't. And they have a group of deacons on their side. It'll be a hard-fought decision, but I doubt Anthimus will come out on top."

"Where will you put a cathedral if you build one?" Irene asked as she put away their mugs and the calda urn. "Do you need to keep it kind of hidden?"

Andrew made a face. "One of our converts has offered us some land," he said. "It's on a knoll overlooking Diocletian's palace. So, no, it won't be hidden. Diocletian will see it every time he goes out his front door."

——— **DIOCLETIAN** ———

"I have decided to appoint Maximian to be Caesar[4] of the western part of the empire," Diocletian said after calling the meeting of his war council to order. "We will divide the armies, and he will take charge of Carinus' troops."

No one, not even Hiram and Afranius, had known of

---

[4] Diocletian had the title of Augustus, which meant that at this point he was still superior in rank to Maximian.

Diocletian's plans, but all of them knew Maximian. He was an aggressive military man, and he and Diocletian had both fought in Carus's campaign in Persia.

Diocletian continued. "This is no slam against Melinias. I will need him as my personal general, since I have to spend most of my time on administrative duties rather than running the military."

Diocletian looked at Hiram. "You can arrange for the ceremonies. I'd like to appoint Maximian next week." He turned to Afranius. "You can also help take care of things."

Later Hiram and Afranius discussed it further. "I wonder if Maximian knew of this before the meeting," Afranius commented.

"Or if Melinias did," Hiram added. "He's the one I would worry about. He could easily have thought he himself would be the one to receive the appointment."

"Diocletian and Maximian have been fellow officers and friends for a long time," Afranius said. "I wonder if they had this planned all along."

"Stranger things have happened before," Hiram replied. "It could be Diocletian's way of making sure Maximian stays out of the way as he consolidates his power."

Afranius shrugged. "We'll probably never know. I'm sure neither Diocletian nor Maximian will be telling us anything about it."

It was a beautiful day a week later when Maximian was appointed Caesar. In many ways it reminded Diocletian of the day only nine months earlier when he had been appointed Augustus. *A lot has happened since then. Things are moving along. I'll have to be careful not to push too fast, but this will be another memorable day in history.*

Diocletian's mind wandered during the ceremony. *I'll wait a year or so and see how Maximian does. If things go well, I'll promote him to Augustus and start preparing for the next phase of my plan. Once the empire is stabilized, I can move on to taxation and the money system.*

His mind jerked back to reality as the high priest of Apollo finished the coronation ceremony and the soldiers cheered. They followed with the crashing Roman salute, the soldiers drawing their swords and slamming them against their metal shields—once, twice, and then a third time.

Maximian acknowledged the salute by flinging his head back and raising his sword to the sky. "I am Caesar!" he bellowed.

"You are Caesar!" the ranks of soldiers echoed. Then once again they cheered.

Diocletian smiled. *He sure knows how to appeal to the rank and file. That's one value of taking a Caesar from the ranks of the common people.*

Maximian's greatest strength was his military expertise. He loved to fight, and leading Rome's armies into battle as a Caesar was his dream come true. His first assignment was to head for the Rhine frontier to fight the Germanic tribes who were invading Roman territory.

Diocletian was happy that Maximian was willing to take

over this part of his duties. He wanted to get on with reforming the Roman Empire. He dreamed of leaving a reformed empire as his legacy to future emperors.

Maximian had hardly vanished over the western horizon when Diocletian called Hiram and Afranius into the tent that served as both his field office and sleeping quarters. "I need to travel to Italy and restructure the imperial government there," he announced. "I'd like to draw up a listing of consuls and appoint a new prefect. Probably most of Carinus' officials can stay in place."

Hiram and Afranius glanced at each other, and Diocletian noticed it. "I know this is unusual," he added. "But they were loyal despite his actions, and I don't think it necessary to punish them just because they happened to be working for the wrong person."

"Are you going to visit Rome and have the Senate ratify your appointment as emperor?" Afranius asked. Earlier emperors had considered this an important step, but of late the Senate had been pushed into the background.

Diocletian dismissed the idea. "No, I don't consider the Senate to have any authority over the emperorship. I may use some senators to fill positions in my government, but only if they have experience or expertise that will make them useful."

He straightened and squared his shoulders. "Besides, I don't have time to go all the way to Rome. I want to be back in Nicomedia for the winter."

He started to gather his scattered notes. "I want to set up Nicomedia as the administrative capital of the east. That will mean a lot of work for both of you."

November 285

With the emperor and his army out of town, it seemed like an ideal time for the Christians to begin work on the new cathedral. Some were uneasy, however. Should they really build it right beside the emperor's palace?

Although Diocletian was impatient to get back to Nicomedia for the winter, early November still found him almost 400 miles west of the Margus River—a thousand miles from Nicomedia.

He was sitting at his desk one day, working with Hiram, when Afranius entered his tent. The interruption irritated Diocletian.

"What's wrong now?" he growled. "Make it fast. I've got work to do."

Afranius saluted stiffly. "Sorry, sir, but a group of Sarmatians is here to see you. Their tribes have been driven off their ancestral land by enemies, and they want you to help them get it back."

He hesitated, gauging the emperor's response. "Either that, or they want pasture rights on this side of the Danube, in Roman territory."

Diocletian frowned. "Were they as demanding as you make it sound? Who do they think they are, ordering us around like that?"

"It was even worse than that," Afranius replied. "They demanded an immediate audience with you and wouldn't take no for an answer."

Diocletian looked up, startled. "Where are they? Are they—"

"They are right outside the door," Afranius interrupted. "Only the presence of six guards kept them from walking right in with me."

Diocletian's brow furrowed. "Send them on their way!" he exploded. "They need to learn to respect their betters. The Roman army can't be expected to settle every little upheaval among the barbarian tribes beyond our borders."

Afranius bowed and left the tent. Understandably, the Sarmatian delegation wasn't happy with his news, and the guards ended up forcibly removing them from the camp. A week later Roman scouts brought news that the barbarians had taken things into their own hands and were trying to annex pasturelands south of the Danube River.

Diocletian was furious at this interruption to his carefully planned schedule. He called his war council together immediately. "Melinias," he barked, "I want those Sarmatians driven back over the Danube River."

He glared at the general, as if the situation were Melinias' personal problem. "And I want it done quickly. I've got too much to do to spend a lot of time on them."

The general nodded respectfully. "Yes, sir, we can do that. It'll take us several days to get ready, and a week or so to chase them back." He hesitated. "Well, it would take longer than that to do it properly, but if you're in a hurry we can teach them a lesson and leave it at that for now. We may need to come back and do it right sometime down the road."

"That's fine," Diocletian agreed. "We don't have time for a full-scale invasion. But they are not going to get away with snubbing their noses at us."

He dismissed the council brusquely. "Do what it takes. I want to be in Nicomedia within a month."

———— MARK ————

Andrew left for work early that morning. "I've got some things that need to be done," he told Irene. "We have a deacons' meeting this afternoon to finalize the plans for the new cathedral."

Irene looked up in surprise. "Are you going ahead this fall already? What's the hurry?"

Andrew grimaced. "Well, we heard that Diocletian is returning to Nicomedia for the winter, and some of the bishops felt it would be better to have the work started before he arrives. That way it will be harder for him to stop it."

"Are they afraid he'll stop it?" Irene asked. "Wouldn't it be better to get his permission?"

"Several of the bishops feel that would be like asking the

devil for permission to do God's work," Andrew replied. "So we decided to go ahead."

"I hope we aren't asking for persecution," Irene said. "I still wonder if we really need a cathedral."

"We've been through all this before," Andrew said. "Nicomedia has the largest Christian community in the whole Roman Empire. We should acknowledge that in some way."

Irene still looked uneasy. "Well, I guess we can't do anything about it," she finally acknowledged. "I just wish we had a better spot for it. To build it right at the emperor's front door is like poking a finger in his eye and expecting him to approve of it."

Andrew knew she was right, but he was tired of her bringing up the subject. Besides, he had said all he could. He was already being blamed for holding back the Lord's work.

"A few of the deacons agree with you," he admitted reluctantly. "And Bishop Anthimus does too. But most of them want to go ahead."

Work on the cathedral soon got underway. It was an ambitious project and would take years to finish.[1] To Irene's consternation, Andrew was appointed as the main construction supervisor.

"Will you be paid for this?" she asked.

Andrew nodded. "I'll get my usual wage. The people I work

---

[1] As far as cathedrals went, this was a minor one. Many of the major cathedrals of later centuries took nearly a century to complete. However, at this time in history, it was unheard of for a Christian building.

COUNTDOWN

for are actually being hired for the job, with the understanding that I can work on the cathedral as needed. They will get paid for the time I need to take off from my other work. They are fine with that."

"It will add to their reputation as well," Irene said. "I suppose they don't mind that, even though they aren't Christians."

"That's true," Andrew said as he got to his feet. "It's also a good opportunity for me. It might open the door for other possibilities."

Mark was just as pleased this morning as his father was, but not for the same reason. He had finally managed to work his way through the writings of Homer and was ready to start working on Virgil and some of the other Latin poets. Irene had promised that he could drop his Greek studies and mainly focus on Latin for a year or so.

"But then I want you to study Greek some more," she told him. "By then you will be old enough to work on the New Testament writings. I'd like for you to do some comparative studies between the Latin and Greek versions of the Holy Writings[2] so you can see the value of knowing both languages. Some of Paul's epistles are good for that."

She smiled at Mark's gloomy look. "Don't worry, there will be other things to do as well," she said. "I'm sure your father

---

[2] The New Testament did not exist as a separate compilation at the time. Because of this, the various books and epistles are called the Holy Writings in this book. Mark's home was unusual in that he grew up with access to these writings. Andrew, as deacon, was custodian of the church's collection of Holy Writings.

will want to teach you how to do some of his work too. But I want you to have a working knowledge of the Holy Writings in both Greek and Latin before you leave home."

They had discussed this before, and Mark knew his mother felt strongly about it. She was disappointed at the lack of interest in intellectual pursuits in the Christian community. Her parents had promoted the study of Greek and Latin during her childhood, and passing this on to Mark was one way she tried to honor her parents, even though they had been pagans.

Lydia still came over several days a week to continue her studies, mostly Latin and numbers. Despite her secret desire to surpass Mark in their studies, she soon realized she might as well forget about that idea, since she had started several years after he did.

———— DIOCLETIAN ————

Still stuck in his camp, Diocletian waited impatiently for Melinias and the army to teach the Sarmatians their lesson. "If they don't return soon, it'll be the end of the year before we reach Nicomedia," he told Afranius. "Winter will soon be here, and we'll be walking in mud."

The army did return several days later. "Are you sure you thoroughly defeated them so they won't return?" Diocletian asked.

"I think they'll think twice before they challenge us again," Melinias replied. "We gave them a rough time and chased them back across the border."

Diocletian looked unimpressed. "That's all you did? I hope it was enough. They'll probably soon come sneaking back."

Diocletian decided to allow everyone a few days to rest before beginning the long march back to Nicomedia. This gave Hiram and Afranius time to implement some of the procedures that Diocletian wanted in place for his stay in Nicomedia.

Every day people came to see him, and each of the visitors had "important" business. It often seemed unnecessary to Diocletian. "Many of these legal questions have been answered many times before," he barked at Hiram as he paced back and forth in his field office. "Make sure you record all our decisions so people can go back to the records. We shouldn't need to decide the answers all over again."

He paused in his walking. "In fact," he said slowly, "once we're settled in Nicomedia and things are running more smoothly, I'm going to assign some people to collect the rulings of past emperors and compile them into an official book of laws."

Hiram was struck by his genius. "I wonder why no one has thought of that before!" he said excitedly. "We are always trying to figure out how questions of law were answered in the past. It would be tremendously helpful to have such a compilation."

Diocletian nodded, pleased at Hiram's response. "Start on it as you have time. See what you can come up with, and I'll get you some helpers once we get settled."[3]

The next day they packed up and started the march to Nicomedia. Diocletian, his guards, and a detachment of cavalry headed out first. Diocletian hadn't seen his family for a year, so he was eager to get back. It would be a fast ride, so they left Hiram behind to travel with the army. As Diocletian

---

[3] Diocletian authorized a compilation of all official edicts and announcements made by previous emperors, going as far back as Emperor Hadrian, who reigned from A.D. 117-138.

New Ideas: November 285

told Afranius, "We can't be stopping every half hour to pick him up and put him back on his horse."

Afranius and Hiram were good friends, but this time Afranius agreed with Diocletian. He too had a wife and family back in Nicomedia waiting for him.

——— MARK ———

Andrew was at the church building site three weeks later when Diocletian arrived. His first inkling that something unusual was afoot came when a detachment of the Praetorian Guard marched through the square. They then mounted horses and rode out through the main gates leading to the Roman road north of the city.

"Must be something special going on," Andrew remarked to several workmen.

Marcellus, the crew foreman, straightened his back and wiped sweat drops from his forehead. The day was cool, but the work was backbreaking. Earlier they had dug a trench around the leveled building site and were now positioning large rocks into the trench. These would become the foundation for the new building.

Four hours later, after the city gates had already been closed for the night, the workers suddenly saw the keepers pull them wide open again. A group of men on horses swept through and pulled up at the palace gates, which were closed as well. Twenty heavily armed guards escorted the group.

The men at the building site stopped their work and watched. "That's the emperor, isn't it?" Marcellus asked. "It doesn't look as if they were expecting him tonight."

The horses pulled impatiently at their bits. "They've had a hard ride," Andrew noted. "Look at the sweat dripping from them. They were in a hurry to get here."

"They're still pretty frisky," Marcellus said. "But I guess the emperor would have access to the best horses in the empire."

The praetorian prefect rode up to the gate and called for the guards while Diocletian and the others waited. A few minutes later, the gates swung open and the horses surged through.

That evening Andrew told Irene, Mark, and Lydia all about it. Irene dished up supper while Andrew started his story. "They rode in just before dark, maybe an hour ago," he said. "They were all riding fast horses that had been running hard. Most of the horses were dripping sweat, and you know how chilly the wind was today. I hope someone cooled them down properly and dried them off."

Andrew pulled his stool to the table, and they bowed their heads while he gave thanks. Then he continued. "I don't think anyone was expecting them, because the palace gates were shut already. There was a lot of excitement when the people in the palace realized who they were." He grinned. "They swung the gates open in a hurry. Diocletian led the way in."

He ladled more soup into his wooden bowl. "Good soup," he said, smacking his lips. "Working outside makes me hungry."

"Did they have any prisoners?" Mark asked eagerly. "Were they in chains?"

Andrew shook his head. "If they have any prisoners, the

army will bring them later. I'm sure the main camp will arrive in a few days."

"I hope they don't have any executions," Irene said with a shudder. "Executions bring back so many bad memories for me."

Andrew and Irene talked more seriously after Mark went to bed. "It's too bad Diocletian has chosen Nicomedia for his capital," Andrew said. "That will make life here more stressful for all of us, I'm afraid."

Irene nodded. "I'm sorry for being so negative," she said haltingly. "But I'll never forget how the soldiers came to arrest my family. They killed them with their swords. My father was killed last . . . he was forced to watch as they killed my mother and younger sisters.

"Every executed person is part of someone's family," she added. "The government doesn't seem to care. And with Diocletian making this his capital, I'm sure more executions will take place here."

She brushed tears from her cheek. "I wish I could forget, but I can't. How long will it be until Christians are executed at the palace? Oh, I wish the bishops wouldn't have pushed ahead with building a new church right now."

Andrew didn't answer immediately because he knew she was right. Then he reached over and took her hand. "I guess we'll just have to take one day at a time," he said comfortingly. "For all we know, Diocletian won't last long. Or he might turn out to be sympathetic to Christianity. Or he might decide to move his capital somewhere else."

DIOCLETIAN

Diocletian wasn't an emotional person, but he was glad to see his wife and daughter. He dismissed most of his men so they could go home to their families. Prisca and Valeria had already eaten, so he just ate a quick supper beside the fireplace in his office. He found his mind going to all the work he had to do in the days ahead.

Prisca brought him a glass of wine, and Diocletian found himself relaxing. "I have a lot of work to do in the coming days," he said. "Do you know of anything that needs attention right away?"

"I think everything is under control," Prisca assured him. "Tomorrow I'd like to show you the finished renovations. I think the workers have a few questions, but they have gotten along very well. They should easily be finished before spring."

"Good," Diocletian replied. "I'm turning Nicomedia into the capital for the eastern part of the empire, so we need to be able to handle all the people that will involve. We will also need more clerks to look after things."

"I think you'll like what they have done," Prisca said. "The business wing of the palace is finished, so your secretary and the prefect can move in right away. There's also room for extra clerks and an open area outside the walls where people can set up camp while they wait."

Diocletian was pleased. Work came first for him, and he could hardly wait to see how everything was progressing. But for now, it would wait until morning.

It was good to be home.

PART III

A.D. 286-287

Can Emperors Be Gods?

What was the character of his brother in empire, Maximian, called Herculius? Not unlike to that of Diocletian; and, indeed, to render their friendship so close and faithful as it was, there must have been in them a sameness of inclinations and purposes, a corresponding will and unanimity in judgment. Herein alone they were different, that Diocletian was more avaricious and less resolute, and that Maximian, with less avarice, had a bolder spirit, prone not to good, but to evil. For while he possessed Italy, itself the chief seat of empire, and while other very opulent provinces, such as Africa and Spain, were near at hand, he took little care to preserve those treasures which he had such fair opportunities of amassing. Whenever he stood in need of more, the richest senators were presently charged, by suborned evidences, as guilty of aspiring to the empire; so that the chief luminaries of the senate were daily extinguished. And thus the treasury, delighting in blood, overflowed with ill-gotten wealth.

Lactantius, *Of the Manner in Which the Persecutors Died,* Chap. 8

A.D. 286

Diocletian wasn't satisfied to be only an average emperor—he wanted to be a great one. He wanted to truly revitalize the empire. After returning to Nicomedia, he plowed ahead with his plans. It was then that he first became aware of the building project on the hill . . .

The palace schedule fell into place quickly. By sunrise every morning, Diocletian was in his office. Hiram and Afranius met him there for a quick meeting to start the day. They discussed important news and upcoming business.

Diocletian did not like people to spring things on him without warning. Because of this, administrative items went to Afranius first. He took care of Diocletian's schedule and made sure Hiram was regularly updated so he could prepare Diocletian for any upcoming problems. Afranius had access to all the empire's records except the ones under the control of the Roman Senate.

Diocletian soon saw that Afranius was overworked. "Afranius, you need more help," he said. "I'm going to appoint several more prefects to help in the administration here. Do you have any suggestions?"

Afranius had already discussed this with Hiram. "How about Aurelius?" he suggested. "He has a lot of legal knowledge and experience. He could help both Hiram and me.

"And Julius has served under several emperors as well," he continued. "Both he and Aurelius would be a lot of help."

Diocletian listened carefully. He knew the men Afranius had suggested. He turned to Hiram. "Draft letters to both of them and ask them to come to Nicomedia. Tell them we need them here by early spring."

It was several months later when Diocletian first heard about the building project on the hill across from the palace. He should have noticed it earlier, but he had been preoccupied with other things.

"What's that project across the valley?" Melinias asked Diocletian and Afranius one day. "Someone seems to be getting ready to put up a large building."

Diocletian frowned. "Hmm. I guess I did notice some action over there a while ago, but I didn't give it much thought."

He turned to Afranius. "Do you know anything about it?"

Afranius nodded reluctantly. "I checked it out earlier."

Diocletian raised his eyebrows. "So what is going on?"

"The Christians are building a new temple, or meetinghouse, as they would call it," Afranius replied. "I'm not sure why they decided to put it there rather than at the other end of the city. They must feel secure about their position in Nicomedia."

"How large is the Christian presence in Nicomedia?" Diocletian asked. "They must have some money to take on a project of that size."

"Yes, there are almost as many Christians as pagans in Nicomedia," Afranius replied. "It's one of the largest Christian communities in the empire."

The emperor's frown deepened. "I thought most Christians were beggars and poor tradesmen. "Where do they get this kind of money?"

Hiram and Afranius glanced at each other uneasily. "Many upper-class people have joined the group over the last twenty or thirty years," Afranius said. "I suppose they are the ones who want a nicer temple or meeting place. I'm sure money is no problem."

Diocletian was startled. "So," he said, weighing his words carefully, "is this a danger to the empire that we need to be considering?" He eyed Afranius. "And why are you so reluctant to talk about this?"

Afranius took a deep breath. "It is estimated that ten percent of the empire's population is Christian," he tried to explain. "They are an important part of Rome. But here in Nicomedia it is closer to forty percent. They are actually quite important to the economy of the city."

He waved his hand in the direction of the project across the valley. "That building will be one of the most elaborate ones in Nicomedia when it is finished. It is actually being built by a group of pagan businessmen who will make a lot of money on it."

Diocletian sat back. "Why are Christians using pagans to build their temple?" He was obviously perplexed.

Afranius shrugged his shoulders. "I'm not sure. But I understand part of the agreement stipulated that they use Christian workers, which isn't a problem. A lot of their work force is Christian anyway.

"A Christian deacon is in charge of the project," he added.

"But . . ." Diocletian paused for a moment. "Aren't people who help the Christians afraid of what the gods will think?" As one who paid more attention to the gods than most Romans, Diocletian had trouble understanding what he was hearing.

Afranius took another deep breath. "Most people don't worry much about the gods," he said frankly. "Money is more important. I suspect that many people are willing to let the gods fight it out among themselves."

Since he had said this much already, he decided he might as well continue. "Anyway, most people know that the Christians are usually law-abiding people. They don't steal or lie, and they work hard."

Diocletian glared at him. "Are you a Christian, or something? I thought they worship an ass's head and drink the blood of infants in their worship. How can you stand here and support such people?"

Afranius stiffened. "Sir, I must protest," he said formally. "I know many Christians, and none of them practice such superstitious nonsense. I am not a Christian, but I have carefully investigated this group to make sure they are not a threat to the empire, or to you, my emperor."

He bowed. Silence descended on the room while the two men waited for the emperor's reaction.

Diocletian tapped his fingers on the tabletop. "All right," he said slowly. "I'll take your word for it, since you are one of my best advisors. But keep your eyes open. And if the Christians have so much money, maybe we need to relieve them of some of it.

"Anyway, you'd better be right about them," Diocletian concluded with a warning look. "Because no one is indispensable—especially if they give bad advice to the emperor."

———— MARK ————

Andrew saw them coming and met them at the edge of the site. "Can I help you?" he asked. He noted from their uniforms that both held a high rank in Diocletian's staff.

Melinias nodded in greeting. "I'm Melinias, general of the army. And this is Afranius, the head of the Praetorian Guard. We were curious about your building project. I heard that you are building a Christian temple here."

"That's right," Andrew replied. "We began the project last fall, but it will take a number of years to complete it."

Melinias glanced back at Diocletian's palace. "Do you have any particular reason for building here where you will overlook the palace? It doesn't seem like the kind of place Christians normally choose for a building."

"Well, one of our members donated the property," Andrew replied hesitantly. "It was the only big enough area available at the time for a building this size." He decided it would be best not to mention the other reasons.

Melinias nodded. "That makes sense, I suppose. A less prominent spot might have been a better idea, but that's your choice, not mine."

He glanced over the site, noting its size. "This is going to be a large building." He looked back at Diocletian's palace again thoughtfully. "Really large," he added. "Even larger than the palace, by the looks of it."

Andrew already knew this, but he didn't want to admit it. "We haven't measured the palace, but I don't think it will be much larger. We're not building it to draw attention."

"What kind of meetings will you have here?" Melinias asked curiously. "What kind of fixtures and furniture do Christians need for their meetings? Do you have a statue of Christos?"

Andrew was unusually thoughtful when he came home that evening. Irene asked him the second time how his day had been before he noticed her question. Even then, he pulled off his muddy boots before answering.

"Melinias is back," he said. "He came over to see what we were doing."

Irene looked up from her work, wide-eyed. "What did he say? Did he seem antagonistic?"

"No, not really," Andrew replied, "but I do wonder what he

thought about it. He said he had heard that this would be the largest building ever built in Nicomedia. But he didn't seem overly concerned.

"He asked what kind of meetings we'll hold there, and what kind of images we'll set up. I told him we have an altar and candles, and some paintings of the Christos and other scenes from our Holy Writings.

"Mostly he seemed curious." Andrew sat down on his stool at the table. "But he did say it might have been wiser to put our building in a less conspicuous spot."

Irene's eyes widened. "Did you tell him you agreed with him?"

"No, I didn't," Andrew replied, "though I felt like it. He seemed like a decent man, but I hope he wasn't trying to warn us."

He walked across the room to where Mark and Lydia were practicing their elocution skills. He chuckled as Lydia intoned pompously, "What indeed has Athens to do with Jerusalem?" She looked for all the world like a haughty, self-righteous Pharisee, looking down her nose at Mark.

Not to be outdone, Mark read the next line just as arrogantly. "What concord is there between the Academy and the Church?"

Andrew smiled. "You have them reading Tertullian, do you?" he asked Irene. "Isn't that a bit of a stretch for them?"

"They don't understand all of it," Irene admitted. "But it is one of the best examples of Latin Christian rhetoric that I have ever read, and I want them to learn from good teachers."

DIOCLETIAN

Spring came early to Nicomedia that year, but Aurelius and Julius, the new administrative prefects, managed to report to work in good time. Diocletian, however, was getting restless.

"I've decided to promote Maximian to Augustus," he announced to his council in early March. "He's been doing well in the west, but he needs extra authority to help him deal with pirates and Gaulic bandits.

"I won't be able to go to Rome to oversee the ceremony myself, as I need to visit Syria and Palestine this spring. Instead, I'm going to send Julius." Turning to Julius, he continued, "I want that to take place in April, so you will need to leave as soon as possible."

Diocletian smiled briefly as he noted the surprised looks around the room. He liked to do this occasionally. An unexpected major decision kept the men around him informed that he, and he alone, had the final word. They could advise and criticize, but he was the one who made the final decision.

Melinias was the only one to comment. "Are the Jews making a problem again, that you have to visit Syria?"

Diocletian shook his head. "Not that I know of. But it's a good idea to remind them periodically who is in charge. They seem to forget too quickly."

That ended the official discussion, but Afranius and Julius talked it over as they prepared for Julius' trip to visit Maximian.

"There is more to this than meets the eye," Julius remarked as they entered his workroom. "Diocletian doesn't give away favors like this just to surprise his advisors."

Afranius nodded as he took a seat across the table from Julius. "Several messengers have come from the west recently," he said. "Maximian has been having some military problems, I think."

Julius looked puzzled. "What would promoting him to Augustus do to alleviate that? Maximian can have all the titles in the world, but it won't help him fight his battles."

Afranius nodded. "That's true, of course," he agreed. "But the military leader in charge of Britain and northern Gaul is making some noise. He's cooperating with Maximian at this point, and if they got their heads together they might be tempted to take the western part of the empire and divide it between themselves. I'm guessing this is a bribe to help Maximian remember the advantages of staying faithful to Diocletian.

"Anyway, keep your eyes open while you're there," Afranius concluded. "See what you can learn."

Diocletian left for Syria soon after Julius left for the west. Afranius and Melinias traveled with him, taking a full cohort[1] of cavalry for security. Aurelius, the other jurist prefect, stayed with Hiram to keep the administration in Nicomedia running. The main body of the army stayed behind as well, under the leadership of one of Melinias' lieutenants.

As the group traveled east, Diocletian's purposes became

---

[1] A Roman cohort had between 360 and 800 soldiers.

clearer. Every emperor kept Persia in the back of his mind, and Diocletian was no exception. Rome and Persia had been at war since before the time of Christ.[2]

The biggest battle had taken place about twenty-five years before Diocletian became emperor. Valerian the Elder, the emperor at that time, had been taken captive by the Persians during the Battle of Edessa—the first Roman emperor to ever suffer this indignity. He died in slavery, though no one knew exactly what happened to him.[3]

It wasn't often that a Roman emperor visited Antioch, and Diocletian received a royal welcome. Half the population lined the streets to watch the ceremonial entry to the city. The governor and Diocletian led the procession, followed by Melinias and Afranius, then the Roman cavalry guard. Local Roman legionaries marched two abreast on each side to keep the crowd from spilling onto the street.

It didn't take Diocletian long to get to business. "I'd like to inspect the eastern boundary," he told the governor that evening. "We have lots of soldiers tied up along the border, and I want to see how secure it really is."

The governor wasn't happy to see Diocletian taking that kind of risk. "We can do that," he said hesitantly. "But I wouldn't want any Persian band thinking they can do a rerun

---

[2] This war lasted almost 700 years and was one of the longest wars in history.

[3] After they killed him, they reportedly skinned him and stuffed him to keep as a souvenir.

of Valerian."

"I'm not worried about that," Diocletian replied dryly. "That's why I brought a whole cohort of cavalry along. If you don't think your troops can keep me safe, we'll show you how to do it."

The governor flushed. "I'm sure the danger isn't that great," he hastened to reply. "But I'd hate to be responsible for any accidents."

Diocletian shrugged. "I can be responsible for myself. We'll spend a few days here, for the sake of the local population, but then I want to head to the border."

Later that evening Diocletian met alone with Melinias and Afranius. "I'm hoping to meet with some Persian officials," he said. "I'll break the news to the governor when we get a little closer. I don't think he has the stomach for anything that seems dangerous.

"However, we won our last battle with the Persians, and we need to remind them about it before they forget."

A.D. 287

Were the emperors of Rome gods or men? Rome had long struggled with this question. Many of its leaders were deified after death, but were they also gods while they lived? Diocletian took religion more seriously than most Roman emperors, but it seemed the more he thought about it the more confused he became.

"Which of Rome's gods is the most important?" Diocletian asked during an early morning session. His chief advisors stared at him, the question dangling in midair.

When no one answered, Diocletian continued. "If you were choosing a patron god or goddess for yourself, which one would you choose? And don't tell me Christos. He's not an option."

Melinias spoke up first. "Mars," he said, not sounding too sure. "He's the god of war and would make a good god for a general, I suppose."

Afranius remembered the sacrifice Diocletian had ordered at the Margus River, before the battle that had removed the last obstacle for Diocletian's plan to rule the Roman Empire. "Jupiter, maybe?" It was just a guess, because no one knew what Diocletian was getting at.

Diocletian's lips tightened. "If this group here can't even decide which one is most important, it's no wonder so many of Rome's citizens ignore the gods—or even decide to worship an ass's head." He glared at the men around the table, as if daring them to defend his caricature of the Christian God.

When no one spoke, he continued. "I wonder what would happen if I declared myself a god?" Again his eyes dared them to respond. "After all, the Senate will deify me when I die, so why not while I'm still alive and can enjoy it?"

Afranius was getting tired of this charade. "I don't think I'd want to be a god," he said bravely. "Everyone would blame me for the bad weather, for the plague, and for anything else that went wrong in Rome. Someone would be bound to come along to see if it was really true—and put a dagger between my shoulder blades."

Instead of erupting in fury, Diocletian laughed and said, "You always were a cynic, Afranius. Remind me to not let you walk behind me if I ever proclaim myself a god.

"But you have proved my point," he continued, suddenly grave. "Romans do not take the gods seriously. One of these times the gods are going to decide they've had enough. They will give us a serious working over to remind us of their existence."

He leaned back on his chair. "I think it's time to remind

the gods that we are still here and that we still have some respect for them.

"And by the way, Jupiter is the most important god in Rome," he declared. "Have you forgotten that he is the king of all the gods? The Greeks called him Zeus, and even then he was the most important god. He is truly a man's god."

The tension lessened in the room and everyone breathed normally again.

"How about Hercules?" Julius asked. "I'd consider him a man's god too. Jupiter was his father, but his mother was human. Even Jupiter didn't do as many mighty deeds as Hercules did."

Diocletian looked at him strangely. "You're right," he said slowly. "I didn't think of Hercules. He is indeed a man's god."

He changed the subject abruptly. "Hiram, could you read to us that letter Maximian sent?"

——— MARK ———

Mark had just turned fourteen. He had read his way through most of the famous Latin writers as well as the Greek poets. He had memorized parts of Virgil and Homer and knew all about the heroic deeds of Odysseus and the Trojan horse. It was from this context that Mark got his favorite greeting for Lydia, "I fear Greeks, even those bearing gifts."

She in turn would roll her eyes and retort with a quote she had found in a Greek poem, "I've no mind to be a Caesar."

Then they would both laugh, though to an onlooker the quips were mystifying. The quotes quickly became a symbol of their growing rapport. Both Mark and Lydia were progressing well in their studies, but Irene wasn't satisfied to merely teach them classical literature. She wanted them to grow in spiritual understanding as well, so the Holy Writings, as well as the writings of Plato and Origen, became the major part of their studies.

DIOCLETIAN

"Can a man be a god?" Diocletian asked one morning several weeks later. "Or perhaps an earthly representation of a god?"

Hiram was the most philosophically inclined person on the advisor team, but even he had to think for a bit. "Could you enlarge on that idea?" he asked cautiously. "If I understand correctly, the Christian religion teaches that Christos was the Logos that Plato spoke about. I've heard that one of their Holy Writings calls Christos the Logos."

Diocletian frowned at this comparison but had to acknowledge its truth. "Well, perhaps a little like that," he admitted grudgingly. "Though I have no doubt that Christos was a fraud. I'm speaking about one of the real gods, like Jupiter."

Hiram was starting to glimpse what might be behind Diocletian's questions. "Well, I suppose a man could adopt a god as his patron god," he finally replied. "That might cause the god to pay special attention to him."

Diocletian eyed Hiram contemplatively. "What about a god adopting a man to represent him on earth? That would be even surer, wouldn't it?"

"Maybe," Hiram replied dubiously. "But how would you go

about persuading a god like Jupiter to adopt a human? How would you get his attention in the first place?"

Diocletian didn't seem to have an answer and changed the subject. But he brought it up again a few days later. "Maybe the Oracle of Delphi[1] could answer my question," he told Afranius and Hiram. "I feel like sending one of you to see what she says."

"Why are you so obsessed with this?" Afranius asked. "You will need to have a better question to ask the priestess than what you've been asking us."

Diocletian walked to the door and looked out across the courtyard. "I've been thinking that if Jupiter could adopt me as his son, and Hercules could adopt Maximian, it would draw the attention of the gods, as well as the Roman population."

Hiram and Afranius talked about it later. "He really seems obsessed by this idea," Hiram said. "Most people would just call themselves a son of Jupiter and be done with it, but he wants to make it official."

They entered Hiram's workroom and closed the door before Afranius answered. "I know," he said thoughtfully. "I wonder if the stories of Christos haven't influenced him more than he wants to admit."

Hiram glanced at the ceiling, then back at Afranius. "Maybe he wants to be a pagan version of the Christos. That would be an interesting twist on things. I could imagine Nero trying that, but I thought Diocletian had more sense."

"Well, Diocletian is just a man, no matter what he decides

[1] The Oracle of Delphi was a priestess at the temple of Apollo who answered questions brought to Apollo. Diocletian asked the Oracle for advice later in his reign, and she ruled against the Christians.

to claim," Afranius replied. "I've been around him long enough to know he's no god.

"And he never will be a god," he added. "This habit of deifying emperors after they die is just a way of making people feel good."

One morning Diocletian made an announcement. "I am taking a new title. Along with my other titles, I will now also be known as Jovius, the son of Jupiter."

Almost as an afterthought, he added, "And Maximian will receive the title Herculius, the son of Hercules."

He turned to Hiram. "Please prepare the necessary public announcements."

—————— MARK ——————

After the usual small talk about the cathedral building project, Andrew casually dropped a bombshell into the middle of their supper table conversation.

"Well, our emperor has promoted himself," he announced. "I saw a notice today that Diocletian has taken the title of Jovius, the son of Jupiter."

Irene almost dropped the pot of lentil soup she had just lifted from her charcoal stove. "He has made himself a god?" she asked, shocked. "Why, that means he is an antichrist."

Andrew sat back and looked at her quizzically. "What are you talking about?"

Irene set down her bowl and walked over to the little closet where they kept their library of scrolls and papyrus books. She picked up one and opened it. "Listen to this," she said when she had found what she was looking for. "Let no man deceive you by any means: for that day shall not come, except there come a falling away first, and that man of sin be revealed, the son of perdition; who opposeth and exalteth himself above all that is called God, or that is worshipped; so that he as God sitteth in the temple of God, shewing himself that he is God."[2]

She closed the book carefully and put it back on the shelf. "That is from the writings of Paul to the Thessalonians. I have had a strange feeling about Diocletian from the very start."

Mark could see that his father hardly knew what to say. Even though he was a deacon in the church, he was less knowledgeable of the Scriptures than his wife. Building a cathedral was more natural for him than holding his end in a spiritual discussion.

Mark was more like his mother. "Why did you call him an antichrist?" he asked.

Irene sat down at the table across from Andrew and waited until he had said a simple grace before she replied. "The Apostle John wrote about antichrists. When a ruler starts to consider himself a god, it is always a danger sign for God's people."

Andrew stirred uneasily. "There was more to the announcement," he admitted. "Maximian is now entitled Herculius, the son of Hercules. So how does that fit into your idea?"

This stopped Irene for a bit, and she was deep in thought for the rest of the meal. But after supper she came back to the subject. "Have you ever read the Revelation?" she asked Andrew.

Andrew shook his head. "I prefer the Gospels. They are more

---

[2] 2 Thessalonians 2:3, 4

practical, and I'm a practical person."

Irene smiled. "Well, it's probably good that one of us is practical. I tend to get carried away with ideas. The Revelation talks about two beasts who will set themselves up against God's people."[3]

Andrew cocked his head. "I'll leave that to you to figure out. One of the bishops was talking about the Revelation recently, and he wasn't sure that it is one of the inspired books."

Irene nodded. "I know that some in the church question it, along with a few other books, like the letter to the Hebrews and Peter's second letter. But I think they are from God. I've been blessed by them."

Irene brought up the subject again a week or two later. "I wonder if this is Diocletian's way of trying to bridge the gap between pagans and Christians," she told Andrew and Mark.

"Where did you get that idea?" Andrew asked.

Irene smiled. "You never were a pagan, so it might not hit you like it does me. But tell me, what do you know about Hercules?"

Andrew looked at her oddly. "Not a lot, really," he said. "If I recall correctly, Jupiter was said to be his father."

"And who was his mother?" Irene asked.

Andrew stiffened as he caught where she was going. "Wasn't she the betrothed wife of someone?"

Irene nodded. "Hercules was the son of Jupiter, called the greatest of the gods, and his mother was a human. She was betrothed to a husband but not yet married." To make her meaning clear, she added, "In the same way, Christos was the

---

[3] Revelation 13

son of the only true God, and his mother Mary was human.

"Diocletian is calling attention to this parallel," she said. "Do you suppose he really feels that this will heal the schism between the Christians and the pagans?"

Andrew grimaced. "If he does, he is badly mistaken. The differences between Christos and Hercules are so vast that no one acquainted with both would ever accept the parallel.

"And in the old myths Jupiter was as great a sinner as the worst of men," he added. "No Christian would ever accept him as a parallel of the true God."

Several days later Lydia seemed troubled. "My mother is sick," she told Irene and Mark. "I'll have to stop coming for lessons."

Irene looked up from her sewing. "I'm sorry to hear that," she said gently. "But your mother comes first. You have done well with your schooling. And even if you have to stop now, you have a good start for life."

Lydia sat down and watched Irene work for a few minutes. "I'm really glad for what I've learned," she said. "Especially the studies you've given me from the Holy Writings. It has made Christos and the church much more real to me."

Irene smiled at her. "That is one of the blessings of education," she said softly. "I hope you never get tired of learning from the writings."

Lydia smiled and replied wistfully, "I wish I could have my own copies of some of the books, but that isn't likely to ever happen."

"We don't have nearly all of them either," Irene said. "A

number of these are copies that belong to the church and are stored here for safekeeping.

"We'll miss you, Lydia," Irene added, giving her a parting hug. "I've enjoyed having another lady in the house."

Several days later Lydia tapped on their door again. "My mother died this morning," she said brokenly. A tear ran down her cheek and dropped from her chin.

Irene drew her close in a comforting hug. "Do you need help to get her ready for burial?"

Lydia shook her head. "My brothers and their wives are looking after it. I just wanted to let you know. We'll bury her later this afternoon. One of the bishops is coming to take care of the ceremony."

With Lydia no longer coming to their house, both Irene and Mark realized how much they had enjoyed having her there.

Several months later, Lydia's father Hamas died as well. He had been ailing for some time and also never recovered from the loss of his wife. Lydia moved in with her brother and his family for the time being.

PART IV

A.D. 293

Dividing the Empire

While Diocletian, that author of ill, and deviser of misery, was ruining all things, he could not withhold his insults, not even against God. This man, by avarice partly, and partly by timid counsels, overturned the Roman Empire. For he made choice of three persons to share the government with him; and thus, the empire having been quartered, armies were multiplied, and each of the four princes strove to maintain a much more considerable military force than any sole emperor had done in times past. There began to be fewer men who paid taxes than there were who received wages; so that the means of the husbandmen being exhausted by enormous impositions, the farms were abandoned, cultivated grounds became woodland, and universal dismay prevailed. Besides, the provinces were divided into minute portions, and many presidents and a multitude of inferior officers lay heavy on each territory, and almost on each city. There were also many stewards of different degrees, and deputies of presidents. Very few civil causes came before them: but there were condemnations daily, and forfeitures frequently inflicted; taxes on numberless commodities, and those not only often repeated, but perpetual, and, in exacting them, intolerable wrongs.

—Lactantius, *Of the Manner in Which the Persecutors Died,* Chap. 7

A.D. 293

Diocletian had managed to stay in power for nine years now, longer than most Roman emperors. But it was no time to relax. In his quest to consolidate power, he cared little how it affected the lives of others. No one was exempt—not even his own family.

Diocletian was up to his armpits in work, and he was getting tired of it. He needed help, and he needed it now. In his last meeting with Maximian, the two emperors had agreed on the need to appoint Caesars to lighten the load. Now, with his heavy work schedule, Diocletian realized it was time to do it.

There was just one problem: It meant he would have to talk to his wife and daughter . . .

Diocletian needed to bind his chosen assistant to himself

with the closest alliance possible. Since he had no son to appoint, his daughter Valeria would have to marry the man he chose. Somehow he would need to get the cooperation of both Prisca and Valeria.

It never entered Diocletian's mind that his daughter might try to refuse. Roman women were used to obeying their men, for better or worse. He thought of the eighteen years he and Prisca had been married. This was unusual, for most emperors had a succession of wives, or even several at a time.

He smiled as he thought of Prisca. She was a soldier's dream come true when he married her. Dark-haired and slender, with soft dark eyes, a ready smile, and a sweet temperament. What more could a man want? And the years had been good to her—she was still as pretty as she had ever been. Most people would have taken her as being fifteen years younger than he was. He realized with a start that he wasn't even sure how old his wife was. He had never asked her, but he would have guessed her at about fifteen or sixteen when they had gotten married.

His mind wandered to his daughter, and he wondered for the first time how she would feel being married off as a political pawn. But surely she had been expecting it. Any daughter of an emperor knew she would marry someone her father needed an alliance with. Galerius was old enough to be her father, but it couldn't be helped. At least she wasn't being asked to marry some foreign king a thousand miles away.

He shrugged. He might as well get it over with.

COUNTDOWN

It took a special woman to be an emperor's wife and stay married to him. Emperors were notorious for cheating on their wives and replacing them as they tired of them. Prisca had been married to Diocletian long enough to give him a seventeen-year-old daughter, and she was still the most important woman in his life. But most Roman women expected certain indiscretions on the part of their husbands, and in that Diocletian was no exception. Prisca was grateful that he was careful about his indiscretions and didn't involve his wife and daughter in them as some emperors had done.

Prisca did not try to assert herself and manipulate Diocletian. She quietly submitted to his ideas and did what she could to keep him happy. She did not grumble when he spent months at a time away on business or when business disrupted his home life, as it often did. She had long ago learned that Diocletian usually worked in his office until late in the evening and often didn't retire until after midnight.

So when her husband unexpectedly showed up early in their living quarters that evening, Prisca knew something was afoot. She had been expecting a meeting like this at some point, but that didn't mean she was ready for it. She had also tried to prepare her daughter for the inevitable but hadn't succeeded.

———— MARK ————

Mark had grown from childhood to manhood during the past five years. He had finished his formal education and was employed full-time for the men his father worked for. He had also taken on various responsibilities at church. As a result of Irene's efforts, he was one of the best educated Christians in Nicomedia.

The new cathedral was about halfway finished and was one of the up-and-coming projects in town. There had been no more feedback from Diocletian or his officials. But what would happen when it was completed?

Irene had prepared a simple supper. It was a quiet meal. Andrew remarked that Diocletian had returned that afternoon, and Mark commented on the weather. Irene talked a bit about the high prices at the marketplace, but mostly they kept their thoughts to themselves. Mark seemed especially preoccupied, and Irene glanced at him quizzically several times during the meal.

After the meal, Mark pushed back his empty bowl and stretched. He seemed to have reached a decision. "I am thinking it's about time for me to get married," he announced.

Irene and Andrew looked at each other, wordlessly inviting the other to respond. As usual, Irene spoke first. "Do you have someone in mind?" she asked cautiously. "And what made you decide this so suddenly?"

"Well, it isn't really suddenly," Mark replied with a smile. "I've been thinking about it for a while. But . . . I met Lydia today . . . at the market.

"I went back to the warehouse to get a tool and met up with her on the street. We got to talking. I've seen her at church meetings occasionally, but I don't think we've talked for three or four years."

Andrew chuckled. "I can guess what you said to her."

Irene and Mark looked at each other and chanted in unison.

"I fear Greeks, even those bearing gifts."

They all laughed, and Mark continued, "And she said, 'I've no mind to be a Caesar.' She's still the same Lydia." He lapsed into silence.

Andrew spoke first this time. "I always figured your friendship would lead to this someday. And unless she's changed a lot, I have no problem with it. Where is she living?"

"She's staying at her brother's house," Mark said. "She's a caretaker and teacher for their children."

Andrew glanced at Irene. "I should look up her brother and speak to him about it, I guess. Her father isn't living, so her brother would be next in line, I suppose."

Irene nodded. "I always liked Lydia. She was like the daughter I never had."

——— DIOCLETIAN ———

The discussion at the palace did not go quite so smoothly.

The servants had cleared away the food, and Diocletian and his family were gathered around the fireplace in the cozy sitting room drinking their after-dinner wine.

"Did your travels go well?" Prisca asked. "I suppose you attended many meetings and fancy dinners."

Diocletian nodded. "Too many. Maximian seemed determined to show me how civilized Milan is compared to Nicomedia."

He turned his eyes on the flickering flames in the fireplace. Now that he was home, he was finding it harder to settle his daughter's fate than he had expected.

Valeria tossed her head. "Did you bring us any gifts?" she

asked artlessly. "You know that women like to be remembered and rewarded for their patience in staying at home while the men roam the countryside."

Prisca smiled. "Men tend to forget their women as soon as they walk out the door," she told her daughter. "Don't get your hopes too high."

Diocletian was a bit nonplussed. He hadn't even thought of bringing gifts. Too late he realized that a bit of jewelry or some fancy clothing might have made his announcement easier.

"I was quite busy," he replied lamely. "I didn't go away to sightsee."

Valeria hadn't expected a positive response. Her father spent very little time with them, and she hadn't missed him any more than he had missed her while he was gone. She took another sip of wine and wondered how soon she could excuse herself without being impolite.

Diocletian had already forgotten her question. "Maximian and I discussed our plans for the future of the Roman Empire," he began. "We are taking steps to appoint several Caesars to be junior emperors."

Prisca took a deep breath and set down her wine glass.

So *that* was why they had been favored with Diocletian's presence this evening.

Diocletian drained his glass before continuing. "I'm planning to appoint Galerius as my assistant. He's a good soldier and an ambitious leader."

Valeria yawned. Prisca looked at her sharply. She wasn't catching on at all. Her father was talking about her future husband—and she was totally in the dark.

Diocletian looked relieved. Maybe this wouldn't be as bad as he had feared. Valeria seemed to be taking his announcement well. "We've got some time, and Galerius has some personal affairs to look after," he continued. "Do you think next spring would work for the wedding?"

"Wedding?" Valeria asked. "What are you talking about? What does Galerius' wedding have to do with us?"

Diocletian looked startled. "Why, why . . . *your* wedding," he stammered. "Surely you knew this was going to happen someday."

Valeria's face reddened as his intent dawned. "You sit here and announce my wedding as if it were just another business deal!" she exploded. "Do you think I'm going to marry some soldier friend of yours just so you can appoint him Caesar?"

Her outburst was beyond Diocletian's comprehension. He looked at Prisca but soon realized he wasn't going to get any help from her. "Well, I assumed you were expecting this," he said, looking back at Valeria. "You're an emperor's daughter, and this is part of your family duty."

If looks could kill, Diocletian would have been floundering on the floor. Valeria's eyes blazed fire as she glared at him. "Did it ever occur to you that I might want to have some say about this?" she asked coldly.

"Did it ever occur to you that I am your father and also the emperor of Rome?" Diocletian retorted, refilling his empty wine glass. "This is not open to negotiation or discussion. It is going to happen. I'm just asking when would be a good time."

This was real. Her father had signed away her life to some stranger, and there was nothing—absolutely nothing—she could do about it.

Valeria sat quietly for a moment, then asked in a small voice, "How old is this man, and what kind of person is he?"

Diocletian relaxed. The worst was over. "He's probably about forty," he told her. "He'll make you a good husband. Anyway, if he doesn't, he'll be too busy to be home enough for it to matter."

Valeria's eyes glittered. "That's old enough to be my father!" she exclaimed. "Why isn't he married already?"

Diocletian looked at her. How naive was his daughter anyway? "He is married. He'll need to divorce his wife. That's part of the deal."

Prisca stirred but didn't speak. This was news to her as well, but neither she nor Valeria would benefit from rebelling.

Valeria looked as if Diocletian had just hit her over the head with his sword. Like any seventeen-year-old girl, she had her dreams. Even now, a handsome young face flashed into her mind—smiling eyes, white teeth, hair flying in the breeze. It was like rubbing salt in her wounds.

This was the end of her girlhood. Valeria would always look back on this evening as the night she finally grew up. She sat there, silent at last, with the remains of her sandcastle crumbled about her feet.

A tear ran down her cheek.

MARK

Andrew didn't waste any time. He was almost as eager as Mark was, now that the decision had been made. They should have looked after this a few years ago, he realized. Lydia could easily have married someone else before this.

Andrew had visions of getting to Lydia's home only to discover that someone else had gotten there ahead of him. Irene laughed at him. "I'm sure God has His hand in this," she assured him. "Another day isn't going to make that much difference. Mark is younger than most young men when they marry."

"But Lydia is older than most girls when they wed," he replied. "I'm going to find her brother tomorrow and speak to him."

A Roman betrothal was a legal contract just as important as the marriage contract. One of the most important parts was the value of the dowry the bride would bring with her. Normally, in cases such as Lydia's, part of her father's inheritance was kept for her dowry to ensure a good marriage. Unfortunately, her father had died penniless, so her prospects of a good marriage were quite slim.

Lydia's brother was not surprised to see Andrew on his doorstep and stepped outside to talk in private. Lydia had told the family of meeting Mark on the street and the renewal of their old friendship.

Andrew came to the point quickly. "My son Mark is interested in marrying your sister Lydia," he said. "Would this be of interest to you and the rest of her family?"

The brother hesitated. "Do you realize she will not be able to supply a dowry?" he asked. "We have been approached before, but no one has been willing to take her without a dowry."

Andrew wasn't surprised. He had assumed this was probably the reason Lydia was still unmarried. "We realize the circumstances," he replied, "but my wife and I have no other children, and we are willing to supply the dowry ourselves."

The brother looked surprised but quickly seized the opportunity. "In that case, I am sure we will sign. Do you have a betrothal contract along?"

"You mean you're not going to counsel with the rest of the family?" Now it was Andrew's turn to be surprised. "We can wait a few days."

Lydia's brother gave him a crooked grin. "That would be the normal procedure," he agreed. "But in this case, my brothers would surely ask me why I didn't snatch the opportunity when it arose. They will not have any problem with your offer, but they might be afraid you will back out in the meantime.

"If you don't mind waiting for a few minutes, I *will* talk to Lydia, however," he said. "I don't expect her to object, but I want to be sure."

This was not the normal procedure either, but Andrew would have done the same. He didn't have to wait long. The brother soon returned—and behind him was Lydia.

She had become an attractive young woman. Her flushed cheeks emphasized her dark hair, and her smile was radiant.

—— DIOCLETIAN ——

Valeria would gladly have given up her status as the emperor's daughter for a position such as Lydia's. How foolish and naive she had been to ever dream of a marriage of love. Women of her class were almost always tied to a marriage of convenience. In most cases, their husbands found love in other places than at home.

Prisca's situation was somewhat unique. Her husband loved her, or at least had loved her when they married. But love was not normally an expected part of Roman marriages.

Valeria had no idea who her husband-to-be was. The betrothal contract needed to wait until Galerius had divorced his wife, and he seemed in no hurry to do so.

It was a nerve-wracking time, but Valeria realized that rebelling would not help her cause. When Galerius and his guards finally arrived in Nicomedia for the betrothal ceremony later that fall, she managed to secrete herself in a hidden nook within Diocletian's palace. The men walked in, greeting Diocletian more as a fellow soldier than an emperor. Her heart sank when she figured out which man was Galerius. Somehow she had harbored a bit of hope that he might be a "prince charming" after all and that her marriage might still fulfill her childhood dreams. But her heart chilled when she saw him.

Galerius was twice her age and balding. Even worse, he was crude. The joke he was telling his buddies made her ears burn. But his eyes were what stood out to her the most. Never had she seen such cold eyes. Here was a man who would have no qualms at all about stamping out the life of an innocent woman or child.

She shuddered, and something died within her.

——— MARK ———

Mark and Lydia were married about six months after their betrothal. They lived in a small apartment close to Andrew and Irene. It was a happy union and both were overjoyed at this culmination of their childhood friendship.

Lydia still spent time helping her brother's family, and the older children came regularly to her house for lessons in simple reading and calculating. In return, her brother paid what he could to help them get a start in life, even though the marriage contract stated that Andrew would supply the nuptial dowry.

Mark borrowed scrolls and parchment books from his parents and spent some of his evenings in study. Both he and Lydia were especially interested in the Holy Writings of the apostles. Lydia never tired of reading the Gospels and using their simple stories in her teaching.

Mark took his Christian life seriously. He tithed faithfully, he fasted during Lent and before the Eucharist,[1] and he did his other church duties. He especially studied the Holy Writings. Lydia would shake her head when he read to her from Paul's letter to the Romans, or from the book written to the Hebrews.

"Do you really understand that?" she asked him one day after he had read to her a passage dealing with high priests in the old covenant. "I like the stories in the Gospels, where Jesus blesses the children and heals the sick."

Mark looked at her thoughtfully. "I suppose it's partly the difference in our personalities," he said after a pause. "I enjoy the Gospel stories too, but the teachings of Paul thrill me. Some of the pagan poets may have been better writers, but their works are very shallow compared to Paul's writings."

He smiled. "My mother struggles with that. She loves the Holy Writings, but the writings of her forefathers are also special to her."

---

[1] A term used by the early church for Communion.

DIOCLETIAN

Valeria married Galerius the next year. The whole city celebrated with them, drinking the free wine and eating the free food. The poorer class no doubt wished Diocletian had more daughters of marriageable age. And so did the soldiers, especially some of the officers who would have liked to hold a special office.

Galerius treated the whole affair as a big joke. Not only did he gain the position of Caesar out of the deal, but he also acquired a beautiful young bride. The novelty of all this kept him cheerful for a few weeks, but then he started longing for the wide horizons and the tough life of the army camps. He soon found reasons to take him away from Nicomedia.

And Valeria? She stood at the gate of Diocletian's palace and watched Galerius ride off with his fellow soldiers, much as she had first seen him come. If she shed any tears, it was because of the final burial of her childhood dreams. Overall, she was glad to see Galerius leave. Now life could get back to normal.

At least as normal as it could get.

Valeria had seldom bothered with serious thoughts until she learned about the plans her father had made for her. But betrothal and marriage had changed her. Prisca noticed that she had become quiet and troubled. Several weeks after Galerius left, she spoke to Valeria about it.

Valeria was passing through the living area to reach her

personal quarters when her mother stopped her. "Are you doing all right, dear?" she asked. "Is something troubling you?"

Valeria sank into a soft chair across from her mother, and Prisca laid down the needlework she had been working on. Valeria gathered her thoughts before replying. "I suppose I'm doing as well as can be expected," she said slowly. "I've had a rude awakening, and I was stupid to expect anything else."

"I never had to face what you did," her mother replied softly. "I wish I could have spared you from it."

Valeria stared into the fireplace and watched the dancing flames. A knot in the burning wood snapped, and she woke from her reverie. "It's not just that. I've been thinking a lot about life in general. Somehow life seems so useless. I have nothing to live for now that my dreams for a happy marriage are crushed."

She brushed back a few unruly locks of hair from her face. "Don't you ever wonder what we're here for?" she continued. "We get up every morning, do our hair, get dressed, and eat breakfast. Then we sit and do needlework. We don't help with the work or the cleaning. We're just useless ornaments—fancy birds living in a cage."

She got to her feet and stood in front of the fireplace, turning her back to the fire so she could watch her mother's face. "You know what I mean," she said. "We don't really have friends here in town. No one else is in our class, so the only people we entertain are my father's friends."

She turned and stared into the flames again. "I hate Galerius," she said bitterly. "He isn't interested in anything but being a Caesar and eventually replacing my father as emperor. He doesn't notice anything beautiful—like a sunset or a picture or a song." She blushed and continued softly, "He doesn't even notice me, at least not most of the time. I'm just a new toy that he's already tired of."

She abruptly changed the subject before her mother could answer. "I'd like to visit a church of the Christians sometime," she said. "They seem to be the only people who really know what they believe. At least they have something to live for; I don't."

Prisca's eyes opened wide and she looked cautiously over her shoulder. "Don't ever say that when the servants or your father are around," she warned, almost in a whisper. "It would be very dangerous to be overheard."

"But why?" Valeria asked. "Some of the friends I had when I was younger were Christians, even though no one knew it. Most of the things people believe about them aren't even close to being true."

Prisca shifted uneasily. "I know," she replied softly. "Some of the palace servants are Christian, and a few have talked to me about their beliefs. I would be happy to join them, but it's impossible. Your father dreams of getting the pagans and Christians together, even though his attempts to do so have always failed."

Valeria gathered her skirts together before replying. "Galerius is very much against the Christians. He thinks the empire should destroy Christianity once and for all. His mother is a pagan priestess and has persuaded him that they are the greatest danger the empire faces." She shuddered. "If Galerius ever becomes emperor, he will start a bloodbath."

PART V
A.D. 295

Teaching Latin

I relate all those things on the authority of well-informed persons; and I thought it proper to commit them to writing exactly as they happened, lest the memory of events so important should perish, and lest any future historian of the persecutors should corrupt the truth, either by suppressing their offences against God, or the judgment of God against them. To His everlasting mercy ought we to render thanks, that, having at length looked on the earth, He deigned to collect again and to restore His flock, partly laid waste by ravenous wolves, and partly scattered abroad, and to extirpate those noxious wild beasts who had trod down its pastures, and destroyed its resting places.

—Lactantius, *Of the Manner in Which the Persecutors Died,* Chap. 52

9

June 295

Diocletian was a man with many interests, but his top priority was advancing the Roman Empire. To have a unified empire, he decided, they needed a unified language. They needed to speak Latin, not all these other barbaric languages. Something had to be done.

Diocletian's education had been hit and run. He spoke Latin well. He could also read it, though not as well as he could speak it. His handwriting was indecipherable for anyone but Hiram or himself, so Hiram took care of his official correspondence. He got along with communicating in Latin and had picked up some Aramaic during his years as a soldier, but any other language was barbaric in his opinion.

Diocletian swallowed his comments until Afranius had ushered a delegation from Syria out the door. Then he exploded.

"Every Roman citizen should know how to speak Latin! I feel like posting a sign outside the gate that all communication within this palace is to be in Latin, and Latin only."

Afranius and Hiram had heard this complaint before, so neither replied.

"Do these people expect to come in here and speak Greek or Persian or Syriac and have me understand them?" The answer was obvious, so he didn't wait for a reply. "We've got to do something to teach these barbarians a civilized language."

He drummed his fingers on the desktop. Suddenly he turned to Hiram. "Do you have any idea who would be a good teacher of Latin?"

Hiram leaned back in his chair and rubbed his chin. "Probably Lactantius. He lives in Numidia, in North Africa, as far as I know."

"Does he also know Greek and Aramaic?" Diocletian asked. "He's well educated?"

Hiram nodded. "Absolutely! He probably knows half a dozen languages, but he's especially good with Latin and Greek."

Diocletian glanced at the ceiling, as he often did when deciding what course to take. The ceiling evidently approved of his thoughts. "Write him a letter," he said to Hiram. "Tell him we need a teacher of Latin in Nicomedia. We'll make a place for him here in the palace. We can at least do that much to stamp out Greek here."

Abruptly he got back to business. "Are there any more delegations I need to meet this afternoon?"

LACTANTIUS

Six weeks later the imperial mail runner left a message for Lactantius in the local Roman outpost in Cirta, a city of Numidia[1] with almost 50,000 people, close to the Mediterranean. Lactantius had just dismissed his afternoon class when the portly local magistrate came puffing up the street.

"What's the rush?" Lactantius asked. "I don't often see you moving this fast."

The magistrate's face flushed an even deeper red. "Y-You have an official l-letter from the emperor," he said, trying to catch his breath. "I w-wanted to let you know r-right away."

Lactantius brushed back a few stray locks of hair from his forehead. He was in his mid forties,[2] tall and lean, with a scraggly brown beard and a full head of hair. In appearance and in personality, he was the opposite in almost every way from the sputtering, puffing, self-important magistrate.

"Well, I'm sure the emperor's letter could have waited another day," he said, chuckling. "It probably took over a month to get here from wherever the emperor was when he sent it." He glanced at the sky to judge the time before continuing.

"I don't suppose you brought it with you?" he asked. He saw from the perplexed look on the magistrate's face that

---

[1] Cirta was in modern-day Algeria in northern Africa.

[2] There is some disagreement about when Lactantius was born. Some feel he was very old (in his 80s) when he vanished from history in A.D. 325 or 326. That seems unlikely, and I have gone by the tradition that he was born around A.D. 250. This would make him about five years older than Diocletian.

he hadn't even thought of that.

"Well, I have a bit of time before supper," Lactantius continued. "I'll walk back with you and see what favor the emperor is asking of me."

The magistrate had a hard time keeping up with Lactantius' long strides, and he was still too short of breath to converse. Lactantius, despite his pretense of a moment before, was curious about the emperor's message and set a rapid pace.

The local barracks for the Roman guard doubled as the imperial post office. The magistrate bustled toward the door, to the amusement of several soldiers sitting on a rough wooden bench. Lactantius noted their half-stifled grins and smiled at them. The magistrate looked for all the world like a small, overweight banty rooster. But he had pricked the man's balloon enough for one afternoon, so he simply thanked him for the document and stuffed it inside his doublet without further comment.

The magistrate looked disappointed, but Lactantius had no intention of enlightening his curiosity. The emperor's message was for him, and him alone. If he told the magistrate what the scroll contained, half the people in town would know about it by morning.

Lactantius broke the news to his journal that evening.

The emperor wants me to move to Nicomedia. Seemingly, he assumes that his invitation is a great favor, and he is anxious to have me set up a department to teach Latin to the barbarian

*population there. Most Nicomedians speak Greek or Syriac
rather than the majestic Latin of Rome.*

Lactantius laid down his pen and walked to the doorway of
his two-room hut. The emperor had said nothing about paying
his expenses. *I wonder who did me the "favor" of bringing me
to the emperor's attention,* he mused. *He hasn't really left any
room for refusal. I wonder what he would say if I told him I
consider Latin to be more barbaric than Greek. Oh well, it
could be an interesting venture. The emperor's letter will probably give me enough clout to arrange passage on an imperial
vessel. That would help with the cost of the trip.*

He shrugged as he shut the door for the night. *I'll need to
shut down my classes at the end of the month. He must be the
impatient sort. He hasn't left much time for me to get things
in order here.*

———— MARK ————

Had Diocletian realized it, he could have hired a few teachers
of Latin locally rather than importing one all the way from
Africa. Now that Mark was no longer living at home, Irene had
started taking in some students, and Lydia was teaching Latin
and ciphering to her nephews. And Mark himself excelled even
his wife and his mother in both Latin and Greek, as well as
in his studies of the Holy Writings. In this, he also excelled
Lactantius, a pagan with little interest in the Christian writings, other than perhaps some academic curiosity.

Mark had borrowed from his father the church's copy of

Paul's epistle to the Romans. He had finished his reading for the evening and was wrapping the precious manuscript in a soft, purple, velvet cover. He watched as Lydia finished cleaning up the little sitting area that doubled as a classroom during the daytime.

"I wonder if anyone has the original manuscript Paul wrote," he said pensively. "I think this one has a few errors."

Lydia looked up, surprised. "I thought this one was pretty old. And it's in Greek too."

"But it's not the original," Mark said. "The copyist initialed it at the end and noted that he had copied it from one in Alexandria. The copy he used as a master was a copy of still another one. I guess it's no wonder these writings have a few errors."

He tied the leather thongs carefully around the cover and laid the scroll reverently on the table. "I wish I could see the original," he said wistfully. "Just imagine being able to see Paul's handwriting."

Lydia smiled at his intensity. "Maybe the church in Rome has the original manuscript," she suggested. "Surely they would have kept it in a safe place."

"I surely hope so," Mark said. "But they might not have realized what a treasure it was. It must have taken Paul weeks to write it. I wonder how many copies are in existence."

Lydia watched as he put the scroll safely in a cupboard. "How many Holy Writings are there? And how do we know if a writing is inspired or not?"

"I'm not sure," Mark replied. "I should ask my mother if she knows. A few books, like Hebrews and the Revelation, are disputed by some. So is the Shepherd of Hermes and the Gospel of Thomas."

"I wish we could get a copy of all of them fastened together in one book," Lydia said. "But someone would need to decide which books belong in it and which don't."

"I suppose it will happen someday," Mark said as they prepared for bed. "But it will take a lot of discussion to decide which ones to accept."

—————— LACTANTIUS ——————

Lactantius shut down his school, settled his affairs, and packed his extensive library of scrolls. He had very little else worth taking along, as he sold the bit of furniture he had inherited from his parents. Then he made another trip to the barracks to talk with the magistrate.

The magistrate seemed pleased to see him. "How can I help you today?" he asked, rubbing his hands together. "I trust your communication from the emperor was satisfactory?"

Lactantius grinned at the magistrate's obvious attempt to find out what the letter had been about. "It was fine," he replied. "But the emperor wants my help, and I have to go see him. I thought you might have some advice on the best way to travel to Nicomedia."

"Well now . . . hmm . . . you know, I've never been there," the magistrate admitted. Lactantius almost smirked but controlled his expression just in time. Of course the magistrate had never been to Nicomedia. He probably had never been farther than a day's journey from Cirta.

But the magistrate's eyes brightened. "We have a shipment of mail going to Nicomedia before long. I could arrange for you to travel with it. It's going by an imperial vessel."

The smile on Lactantius' face grew broader. This was exactly what he had been after. "Do you have authority to write me a permit to travel with the mail?"

"Oh yes, I can do that," the magistrate assured him. "I'll have it prepared right away, and you can pick it up next week when the shipment leaves."

Lactantius looked duly impressed at the magistrate's authority and passed him a nice tip. He waited until he was down the street and around the corner before he started to laugh. *Well, there's my free trip to Nicomedia,* he grinned. *I'll have to put in a good word for our magistrate with my friend the emperor when I get there.*

He was still chuckling when he arrived at his home.

A brisk wind caught the sails, and the ship was on its way. Lactantius stood at the rail watching the shoreline as it gradually receded. He spread his legs to keep his balance as the ship hit the first swells coming off the Mediterranean. He breathed deeply, savoring the brisk, salty air. *Sure beats the heat and smell of the city. I'm going to enjoy this trip to the fullest.*

He worked his way across the deck to the little cabin he shared with Nestor, the ship's first mate. Imperial post vessels weren't intended for run-of-the-mill passengers, and it had taken him a bit to persuade the captain that he had a permit to travel with them. He had been prepared for this, of course. A bit of silver in the right palms went a long way, and that proved true even of a captain of the emperor's ships.

Lactantius grinned as he remembered the dismay on the first mate's face when he saw the boxes of scrolls he had stashed in his cabin, but a little more silver had smoothed that out as well. They were friends already. Unquestionably, Lactantius' personal invitation from Diocletian helped too. Most people had never met anyone who was on a first-name basis with the emperor. Lactantius, of course, didn't bother to enlighten them with the fact that he didn't know the emperor any better than they did.

The ship lurched as a rogue wave hit it sideways, and Lactantius almost lost his balance. He caught himself on a rope and sat down on a wooden storage box. *Might as well enjoy whatever sunshine is left. I should be able to get some inspiration for a few ballads or sonnets out of this trip. No use letting my mind get rusty or lazy.*[3]

Dreamily he watched the sun drift closer to the horizon, brilliantly highlighted against the rapidly deepening twilight. *Every writer or teacher of rhetoric should take a sea voyage. This is going to inspire me for months to come.*

The sun had almost drowned itself in the western waters when his cabinmate came to find him. "You want a bite to eat? Or maybe you're seasick?"

Lactantius pulled himself to his feet. "No, not yet," he said

---

[3] Supposedly Lactantius did write the story of his journey, but unfortunately it has been lost, along with his other writings from his pagan period.

with a grin. "Sorry to disappoint you."

Nestor laughed ruefully. "Don't worry, it'll get you yet. We're bound to get a good blow or two before we get across Our Sea."[4]

Lactantius had heard enough about the Mediterranean to know that this prophecy would probably come true. But he also had enough of an easygoing personality not to worry about it until it happened. He was on this trip partly for adventure and would have been disappointed if a storm didn't materialize. He glanced once more toward the blazing panorama of the sunset, then followed the mate to the galley in the stern.

The cook dipped out a soupy concoction with some hardtack floating in it and handed a steaming bowl to each of them. "Eat up," he said. "This is the best it's going to get until we take on new provisions in Alexandria."

Lactantius eyed the strange mixture uneasily, then took a bite. It tasted better than it looked, and he cleaned it up with only a little less enthusiasm than his shipmate. Both washed it down with a hot mug of calda.

It was almost dark when they exited the galley, and Lactantius headed straight for his bed. Nestor had to work the first half of the night, so they parted at the cabin door. "I'll try not to wake you when I come to bed," the first mate promised. "Leave the bottom bunk for me."

Life quickly settled into a monotony, and Lactantius dug out his scrolls and writing materials. *Might as well start recording my impressions.* He set up a make-shift desk with several of his boxes of scrolls and pulled out his ink bottle and

---

[4] The Romans called the Mediterranean "Our Sea" from the time of Caesar Augustus until the fifth century. Totally surrounded and controlled by the Roman Empire, it was truly a "Roman Lake."

a new quill pen he had made. He was a prodigious reader; he would pattern his ode to the journey after one of Cicero's masterpieces.[5]

A week later, Lactantius was deep in thought when Nestor stuck his head in the door. "Sorry to disturb you. But would you want to see the island of Malta, where Paul was shipwrecked?"

Lactantius had learned that the mate was a Christian, and he himself was acquainted with Paul's history from his studies under a Christian apologist in Numidia.[6] He joined Nestor and a few others at the rail while the mate pointed out the shoreline where Paul had probably been shipwrecked.

MARK

Mark and Lydia rose several hours before sunrise on Thursday morning. They planned to attend a morning prayer vigil in one of the company warehouses. Mark often rose early to pray and meditate, but Lydia found the early mornings difficult.

Mark placed a kettle of water on the charcoal stove for a quick mug of calda. Lydia emerged from the curtained-off sleeping area, still rubbing her eyes. She yawned desperately. Mark chuckled. "Here," he said, handing her a pot of cold water. "Wash your face with this. It'll wake you up."

Lydia did as he told her, gasping and spluttering as she splashed the water on her face. "Oh, that's cold," she moaned,

---

[5] Cicero was a Roman orator and writer who lived from 106-43 B.C. He is known for his skillful, precise way of writing and speaking. Lactantius has been called the "Christian Cicero."

[6] Lactantius studied under Arnobius, who was a somewhat unorthodox defender of Christianity with more zeal than knowledge, it appears. Lactantius shows little if any influence from his teaching.

shivering. "I don't see how you can bounce out of bed this time of the morning. I could have slept for hours yet."

Mark shrugged. "It's just how I'm made. My father is the same way."

He opened the door and glanced at the stars, assessing the time. "We'll have to leave in a few minutes, or we'll be late," he said. "Let's drink our calda before we go."

A short time later Lydia followed Mark out into the darkness of the street. They stood in front of their little apartment, getting used to the darkness. Mark looked into the sky. "There's Orion," he said. "See the belt and sword?"

Lydia just shivered. "Why do we have these early morning vigils anyway?" she asked. "I'd rather go in the evening."

Mark took her by the arm, and they started to walk down the street. "It goes way back to the beginning of the church," he said. "Many Christians were slaves and had to work from dawn till dusk, seven days a week. So early morning was the best time for Christians to gather."

Lydia shivered again, and Mark pulled her closer. "That night wind is chilly," he noted before continuing. "The pagan masters mostly didn't care as long as the slaves were awake enough to do their work in the daytime."

He paused while they maneuvered their way past a heap of garbage beside the street. "It did make for some strange stories though. The pagans couldn't believe that people would voluntarily go to a worship service that time of the morning, so word got around that the Christians had all kinds of immoral orgies, and sacrificed babies and drank their blood."

"And worshipped an ass's head," Lydia added.

"Yes, that was another one, and it still hasn't died," Mark said. "I think the rest of the stories have mostly died, but that one still hangs on."

The warehouse loomed in the darkness before them, and Mark cautiously led the way to a door at the back. "Come quickly," he whispered. "Just in case . . ."

It had been years since any soldiers had interfered in a Christian service, but some of the older worshippers still vividly remembered it. Even now, their meetings were not officially sanctioned and local opinion could turn against them at any time. After having relative freedom for over thirty years, however, few expected it to happen. Still, one never knew. And in the predawn darkness, it somehow seemed a bit more likely than usual.

——— LACTANTIUS ———

"What was Paul really like?" Lactantius asked Nestor. "Didn't he prophesy that everyone on the ship would make it safe to land that day?"

Nestor nodded. "Not only that, but a poisonous snake bit him when he was putting wood on the fire. Everyone expected him to fall over dead, but he didn't."

Lactantius eyed him skeptically. "I had a teacher back in Numidia who had all kinds of stories like that. But how many of those old stories are just stories?"

Nestor shrugged. "I can't really say," he admitted. "But there are so many of them that it does seem that at least some of them must have happened."

Lactantius didn't look convinced. "The pagans have all kinds of stories like that too. But they usually happened to their gods, not to humans. Somehow that seems a little more likely."

"Well, Paul resisted the idea that he was a god," Nestor said. "In fact, one time when he healed a man, everyone thought he must be Jupiter. The priests even hauled out the sacred bull and tried to sacrifice to him."

Lactantius grinned, picturing the itinerant Jewish preacher trying to work his way out of that one. "So what happened? I suppose he refused to let them do it."

Nestor nodded emphatically. "He certainly did. It took Paul a bit to figure out what was going on, because he didn't understand their language. But when the priest found out that he was only a man, they realized how close to blasphemy they had come. They were terribly upset and ended up stoning him. It seems some of Paul's Jewish enemies took advantage of the situation."

Lactantius raised his eyebrows at this. "But he survived it, apparently."

Nestor glanced at him before answering. "Yes and no," he said reluctantly. "They left him dead on the junk heap outside the city. His friends gathered around him to pray. They were shocked at the turn of events. But suddenly he came back to life, got up, and walked into the city with them."

"Now wait a minute," Lactantius replied. "Are you sure he was dead? Maybe he had just fainted."

Nestor backed down a little. "Well, I wasn't there, but Luke recorded it in his history of the Acts of the Apostles. Maybe he states that they thought he was dead. I'm not sure."

Silence fell between the two men. Lactantius walked to the door and looked out into the darkness. In the distance he could see a spark of light, perhaps from some lonely fishing boat from Malta.

Finally he turned to Nestor again. "Well, I guess there's no way to really prove how it was, but I'd like to find some of Luke's writings and read them for myself. That way I could judge better."

The storm caught up with them the next afternoon. It was not as bad as the storm that took Paul's ship to a watery grave, but still the worst that Lactantius had ever experienced. The sailors saw the cloud formations on the horizon several hours before it arrived and knew it was coming. Lactantius watched their preparations with a professional but somewhat detached interest.

The wind had picked up and the ship was pitching in the waves when the first mate found Lactantius still sitting out on the deck. "You'd better head for the cabin," he instructed. He had to lift his voice over the roar of the wind and waves. "This isn't going to be any kind of picnic out here."

Lactantius cocked his head and grinned. "I'm not seasick yet!"

Nestor bent over and yelled into his ear for added emphasis. "You will be, and soon! But you'll never be able to hang on to your seat here. If you don't want to be washed overboard, get into the cabin while you still can."

Seeing that the mate was serious, Lactantius worked his

way across the deck, losing his footing several times. One time he was saved only by catching hold of a piece of rigging. All in all, he was thankful to reach the cabin. *That was a close call,* he realized. *I could be floating on the waves a half mile away by now.*

Even in the cabin, riding out the storm was far from a picnic. Lactantius dismantled his makeshift desk and put the boxes of scrolls on the floor, landing flat on his back several times during the process. Finally he decided to tie himself to the bed.

The next hours were a nightmare. Lactantius lost track of how often he hung his head over the side of his bed and vomited. All he knew was that the storm seemed to last forever, and he was sicker than he had ever been before.

The wind had died down by morning, but the ship continued to lurch. Lactantius was still sick but so thirsty that he was trying to get up when Nestor opened the cabin door.

The mate took a long look around the cabin, which looked as if it had been through a war. Finally his eyes rested on Lactantius. "I see you did get seasick." He wrinkled his nose at the smell.

Lactantius rolled his eyes and managed to sit on the edge of the bunk. "Looks like it. Smells like it too, I guess. Sorry to mess up your cabin like this."

Nestor snorted. "I'd have been surprised if you didn't. Most of the crew was sick as well." He grabbed the doorjamb as the ship pitched unexpectedly. "It was a pretty tough blow. We lost some rigging and a couple of lifeboats. Fortunately, no one got washed overboard."

He stepped over to Lactantius and helped him to his feet. "Come outside for some fresh air. I'll get a bucket of water and swab down the floor in here." He took another look at Lactantius. "Looks like you need some washing up too," he added.

He was as good as his word and soon came back with a bucket. "Here, hang on to this rope," he told Lactantius, pointing to a rope hanging from the boat's rigging. "Now, hold your breath." He poured the bucket of cold sea water over Lactantius' head, then a second one over the rest of him.

August 295

As their responsibilities increased, Mark and Lydia learned to trust God in a new way. Lactantius, on his way to Nicomedia to be a teacher of Latin, also learned more about God—as well as the Mediterranean Sea.

"**D**id you ever hear back from your Latin friend?" Diocletian asked Hiram one day in late July as he walked by his work area. "He should be here by now, shouldn't he?"

Hiram looked up from his work. "He wrote back and said he plans to arrive in August. He's coming with the monthly mail shipment from Carthage."

Diocletian's eyebrows lifted. "The mail shipment? Who gave him permission to do that?"

Hiram shrugged and picked up his pen again. "I don't know, but what else was he supposed to do? We didn't offer to pay his way, and rhetoricians aren't noted for having a lot of extra cash."

Diocletian's forehead wrinkled. "He must have some well-seated friends. Mail ships take passengers only in exceptional circumstances."

Hiram dipped his pen into a pot of ink. "Well, I guess if you get a letter from the emperor ordering you to make a two-month journey to work for him and don't have money to pay for the trip, you could probably be excused for considering it an exceptional circumstance."

"All I can say," Diocletian replied tersely, "is that he had better be a good teacher."

———— MARK ————

Mark and Lydia had their own set of exceptional circumstances. These had to do with money as well. Mark broke the news one evening after supper. "Bishop Anthimus asked me if I would consider training to become a presbyter in his bishopric."

Lydia slowly laid down the garment she was mending and looked at him searchingly. "But why would he ask you?"

Mark took a deep breath. "I'm not sure. He said something about my knowledge of the languages of the Holy Writings and my understanding of their content."

Lydia looked baffled. "But your age—you are much younger than presbyters normally are. That . . . that means he wants to prepare you for a position as bishop." She saw immediately, by the expression on Mark's face, that he had already thought of that.

Another thought flashed through her mind. "But what will we live on, Mark? Don't presbyters have to quit their jobs?"

Mark had been through all these thoughts already. He just had a few hours' head start on her. He merely nodded.

Lydia's shoulders sagged. "But I can't make enough income from teaching to keep us alive. And I was hoping that eventually we'd have some children. How do presbyters manage to make a living?"

Mark lifted his shoulders and dropped them again. "I asked him that. He said that God provides. People give gifts of money or food. He said Paul wrote that the laborer is worthy of his hire,[1] and that a faithful presbyter doesn't need to worry."

Lydia got to her feet to put away her sewing. "I suppose Anthimus would know." She put her hand on Mark's shoulder and looked down at him. "After all, he's lived that way for a long time."

Mark nodded. "Yes, and he's a very caring person. Not at all arrogant like some of the other leaders tend to be. He encouraged me to take the gifts God has given to me and use them for His kingdom.

"If we accept this, he wants me to quit my job and start meeting with him and several others soon. He wants me to take a year's training, then work as his assistant for a few years. Then, if everything goes well, he would assign me to start a new congregation."

Lydia watched her husband get to his feet. He seemed to

---

[1] A saying of Jesus (Matthew 10:10) quoted by Paul in 1 Timothy 5:18.

have aged several years in the last few hours. "How soon do we have to give our answer? Or did you already tell him you'd do it?"

Mark shook his head. "I told him we'd pray about it and let him know on Sunday."

LACTANTIUS

It took Lactantius several days to recover, but by the time the ship had crossed most of the Mediterranean and was approaching the Aegean Sea, he was back to normal. He set up his makeshift desk again and was working at another lengthy composition. This one focused on the recent storm and poked fun at his first experience with seasickness.

Nestor came to remind him it was suppertime. He glanced over Lactantius' shoulder. "You wrote all of that today?" He lifted his eyebrows. "What are you going to do with it when you're done?"

Lactantius unfolded himself stiffly from the box he had been sitting on and stretched. "Oh, I might use it as a Latin lesson sometime." He rolled up the scroll and tied a leather thong around it. "Some student will enjoy reading it."

He cocked his head and listened as the sound of music wafted through the door. "Are the sirens[2] singing tonight? Or have the guards just gotten lonely?"

Nestor chuckled. "I've spent most of my life on the water,

---

[2] Sirens were imaginary creatures in Greek mythology, half bird and half woman. In the stories, they lured passing sailors to their islands, and, subsequently, to their doom. The sirens were fated to die if anyone should survive their singing. When Odysseus passed them by unharmed, they hurled themselves into the sea and were drowned.

COUNTDOWN

but I've never seen a mermaid, let alone a siren. Those are fables invented by Homer to make his stories more interesting for the poor scholars who are forced to read them."

Lactantius grimaced as a particularly discordant note floated in the door. "That singing certainly wouldn't entice me to jump overboard to my doom, as Ulysses was supposedly tempted to do. Must be he heard something else!"

"No doubt," Nestor agreed.

"By the way," Lactantius asked, rising from his seat, "are pirates a big problem? Do you ever get attacked?"

The first mate shrugged. "Oh, it happens, but it's been a while. That's why the mail ships always have some soldiers on board. About a year ago, one of the mail ships was boarded by pirates who killed the whole crew. But mostly it's been pretty safe."

They walked to the railing and Nestor studied the distant shoreline. "See that land over there?" He pointed at what Lactantius had thought to be a distant fog bank. "That's Crete. About thirty years ago, Gothic pirates attacked both Crete and Cyprus and took thousands of captives. But they were pushed back, and it's been pretty quiet for the last several decades."

The night breeze picked up as they watched the shoreline of Crete fade into darkness. Lactantius brushed back a few locks of hair that insisted on blowing into his eyes. It was the time of evening that brooded introspection, and he started to quote, "Day by day, what you choose, what you think, and what you do is who you become."[3]

Nestor glanced at him and countered, "When I consider thy heavens, the work of thy fingers, the moon and the stars, which thou hast ordained; what is man, that thou art mindful of him? and the son of man, that thou visitest him?"[4]

Lactantius straightened in surprise. "So, you've got a bit of philosopher in you, do you? Who wrote that?"

Nestor watched the moon as it rose slowly in the eastern sky. "That greatest poet of them all," he replied softly. "King David, the sweet singer of Israel."

Lactantius nodded. "Ah, the Psalms. You're right, they are melancholy but deep. I don't have a copy, though I'd love to have one. But Hebrew is one language I have never learned."

"They are also available in both Latin and Greek translations," Nestor replied. "But I have been told they are the most beautiful in the original Hebrew."

Lactantius nodded. "That is always true." He glanced at the stars again. "I wonder what it must feel like to write words so beautiful that people quote them a thousand years after they're written."

——— MARK ———

It was a long week for Mark and Lydia. Lydia had a lot of questions, but she didn't want to add to Mark's pressure. Finally on Friday evening they talked it over again.

---

[3] Heraclitus — Greek philosopher from 500 B.C.

[4] Psalm 8:3, 4

"How do they go about choosing a presbyter?" Lydia asked. "Does the bishop just decide who he wants?"

Mark laid down the scroll he had been reading. "He can, in an emergency, but normally he brings up the need in a meeting with the clergy. He may suggest a name, or they may suggest one."

"Were you the bishop's choice or a suggestion from the group?" Lydia wasn't sure why this mattered to her, but it did. "I talked to your mother, and she knew that the bishop had asked you."

Mark nodded. "He said that they had discussed a short list of names. He didn't tell me who else they were considering, and he didn't say who suggested my name."

He paused. "Our names will be brought before the congregation for final approval once all of us have agreed to his request. He said group approval is very important, and he won't go ahead with it unless most of the congregation is in favor and no one brings up a Scriptural objection. Apparently that is especially true in the ordination of a bishop. A bishop cannot just choose someone to be his successor."[5]

Mark gave a positive answer, and several weeks later the names of the prospective presbyters were announced. One was almost immediately rejected by the congregation because of

---

[5] There were some differences from area to area. During the fourth century, the church transitioned from ordination being a prerogative of the congregation to becoming controlled by the bishops. —Everett Ferguson: "Ordination in the Ancient Church (III)," under heading "Ordination in the Second and Third Centuries," pp. 67 ff.

his bad reputation in the city. The three remaining nominees spent a week in prayer and fasting before being consecrated the following Sunday.

Mark was acquainted with the Holy Writings, but as a presbyter, he needed to memorize many of the ceremonial passages that were part of the special services of the church.

Dedication Prayer for Presbyter

O God and Father of our Lord Jesus Christ, look upon this thy servant and impart to him the Spirit of grace and counsel, that he may share in the presbyterate and govern thy people in a pure heart.

As thou didst look upon the people of thy choice and didst command Moses to choose presbyters whom thou didst fill with the Spirit which thou hadst granted to thy minister,

So now, O Lord, grant that there may be preserved among us unceasingly the Spirit of thy grace, and make us worthy that in faith we may minister to thee praising thee in singleness of heart,

Through thy Child Christ Jesus through whom to thee be glory, might, and praise, to the Father and to the Son with the Holy Spirit in the holy Church now and forever and world without end. Amen.

He started on this the next week. He rose early to read and pray, then left to meet with Bishop Anthimus and the other two trainees. This was also his first week without work or income.

The lack of a regular income bothered Lydia the most. In

theory, it was good to live by faith and expect that God would meet their needs. She had no problem with that. But in practical terms, when she ran out of money and needed bread on the same day, things looked a little different. One evening she met Mark at the door, almost in tears.

"What are we going to do? I scraped together enough food for some supper tonight, but we don't have anything in the house for tomorrow."

It was a quiet meal that evening. Mark led in the prescribed grace but added some words of his own at the end. "Lord, you know we are looking to you to meet our needs. You know better than we do what those needs are. Maybe you want us to learn to live on less so that you would receive more glory. Help us lay aside our fears and our wants and learn to live by your grace."

Lydia looked at him thoughtfully. "Do all our presbyters live like this? Is this what they go through every week?"

Mark nodded. "As far as I know, they do."

Lydia clenched her hands in her lap. "I wonder if they ever get used to it. I never thought of it before. We should have shared more with them."

Mark nodded. "I know. I've been thinking the same thing. I'm sure God will provide, but it will be good for us to realize that what we have is from Him."

Lydia had just opened her mouth to reply when someone tapped on the door. Mark's father, Andrew, opened it and poked his head inside. He grinned at them. "I can't stay. I worked late tonight. But some people brought groceries to the church for you today, and I thought I'd deliver them on my way home."

He placed several bags on the floor and was gone before Lydia or Mark could respond. It took a few moments to sink in, then Mark walked to the door, picked up the bags, and brought them to the table.

Bread. Beans. Fruit. Cured meat. Eggs. Enough for a week at least, and maybe more.

LACTANTIUS

The last several days on board were the longest for Lactantius. He had enjoyed his voyage and the inspiration it added to his writing, and especially his time with his cabinmate. It gave him a chance to ask questions about Christianity in a safe environment. But he was ready to put his feet on solid ground again.

"We're only a day and a half from harbor," the first mate told him. "You'll have to walk the last couple of miles to the palace from there."

Lactantius got up from the box he had been sitting on while watching the changing twists and turns of the shoreline. The channel had narrowed as they navigated through it, and at times he could see land on both sides of the ship. "I'll be glad to walk for a while," he told Nestor. "This ship is getting monotonous."

Nestor grinned. "So how do you plan to get all your boxes and luggage to the palace? With the mail?"

"Sure," replied Lactantius. "Why not? My invitation to visit the emperor has given me free passage this far. There's no reason it can't take me all the way to the palace."

Nestor chuckled. "You've got a lot of gumption. It'll be interesting to see how long it lasts once you're on the emperor's staff."

Lactantius sobered, dropping his pretense of lightheartedness. "I've had second thoughts a number of times," he admitted. "Hopefully there will be a few students interested in Latin. But Nicomedia is a Greek city, and I'm afraid they might be on the scarce side."

He glanced at the sun sinking in the western sky. "After all, if there was really a need for a teacher of Latin in Nicomedia, some enterprising teacher would have been there long ago. But I guess I'll find out soon enough."

The first mate had to get back to work. "I sure hope it goes well for you. As you said, it should be an interesting situation.

"I'll be done in a few hours, so if you have any more questions about Christianity, we can talk about them."

Lactantius did have some questions. He had never been a particularly pious person and worried very little about the gods. If they even existed, he doubted that they spent much time worrying about his opinions or needs. But he could see that Nestor valued his relationship with Christos very highly. This puzzled him. The mate was obviously an intelligent person, not the type to be caught up with myths and conspiracies.

Lactantius lit a candle in the cabin and read to pass the time until Nestor finally returned to the cabin several hours later.

"I've been thinking," Lactantius said, leaning back against the cabin wall and crossing his legs. "Arnobius, my teacher, claimed to be a Christian, yet he seemed to believe that the pagan gods also existed. He considered them inferior to the Christian God, but in his writings he gave many comparisons between them and your God."

He uncrossed his legs and leaned forward. "I asked him why I should follow his God rather than the pagan gods, and he never gave me a good answer. His idea was that all the good people followed Christos, and that should be reason enough."

Nestor settled himself on the bottom bunk a few feet away from Lactantius. He had picked a few apples from the barrel in the galley room, and he handed one to Lactantius before biting into the other one. "It's about time to restock. These apples have been picked through too many times. I had a hard time finding any good ones."

He looked at Lactantius. "So how can you tell if I just gave you a good apple or a bad one?"

Lactantius grinned and took a cautious bite. "Best way is to eat it." He chewed for a moment. "And this one is the best one I've had all week."

Nestor took another bite. "Well, I guess gods are like apples. Some are better than others, and sometimes the only way to find out is to try them."

Lactantius cocked his head. "So, you are telling me that without trying the Christian God I'll never know for sure if He is what He claims to be? Or what you claim He is?"

Nestor nodded. "Something like that, I guess. Though it would need to be an honest trial, without preconceived notions.

"I'm not sure Arnobius was right though," the first mate continued. "I don't think the universe has room for more than one God. If one god is subservient to another one, how can he be a god? He might pretend to be a god, or claim to be one, but in reality, I don't see how more than one can really be God."

He paused, thinking his idea through a little more. "The Holy Writings indicate there are supernatural beings besides God. Take, for instance, angels. Or the devil and his demons. I wouldn't call any of them gods, but some of them have enough power that some people might consider them gods."

Lactantius had been listening closely. "I'm still not persuaded in the existence of any supernatural beings," he finally said. "If they do exist, they don't pay any attention to humans. I think most of them were invented by cranky old ladies who ate too many green apples."

Nestor joined his laughter but sobered down quickly. "How do you account for the universe? The stars? The sun? The water we are sailing on? Your own existence?"

Lactantius took one last bite from his apple before getting up and walking to the door. He opened it and tossed the core over the railing. He gazed at the starlit sky. "I know. That's the one thing that troubles me. It seems there should be a reason for our existence."

He closed the door and sat down again. "But let's say for the sake of argument that the existence of the universe requires the existence of a god. How can we decide who that god is? The stories about the Greek and Roman gods are all myths. No one has ever seen them or talked with them outside those accounts. The Roman gods are just renamed Greek gods. And the Greek gods were Persian gods with different names. How far back do these stories go, anyway? And where did they start?"

Nestor waited until Lactantius had finished his outburst. "But there is one God who has talked with people," he began. "Jesu Christos was God, but He came to earth and was born as a baby. He grew up to be a man and a teacher. He was both God and man. Because He was God, He did miracles and healed many people. Because he was a man, He understood the needs of the world around Him and taught us how to find God and live for Him."

Lactantius drew his eyebrows together, thinking deeply. "Your Holy Writings—do they record these accounts and His teachings?"

Nestor nodded, and Lactantius continued. "But how do we know that we can trust the men who wrote those books? Or Christos, for that matter? Aren't you just replacing one batch of mythological accounts with a different batch?"

"I'm sure you've read many of the myths about the Roman and Greek gods," Nestor said. "You should get some of the Holy Writings and read them. Take the writings of Luke. He wrote an account of Christos' life. He also wrote about the beginning of the Christian church. Get those writings and compare them with what you know about the pagan gods and their followers. The differences between the teachings and actions of Christos and those of the pagan gods are enormous. You are a thinking person, and it will soon be obvious to you which to believe."

Lactantius nodded. "That's a good idea. I'm sure someone in Nicomedia will have copies of the Holy Writings. It has a large Christian community. That will make a good project for this winter."

DIOCLETIAN

Afranius and Julius had just finished sorting some outgoing documents with Hiram when they heard a commotion in front of the palace. A soldier entered Hiram's office a few moments later. "The mail train has arrived, sir. I thought you would want to know."

Hiram bounced to his feet. "Yes, I do. Thank you very much." He glanced at Afranius and Julius. "I wonder if our friend Lactantius has arrived with the mail train."

"Have we figured out where to put him?" Afranius asked. "And supplied him with a bed and a table and a few chairs?"

Hiram nodded. "Everything is ready for him. We are giving him a small outbuilding on the far side of the parade ground. It has living quarters, a little work area for his writing, and a room large enough for him to take in a few students."

"I'll let you two look after him," Julius said. "I have a few items I need to prepare for the emperor to look at during our early morning session."

Outside, Hiram and Afranius watched several loaded donkeys enter the palace court. "That will be him," Hiram said. "I haven't seen him for a long time, but he hasn't changed much."

The two headed across the courtyard. Lactantius was looking around and acquainting himself with the new surroundings. When he saw Afranius and Hiram coming his way, he turned to meet them.

Hiram was all business. "Lactantius, I presume?"

Lactantius nodded. "That's right. I hope you were still expecting me."

"Yes, we were. You are right on schedule. The emperor will be pleased at your arrival." Hiram looked at the donkeys with a critical eye. "These are your belongings?"

"Yes, that's right," Lactantius replied. "Mostly scrolls and writing supplies. I assumed that lodgings and furniture will be supplied. If not, I will need to do some improvising."

Afranius smiled. "Hiram has everything ready for you. He's very organized. Follow us and we'll show you your living quarters." He glanced at the donkeys again. "Do the donkeys also belong to you?"

Lactantius lowered his voice. "No, they belong to the mail service. They are quite anxious to have them back, and I am happy to give them back to them. I am not fond of donkeys and never will be. These two have not been an exception."

Afranius led the way to the building where Lactantius would be staying. "You can take your meals in the guards' mess hall. That will save you needing to prepare your own meals. Hiram and I eat there as well, and the food is normally quite good."

He paused before adding, "You might want to say as little as possible about traveling with the mail. Diocletian is a bit old-fashioned with money and doesn't like to spend more than he has to."

He glanced at Hiram. "We understand why you traveled that way, of course. But it might be better that we don't find out how you arranged it.

"We meet with the emperor at 6:00 in the morning. It would be good for you to be at that meeting so we can discuss your work."

The two donkey attendants had already unloaded his

belongings in front of the outbuilding, and after Lactantius dismissed them with his thanks, he turned to Afranius again. "I am curious about that. Latin isn't the native language of many of the people in this area. How great a demand will there be for my services?"

Afranius and Hiram looked at each other, but Hiram answered. "As I said in my letter, Diocletian wants to promote the use of Latin. He doesn't feel comfortable with any other language even though he can speak some Greek. He is trying to make a statement by having you here. You'll probably have some students, but I'm not sure how many."

Lactantius glanced at the sun, gauging the time. "Maybe I should spend my time teaching the emperor Greek. That might be more useful."

Hiram smiled. "Perhaps, but I would advise you to get to know him a bit before you suggest it. He may want to use you as a translator sometimes, but I don't think he has any intention of you tutoring him."

MARK

"The emperor is promoting the teaching of Latin in Nicomedia," Andrew announced as he and Irene joined Mark and Lydia at their supper table. "His new Latin teacher has arrived from Numidia. He came with the mail pack train."

"That's interesting," Mark said. "I heard several months ago that the emperor had asked a teacher to come to the city. But why Latin?"

"I've heard that the emperor hates Greek," Irene replied.

"He hates any language except Latin. This is his way of telling Rome and especially Nicomedia that he wants us to speak Latin."

Mark took a drink. "I'd be interested in meeting this new teacher and asking him some questions about Greek. I wonder if he knows Hebrew."

Andrew put down his spoon. "He is welcoming visitors every afternoon from now until the weekend so people can meet him. I suppose he hopes to pick up some students that way."

Lydia smiled at Mark. "There's your chance," she said. "I'm sure he'd enjoy meeting you. You could try out your favorite quote on him."

LACTANTIUS

Even though Diocletian was promoting Latin, that didn't automatically translate into students for Lactantius. Hiram suggested to the emperor that they put up notices at the marketplace and a few other places to promote an open house.

The posters did bring a few people. Some of them signed on, though not as many as Lactantius or Hiram had hoped. However, the most far-reaching effect of the open house was Mark's decision to stop by.

Lactantius saw him walking across the parade grounds and came to the door to meet him. Mark introduced himself and welcomed Lactantius to Nicomedia.

"My mother was highly trained in languages," Mark told him. "She has always loved the classical literature of Greece and Rome and has taught me to read and analyze them. Rhetoric is an interest of mine." He didn't mention the Holy Writings, since he didn't know how Lactantius felt about Christianity.

This young man interested Lactantius. "We could have many educational discussions, I'm sure," he told Mark. "I love languages and literature. Teaching rhetoric is one of the practical ways to make a living from those interests."

He glanced more closely at Mark and noted that he was dressed in the clothing of an ordinary working man, though he didn't seem to be one. "Are you a teacher? What have you done with your education?"

Mark was reasonably sure that he could safely speak to Lactantius. "I am in training for a presbyter in the local Christian community," he confided. "I have studied the Holy Writings in both Latin and Greek. My work as a presbyter is quite like that of a teacher, except that teachers get paid and presbyters don't."

This explanation startled Lactantius. He had never met a Christian leader, and this was a rare opportunity. This young man had the qualifications and the abilities to help him answer his questions. But he needed to take a few precautions.

He lowered his voice. "Why don't you pull the door shut? We can talk better that way."

Mark did so, curious as to what Lactantius wanted to discuss.

"I shared a cabin with a Christian during my journey from Numidia," Lactantius continued. "I am not a pious person and don't have much interest in the gods. Nor do I believe that the gods—if they even exist—have any interest in me. But we discussed some things that I would be interested in hearing your opinions on."

Mark nodded. "Sure, I'd be happy to discuss them with you." He glanced at the window.

Lactantius noticed his glance. "We are safe here, I think. No one comes to see me, and my open house is over. I will soon need to join the others for supper, but until then we are free.

"But first, weren't some of your Holy Writings written by a doctor named Luke?"

Mark nodded, and Lactantius continued, "I would like to read those books. Luke seems to have been an educated man who wasn't a Jew. I would like to evaluate his impressions of Christianity."

"Yes, Luke's writing is good," Mark replied. "He wrote the story of Christos from a Gentile perspective. He also wrote an account of the first thirty years of the church, up until the imprisonment of Paul."

Lactantius leaned forward eagerly. "We passed the island of Malta on my way here. My cabinmate told me the story of Paul's shipwreck and pointed out the area where it happened."

Mark smiled. "I might be able to loan you a copy of Luke's writings," he offered cautiously. "We have a repository of Holy Writings that we sometimes use for that purpose. Of course, it would be ideal if you could have someone make a copy for your library."

Lactantius squirmed. "Unless my income increases dramatically, that would be out of the question for now," he admitted. "It will be a long time before I can pay a copyist for such a long writing."

Mark understood. "I think I can work something out. I'll see what I can do."

Mark got to his feet. "Well, I have to go. I'll talk to my wife and maybe we can have you come over for a meal sometime. I could show you some scrolls that I think would interest you."

He stopped before opening the door. "Do you prefer Greek or Latin? We have both."

Lactantius hesitated. "They were originally written in Greek, weren't they? I'd rather read them in their original rendering. I know I'm supposed to be promoting and teaching Latin. But when it comes down to it, Greek is better for conveying ideas and concepts."

Mark nodded. "I agree. I read both equally well, but I'm never sure if the translator got the right feeling into his rendering. I find that when I compare the two, the original has more clarity."

A.D. 296-300

Life soon settled into a routine for Lactantius. He had enough students to pay for his needs, and he got his meals at the palace dining hall. Though it wasn't what he had hoped for, he was surviving. But was it enough to satisfy the emperor?

L actantius started out early, intending to stop at the market on his way to Mark's dwelling for lunch. *I haven't explored Nicomedia much and I'm tired of being cooped up here in the palace,* he mused. *Hiram is friendly, but he doesn't have enough imagination to be a good companion. He just lives for his work.*

He had noticed the building on the hill before, but it caught his eye again as he left the palace. *I wonder what that building is going to be used for?* He wandered across the wide street and up the incline to the building. A group of men were mounting some ornate fixtures on the outside wall, but one of them walked over to meet him.

"Good morning. Can I help you?" The speaker was obviously a supervisor and accustomed to meeting people.

Lactantius watched as the workers carefully lined up what he could now see was a cross. He turned to the supervisor. "I'm new in the area and was just curious what is going on here. I see it must be a Christian temple or meeting place."

The supervisor nodded. "That's right. We've been working on it for some years. It should be ready for use in several years. By the way, my name is Andrew."

"Pleased to meet you, Andrew," Lactantius replied. "I'm the new teacher of Latin at the palace. My name is Lactantius."

Andrew's face lit up. "Ah, so you're the man helping with Diocletian's experiment in Latinizing the local barbarians. I heard that you met my son Mark."

Lactantius looked surprised. "Yes, I did. In fact, I'm on my way to his home to have lunch with him and his wife right now. He said your wife taught him languages and rhetoric."

"She sure did," Andrew replied. "She taught both Mark and Lydia a few years ago, though Lydia was more into the practical areas—ciphering and such like. We had some interesting times around our house in those days. Tell him you don't trust Greeks, even if they come bearing gifts."

Lactantius laughed. "So he's a student of Virgil, is he? I'll have to remember that."

Andrew laughed as well. "Lydia will probably respond, 'I've no mind to be a Caesar.' It's an old joke between her and Mark."

After chatting with Andrew a few more minutes, Lactantius headed on downtown. *The Christians in this city must be quite well to do,* he told himself. *That's sure a fancy building for a Christian meetinghouse. I thought they met in barns and warehouses. Diocletian must be pretty easygoing if he allows them to build right across from his palace.*

Lactantius wandered through the marketplace. He soon decided that a marketplace was a marketplace, no matter where it was. This one was just as dirty and noisy as the one close to his home in Africa. He stopped and listened to a beggar reciting Latin poetry at the top of his lungs. Both the Latin and the poetry were so bad that he finally turned away in disgust.

He bought some fruit to take along for his share of the lunch, but found nothing else that interested him. One stand offered scrolls at exorbitant prices. The seller saw his interest and immediately tried to sell him a scroll. "It's a certified copy of the story of Odysseus," he wheedled. "Really good price for such a valuable scroll."

Lactantius looked at it, more out of curiosity than from any desire to buy it. He already had a copy in his collection. This scroll seemed too short, and he soon saw that it contained only the first part of the epic poem—in very bad handwriting and with many mistakes. He turned away in disgust. When the seller protested, he looked him in the eye. "Sir, you are a fraud. That scroll is rubbish. Homer would have you executed for using his name like that."

The seller protested vigorously. "Homer is a friend of mine

and gave me the scroll himself. I swear it." His assistant nodded his agreement, but Lactantius shook his head in astonishment.

"You must be very old," he said sarcastically. "Old enough to know better. Homer has been dead for over seven hundred years. Maybe you should learn some history before you make such absurd statements."

———— MARK ————

Mark brought several scrolls home at lunchtime. One was Luke's account of the life of Christ, and another was Acts. He also brought John's account of the life of Christ and a copy of the Revelation.

Lydia looked at him dubiously when she saw the scroll of the Revelation among the others. "Why would you give him a copy of the Revelation to read? Even some Christians can't make any sense of it, let alone a pagan."

Mark looked sheepish. "I am curious. Lactantius' mind is an open book at this point, and it will be interesting to see what a pagan scholar thinks of it. At least he won't have any preconceived ideas."

Lactantius arrived soon after Mark. He handed his basket of fruit to Lydia. "I know Mark doesn't trust Greeks bearing gifts," he said, grinning. "So I'll give it to you instead."

Lydia's mouth dropped open. "How . . . where . . . who told you that?" she sputtered.

"The same person who assured me that you had no intentions of becoming Caesar," he replied dryly.

Mark eyed him. "You weren't talking to my father by any chance?"

Lactantius pretended to look surprised. "Where would I have met your father?"

"Well, it was either my father or my mother," Mark replied. "No one else would know that one."

Lactantius relented. "I stopped to look at the new temple the Christians are building. Your father was there, and I chatted with him."

He glanced at the table where Mark had left the scrolls. "I stopped at the market on my way here. A vendor tried to sell me the worst scroll of Homer I ever saw. And then he claimed Homer had personally given it to him."

Mark and Lydia joined in his laughter, but Mark looked incredulous. "He expected you to believe that?"

"I doubt if he could even read," Lactantius replied. "I'll admit it upset me."

Lunch passed quickly as they got to know each other. Then Mark and Lactantius got down to business. Lactantius wanted to see the scrolls and had some questions.

Mark started with Luke's writings. "This scroll tells the story of Christos," he said, picking it up reverently. "He's the only writer who tells the account of Christos' birth in any detail. It is a good choice for you to start with.

"Luke's first scroll ends with the ascension of Christos into heaven." He handed Lactantius the scroll and picked up the second one. "This is his second scroll. It's called the Acts of the Apostles. It starts with the ascension and continues the story until the imprisonment of Paul after the shipwreck at

Malta about thirty years later."

Mark handed over the second scroll as well. Lactantius took it carefully. He knew how big a favor Mark was doing by loaning them to him. He unrolled the first one and noticed the quality of the penmanship right away. "These are valuable copies," he said. "I will guard them with my life. I am very grateful to you for letting me borrow them."

Mark smiled at his eagerness and picked up the third scroll. "This one is a parallel account to the first of Luke's writings. It tells the same story but from a different perspective. Luke was interested in portraying Christos as the Savior and friend of sinners. The Apostle John wrote this in the later years of his life, and he focuses on the person of Christos— His teachings and His character. The two writings make an excellent comparison, and to really know Christos you need to read both."

Mark picked up the last scroll gingerly. "This one is an experiment. Lydia doesn't think I should give it to you, but I'd be interested in your thoughts. It was also written by John, but in the form of apocalyptic literature. Some people think it records the history of the world as God sees it. Others think it speaks of a coming destruction of humanity at the end of time. Still others claim it is meaningless and shouldn't be part of the Holy Writings at all."[1]

"The winter should be short with this much to read," Lactantius said with pleasure. "It will be an educational one too." Carefully he placed the scrolls in his bag, and the

---

[1] The New Testament canon was not finalized until nearly seventy years later. The Council of Laodicea (A.D. 363) still omitted the Revelation, though it had been unofficially accepted in many parts of the church.

discussion turned to other things.

"I've never really believed in supernatural or divine beings," Lactantius admitted. "How can we be sure that the gods exist? And even if they do, why would they pay any attention to us? When I look at the world and the universe, I can see why people might believe it was planned by someone. But does that someone—if he exists—notice me?"

After a pause he continued, "The Christians say that Christos came to tell us who God really is and what He wants of us. They say He loves us, but also that He has a very strict standard and will punish anyone who doesn't obey Him. At least the pagan gods are no better than the rest of us. They commit adultery and kill each other, just as humans do. So if they do exist, they should at least understand us."

Mark smiled. "I suppose your first question is the first one we need to answer. Do the gods even exist? If you conclude that they don't, the other questions don't need to be answered. But if you decide that gods do exist, then you need to address who they are, whether they take any personal interest in you, and what they expect of you."

Lactantius nodded. "But how do you go about deciding if the gods—or the Christian God—exist? What are the criteria?"

Mark leaned back on his stool. "My mother should be here. She thrives on logic. She was raised a pagan and would have some definite thoughts on your questions."

He looked at Lactantius quizzically. "You're a lot older and more experienced in logic than I am. What criteria would you lay down from an intellectual perspective?"

Lactantius rubbed his chin. "Hmm. That's a good question.

Normally, I'd start by looking for physical proof of some sort. At the very least, I'd want some historical evidence. For instance, how do I know Homer was a real person?"

He wasn't really asking Mark, but Mark answered anyway. "One evidence is his writing. We have copies of what he wrote."

Lactantius nodded. "We also have other writers who knew Homer or knew of him. So he doesn't appear to be an imaginary figure."

He pursed his lips, thinking his way through the issue before continuing. "In the case of a god, we'd also expect some supernatural evidence. If a god is no different than a man, then he's just a man, not a god."

"That's a good starting point," Mark said. "I think you will find the needed evidence in the scrolls I've loaned you. John's writings about Christos will give you the eyewitness accounts, and Luke will give you the historical perspective. As to the supernatural aspect, both describe some of the miracles Christos performed. And Luke's writings about the early church tell us how the message of Christos changed people. Why don't you start by reading the evidence? Then we can talk again."

Lactantius got to his feet. "That sounds good. We can't really continue the discussion until I've looked at the evidence. That will take me a while."[2]

---

[2] Lactantius later wrote the *Divine Institutes*, an apologetic treatise aimed to show pagans that it was reasonable to believe in the Christian God. It seems obvious that he went through a time of introspection, which later enabled him to speak to others in a similar situation.

DIOCLETIAN

While Diocletian spent the winter at home in Nicomedia, Galerius was in Sirmium, a city close to the Danube River that served as the capital of the region he ruled. Now it was spring, and Galerius was back in Nicomedia.

After spending much of the night drinking and gambling, Diocletian was suffering from a hangover. He had a serious headache and was in a bad mood.

Galerius, however, was his normal impious self, and his young wife, Valeria, was almost ready to hire an assassin. But he just laughed at her, nonchalantly shrugging off the effects of his night of dissipation.

Prisca was also having a bad day. Normally she and Diocletian had a working relationship, but he didn't cope well with late-night drinking parties, and she took the brunt of it.

The palace was a smoking powder keg that morning and the staff stepped gingerly. Afranius and Hiram arrived promptly for the morning session, but Diocletian was almost an hour late. He glowered at them through red eyes. "What is that teacher of Latin doing these days?" he growled. "Is he doing anything worthwhile, or is he just living off the fat of the land at my expense? How many students does he have by now? He's been here almost a year."

He sat at his normal spot at the table and glared at Hiram. "Send someone to get him out of bed. Or better yet, go yourself. I want a report from him this morning. And it had better be a good one."

Hiram got to his feet, then hesitated. "Lactantius has a morning class with a half dozen or so young men from some of the better homes in the city," he said smoothly. "It starts at seven o'clock, so he will be busy. But I'm sure he will gladly come if you want him."

"He doesn't start until seven?" Diocletian snapped. "He should be at work by six. The rest of us don't get to dawdle around in the morning like that."

Hiram shrugged and left. By now Galerius had entered the room. With cynical eyes he watched Hiram leave. "I think that secretary of yours is getting a bit too big for his britches," he told Diocletian with a growl. "You should give him to me for while. I'd take him down a notch or two."

Diocletian turned on him viciously. "You leave your hands off him, you hear me? Between him and Afranius, they keep this place running. If he left, Afranius would go too. And we can't have that."

As Hiram had told Diocletian, Lactantius had started classes. Hiram had given the number of students to Lactantius' advantage, because only three were in attendance when he tapped at the classroom door.

When Lactantius saw who his visitor was, he stepped outside, shutting the door behind him. He raised his eyebrows questioningly.

"The emperor wants to see you," Hiram said. "He evidently drank too much last night and is in an ill mood this morning. He wants a report from you on your work, and he wants it now." He smiled bleakly before adding, "And he says it had better be a good one."

Lactantius rubbed his chin and glanced toward the sky. "Hmm. Is the report required to be true? Things have actually been rather bleak overall. I've had lots of time for improving myself and furthering my studies, but he probably isn't thinking in such terms."

This time Hiram's smile was real. "Don't tell any lies," he advised, "but it is acceptable to be rather vague. And be optimistic about future possibilities. Maybe toss in a few success stories. You're a master in rhetoric, and you have about two minutes to get ready. You'll make out."

Lactantius wracked his brain as he followed Hiram across the courtyard. He had been expecting something like this sooner or later.

Diocletian was on his feet when they entered the meeting room. He was barking orders at Afranius and at the same time putting Galerius in his place. He stopped abruptly in mid-sentence and turned to face Lactantius.

"What is your schedule? What time do you get up? Why aren't you working before seven?"

Lactantius was tall and lanky and easygoing. He seldom worried about situations he faced, and he didn't worry about this one. If Diocletian kicked him out, something else would show up. This nonchalance, and the fact that he was at least six inches taller than the emperor, was in his favor.

Calmness in the face of confrontation either infuriates an adversary or calms him down. Fortunately for Lactantius, it was the latter. Diocletian waved him impatiently to a chair across the table. "I can't discuss matters reasonably with someone who towers over me," he snapped. "Sit down."

Lactantius sat down. So did Diocletian—to the relief of Afranius and Hiram.

Diocletian started over, moderating his tone. "Tell us about your work, your schedule, and your hopes for the future. Do you feel you are being successful?"

Lactantius would have smiled had he dared. This would turn out all right. He started in carefully. "I normally get up at half past four and have breakfast at five." He omitted the fact that he ate with the officers and staff in the palace dining area. "I then prepare for the day's classes until my students show up for their morning session.

"After that I have lunch and prepare for my afternoon session. That is over by suppertime. After supper, I study or read or play checkers[3] with Hiram."

Lactantius kept his eye on Diocletian and decided this was probably enough detail about his day's schedule. "I wrote a lengthy poem about my journey across the Mediterranean, and I am studying and improving it with my students. We often work at logic and debate, both of which use rhetoric to improve thinking skills. It is a definite advantage to work with youth in these areas. Their minds are pliable and they soak up the information like sponges." He chuckled. "They especially like that it helps them win arguments with their friends."

He noticed the emperor's interest and dug an appropriate illustration from the recesses of his mind. "We were discussing the likelihood of the existence of the gods the other week. I divided the class into two parts and gave them several days to come up with arguments. I didn't care so much about the outcome; I

---

[3] The Romans played many games in which pebbles were moved from one square to another in a grid. These grids are found scratched into floor stones and floor tiles all over the Roman Empire, wherever men or women, or boys or girls, had some time to waste.

was mainly concerned about their use of logic and persuasion."

Lactantius had inadvertently landed on one of the emperor's pet subjects, and Diocletian sat forward. "So what was the conclusion?" he asked.

Lactantius smiled and belatedly remembered an earlier discussion with Hiram about Diocletian's obsession with being an envoy of Jupiter. "Well, the subject was a bit advanced for them," he began. "One young man felt that since he had never seen a god and no god had ever spoken to him, logic dictated that there was no such thing.

"Another student pointed out that man's very existence should indicate something. They finally concluded that unless some strong evidence to the contrary came up, logic would dictate that the odds are in favor of the gods existing."

Lactantius painted his account with a broad brush. In reality, the discussion had gotten very serious, reflecting some of his own thoughts from a winter of studying the Holy Writings. The students had gone home seriously considering that there might be a God who cared quite a bit about them and their choices.

But what Diocletian didn't know wouldn't hurt him. The emperor seemed satisfied. "That sounds interesting," he said. "I won't keep you from your students."

Lactantius nodded his acceptance of the dismissal and left. Diocletian, walking to the other side of the room to get a glass of wine, missed Galerius' remark. "There goes a dangerous man."

But Afranius and Hiram both heard him and glanced at each other. Thankfully, Galerius dropped the subject.

Afranius and Hiram discussed it later, however. "I wonder what Galerius meant," Afranius said.

Hiram lowered his voice. "Galerius heard how Lactantius manipulated Diocletian. He knew what Lactantius was doing even if Diocletian didn't."

Afranius nodded. "It was a work of art, you have to admit. I wasn't at all sure if Lactantius would survive the meeting. At the very least, I expected Diocletian to kick him out onto the street."

"That's why rhetoric is such a strong weapon," Hiram replied. "Someone who has learned the art of persuasion can make a person believe what he wants him to believe. It is much more successful than using force."

——— MARK ———

Irene had wanted to meet Lactantius ever since Mark had told her about their contacts. She felt a kinship with him because of their common background in paganism and education. One day she decided to visit Lydia and drop off some fruit on her way home from the market. She was surprised to find Mark at home.

"Do you have the day off?" she asked. The bishop had drawn Mark into his inner circle as an unofficial assistant. This, along with his regular duties as a presbyter, kept Mark busy, and he was seldom at home in the daytime.

Mark was relaxing at the table, drinking calda. "No, not really," he replied. "Lactantius is dropping by in a few minutes. We've been discussing his study of Luke's writings, and now he's read John's story of Christos and wants to discuss the differences."

Over the winter Mark and Lactantius had built up a mutual

respect and friendship that would last a lifetime. Lactantius hadn't committed himself to the Christian faith but was seriously thinking about it.

Lactantius arrived a few moments later and was as pleased to meet Irene as she was to meet him. "Your son does credit to your teaching," he said. "I have never met a young man with such abilities and understanding. He has been a challenge to me."

Irene looked pleased. "He has an inborn interest in knowledge. He and Lydia were a joy to teach, but he has far surpassed me now."

Lactantius didn't look too sure about this. "It takes a good teacher to produce a student who can do that," he said. "But he told me you were born into a pagan home and were taught pagan beliefs when you were a child. How did you make the transition to believing in Christos?"

Irene hesitated. "It's a long story," she finally said, "and I'm not sure I can fully explain it." She paused, her lips quivering as the awful memories came rushing back. "I remember so well that night when the soldiers came and executed my family. I was still a young girl, only twelve years old—a child, actually—but the horrors of that night will be with me as long as I live. Thankfully, I had been near a door and managed to escape, but through a window I saw them being killed.

"I was taken in by a childless Christian couple after they found me crying in the alleyway. They gave me a home until I married Andrew. My foster parents showed me the love of Christ in their actions. Not only did they accept me as one of their own, but I often saw them give sacrificially to help others. When I compared that with the pagans who—" Irene's voice broke as she struggled for words, "who raped my mother and sisters before lining them up with my father for execution, I knew what I wanted to be a part of.

"I know that not all pagans are bad people, but the pagan gods don't teach love and goodwill like Christos does."

Lactantius understood. "I'm sorry for what you went through. And I agree with your viewpoint of the pagan gods. I always felt it was foolish to believe in gods that don't care about the people who worship them.

"I've read and reread the scrolls Mark loaned me. They very clearly bring out what you are saying. Yahweh is a God who reaches down to help me up, even when I'm unworthy. Gods such as Jupiter brush me aside and tell me to look after myself and work out my own problems."

He laid the precious scrolls on the table and addressed Mark. "I want to thank you again for making these available to me. It was what I needed. I want to take whatever steps are necessary to become a Christian and be a part of your fellowship."

"It's not an easy road, Lactantius," Mark told him soberly. "There will be much opposition from the evil powers that you are denouncing. It will require turning your back on worldly ease and pleasure and, instead, welcoming poverty and hardship—for the sake of Christos."

Lactantius nodded. "That is why I have waited this long to make my decision. I wanted to be sure I was ready, as Christos said, to take up my cross. I know it will not be easy. But my life has not been satisfying. Why should I not look for something more fulfilling?"

Irene probably understood his commitment better than any

of them. "You have made an important choice, my friend," she told him solemnly. "I believe you will not be sorry, even if the road isn't easy."

Mark picked up the scrolls. "I have been praying that you would make this choice. I talked with Bishop Anthimus about it this morning, and he has left his afternoon open for you to come discuss this further if you want to."

LACTANTIUS

Bishop Anthimus was older than Lactantius by at least a decade. He looked frail, almost emaciated, partly from the many days he spent fasting. He had a straggly gray beard and piercing blue eyes that seemed to look straight through Lactantius, but his voice was kind and pleasant.

"I'm pleased to hear of the choice you have made," he said. "Mark has been updating me, and I have spent many hours in prayer for your salvation. You have begun a long road. I'm not sure what Mark has told you about our expectations."

"We've talked about it a little," Lactantius replied. "I understand that I will be taught the faith and be considered a catechumen[4] for several years, and that someone will be my sponsor and stand by me during this time."

"That's right," Anthimus said. "And at the end of your time of instruction, he will be required to vouch that you qualify for baptism. Do you have any questions about this procedure?"

Lactantius hesitated. "I do have a few," he admitted. "I

---

[4] A candidate for baptism.

noticed in Luke's writings that converts were baptized immediately after their choice to follow Christos. I am curious why you require a few years of indoctrination first."

Anthimus smiled. "That is a good question; I see you studied the scrolls carefully. It is true that in the earlier years believers were baptized immediately on their confession. However, at the beginning, most of them were Jewish believers who were already well grounded in their faith. Even when pagans were converted, they were mostly surrounded by Jewish believers who were able to help them on their way.

"Also," he continued, "the danger of death was very real, which made baptism more urgent. But as time went on, the church saw that most of the converts needed more training in discipleship and faith. Some gave up when life got difficult. Others were swayed by false teachers. Because of this, we have adopted this practice over the past several centuries. It has been a blessing to the church to have its members rooted in the truth.

"Sometimes people worry that they might die during the catechesis process and be lost. It is true that baptism is part of experiencing salvation, and if we knew that you were likely to die this week, we would consider baptizing you. But we believe that salvation is a process and that God knows you have undertaken this process. He knows your heart.

"You will find various nuances of belief among us. Tertullian, for instance, believed that the Holy Spirit entered the applicant when he was anointed with oil. I believe that the process of salvation is somewhat of a mystery. Only God knows exactly when it takes place. But He also knows that you are serious about this, and I strongly believe He would not reject a person who is in the instruction process simply because he hasn't been baptized yet."[5]

This made sense to Lactantius, but he had another question. "I know there are some Christians among the palace staff. But I was wondering about my position there as a teacher. It just doesn't seem to me that Christos would have lived in a palace as an applauded teacher of this world's wisdom. Is this something that would concern you?"[6]

Now it was the bishop's turn to hesitate, and he answered carefully. "I've been thinking about that. If the Spirit of Christos has already brought this to your attention, you should follow His leading. Could you make a living by teaching rhetoric in a different setting? What about working as a copyist or a clerk?"

——— MARK ———

As Lactantius' mentor and sponsor, Mark's schedule became even more hectic. They met every morning before Lactantius' classes started for an hour of instruction by Anthimus or one of the presbyters. About once a week they also met with an exorcist[7] appointed by the church to help Lactantius identify and deal with the powers of evil in his life. They also spent time visiting the sick and helping those in need. These practical spiritual exercises were designed to help Lactantius reprogram his desires and aspirations to be more like Christos.

---

[5] I realize that this is not quite the way today's Christians and theologians who have been influenced by fundamentalism would explain salvation. It is, however, how someone in this setting would have believed.

[6] It is known that Lactantius left his position in the palace when he became a Christian.

[7] Exorcists were people assigned by the church to expel evil spirits.

It seemed Lactantius had waited his entire lifetime for this, and he put himself wholeheartedly into his spiritual training. He soon resigned his position at the palace and eked out a miserly income by writing and clerking. But he had never been happier, and he was looking forward to his baptism.

Several years passed. "Do you feel Lactantius is ready for baptism?" Anthimus asked Mark one day. "Has he completed his training successfully? Is he ready for his final entry into the kingdom of Christos?"

Mark's reply was confident. "Yes, I believe he is ready. He has done very well in his training— far beyond our normal expectations. I have no problem recommending him for baptism."

Anthimus was pleased. "You have done very well, Mark. We will baptize him in several weeks, at Easter time. We will also promote you from a trainee to a completely consecrated presbyter at the same time."

This was no surprise to Mark. He had known that his apprenticeship was nearing its end. But he was glad he could share in Lactantius' baptism.

"I will leave the final preparations with Lactantius to you," Anthimus said. "Make sure he is ready to recite the creed[8] with his final testimony."

——— LACTANTIUS ———

Lactantius was a changed man. He still enjoyed literature, but now he spent his free time studying the Holy Writings.

---

[8] This would have been the Old Roman Creed, which was a forerunner of the more commonly known Apostles' Creed.

The church had given him access to its library, especially the books stored at Andrew's house. He often spent evenings with Andrew and Irene or Mark and Lydia. He especially enjoyed discussing the various writings with Mark and Irene.

He carefully studied the Revelation. Mark's description of it had sparked his interest from the beginning, and the two spent hours going through it again. Mark also introduced him to the Jewish Scriptures.[9] Lactantius was particularly interested in the prophetic writings.

"Daniel the prophet speaks of some of the same things the Revelation does," Lactantius told Mark one evening. "Surely there must be a way to figure out the meaning of some of these prophecies."[10]

As his baptism drew close, he spent a lot of time in introspection. "You know, I used to consider myself a deep thinker," he told Mark. "But as I look back over my life, I can see how shallow-minded I was. The teachings of Jesus are so profound, yet so simple to read and understand compared to Virgil and Homer and the other great writers.

"But that isn't the only way I've changed. I still enjoy reading, but I get a greater thrill out of helping some poor person in need."

Even Lactantius' thought processes had changed. He no longer enjoyed using rhetoric to humiliate or overcome others. Instead, he often talked about Christos to those he met. At least half a dozen converts were going through the process for baptism because of his testimony.

---

[9] The Old Testament.

[10] Lactantius was intrigued by prophecies for the rest of his life. He did a lot of writing and built up a theology of eschatology amazingly similar to some of today's ideas.

Easter weekend arrived bright and clear. Lactantius had spent the latter part of the week in prayer and fasting with Mark. While the church gathered for the Easter vigil on Saturday night, Lactantius and several other catechumens met for several hours of prayer and the final preparations for their baptism. They had been waiting for this for several years—now the time was finally here.

Lactantius reminisced as he waited for his turn to enter the baptismal pool. *So this is why God brought me to Nicomedia. I wonder what Diocletian would think if he realized the result of his "Latinization" experiment.*

Then it was his turn. He shivered as he entered the water, not because the water was cold but because of his anticipation. It was almost like a dream, the bishop's hands on his head gently pushing him below the surface of the water— once, twice, three times—then helping him from the pool and pouring warm oil on his head. It was the moment he had been looking forward to for several years.

Then he dressed in fresh white clothing and joined the rest of the little group at the front of the rejoicing congregation. There were songs of praise, readings from the Holy Writings, and testimonies from the newly baptized. He would never forget the memories of this special day.[11]

Neither would Mark.

---

[11] For a comprehensive treatise on the beliefs and practices of the early church about baptism, see Tertullian, *On Baptism,* in the Ante-Nicene Fathers, Vol. 3.

PART VI

A.D. 302

Ominous Rumblings

Narseus, king of the Persians, emulating the example set him by his grandfather Sapores, assembled a great army and aimed at becoming master of the eastern provinces of the Roman Empire. Diocletian, apt to be low-spirited and timorous in every commotion and fearing a fate like that of Valerian, would not in person encounter Narseus; but he sent Galerius by the way of Armenia, while he himself halted in the eastern provinces and anxiously watched the event. It is a custom amongst the barbarians to take everything that belongs to them into the field. Galerius laid an ambush for them and easily overthrew men embarrassed with the multitude of their followers and with their baggage. Having put Narseus to flight and returned with much spoil, his own pride and Diocletian's fears were greatly increased.

—Lactantius, *Of the Manner in Which the Persecutors Died,* Chap. 9

A.D. 299

The Persian Empire had long been a thorn in the flesh for the Roman Empire. Just the year before, Narseh, the king of Persia, had declared war again. Although the Romans had pushed him back and negotiated a new peace agreement, Diocletian and Galerius couldn't agree on what to do next. Maybe they could ask the gods. But what if the gods didn't know? Or refused to answer?

Diocletian liked life to be cut and dried. But somehow, since negotiating a final peace with the Persians, he had hit a stalemate. It irritated him. He liked to feel in control.

It didn't help matters that Galerius had accompanied him to Antioch. Having him around always made Diocletian uptight.

Afranius and Hiram were also there, and they weren't happy about it either. "I'm getting too old to travel all over the country like this," Afranius said over breakfast in Hiram's temporary office. "And it doesn't help that Diocletian's been so cranky the last while."

Hiram wiped his mouth with the back of his hand before replying. "I'd rather be back in Nicomedia too, but at least this is better than being in an army camp."

Afranius chuckled. Hiram had never been fond of roughing it. "Well, at least Diocletian has long gotten over the notion that you could do your work on horseback."

Hiram groaned. "Those were some of the worst days of my life. If he hadn't come to his senses when he did, I would have run off. Or drowned myself. Or something." He jerked his head emphatically.

"But you're right," he added. "Something is bothering him. Of course, he doesn't really trust or like Galerius. And they've been drinking too much again."

Afranius nodded. "Galerius is dangerous, and Diocletian knows it. He's half scared of him, I think."

"I suspect Galerius has plans," Hiram replied, frowning. "Someday he'll either push Diocletian aside or have him assassinated. That's why Diocletian keeps sending him out with the army to fight his wars."

Afranius got to his feet and scratched under his ribs. "My bed is infested with fleas," he growled. "I hardly slept last night. I hope we leave this place before long. If we're going to stay here in Antioch, we should at least be comfortable."

Hiram got to his feet as well. "I have a feeling we're going to stay a while," he said, stretching. "Diocletian doesn't trust the Persians, despite the whipping Galerius gave them. He wants to stay close to the border in case they get restless again."

Afranius chuckled. "I don't think he needs to worry about that. Galerius ran all over King Narseh last fall. Even captured his wife and his concubines and all their children. Then he let him stew for the winter rather than making peace last fall when he wanted it. They were good and ready for our peace terms by this spring."

Hiram followed him across the courtyard to the main building where Diocletian and Galerius were staying. "The terms probably weren't as harsh as Narseh expected," he said. "He seemed eager to agree. I think he expected Galerius to keep his women."[1]

Diocletian and Galerius were already in the room where they met each morning—bickering as usual.

"I'm not planning to stay here any longer than I have to," Galerius said. "I'm heading west as soon as I can. Narseh is beaten for good. He won't show his face west of the border again. But we should have cleaned him up good while we had the chance, instead of giving his wives and children back to him."

Diocletian shook his head. "That would have brought him back on us for sure. We treated him better than he deserved, yet harshly enough for him to know that we meant business. If you push an enemy too hard, you'll upset him to the point that he gets reckless and does a lot of damage."

Galerius rolled his eyes. "I think you're getting soft," he said. "You had no problem making me walk in that military parade by myself in front of you ten years ago after I lost that

---

[1] Some historians take this view, and others feel they were exceptionally harsh.

first battle with the Persians."[2]

Diocletian's eyebrows pulled together dangerously. "You deserved every bit of that," he said. "The way you botched that battle, I should have demoted you and packed you off to the frontier for the rest of your life. If you hadn't been married to my daughter, I would have."

Galerius glared at Diocletian. Obviously, the sting of Diocletian's treatment still festered. "I didn't see you out there showing me how to do it better," he replied. "You were cowering back at home—afraid you'd get captured like Valerian was. At least I was on the battlefield."

Diocletian finally noticed Afranius and Hiram. "About time you got here," he growled. "We need to decide our next move. Sit down." He glared at Galerius. "You too."

Galerius, however, was not in an agreeable frame of mind and shot down most of Diocletian's suggestions. The bickering continued. Galerius wanted to head for home, but Diocletian wanted to stick around for a while in case the Persians acted up again.

Diocletian finally had enough. He pounded the table with his fist. "This is getting us nowhere!" he shouted. "Only the gods know the future. I'm going to call for the haruspices[3] to kill some animals and read their entrails for us. We'll go by whatever the gods tell us to do."

Galerius shrugged. "Suit yourself. I guess I can't fight the opinion of the gods." Afranius glanced at Hiram. Was Galerius

---

[2] Soon after Galerius was proclaimed Caesar, he lost an important battle. Diocletian punished him by making him walk by himself in front of a military parade.

[3] Haruspices practiced divination by inspecting the livers of freshly slaughtered sheep and chickens.

COUNTDOWN

being sarcastic, or was he serious?

Hiram noticed the glance and shrugged as well. *It doesn't matter,* he told himself. *At least they'll come to a conclusion.*

The ceremony was an important one, and all the members of the court were present. Afranius had been through dozens of these ceremonies during his fifteen years of service for Diocletian and wasn't particularly convinced of their validity. He glanced around the group as the priest prepared to slaughter the first sheep. The priests had brought a half dozen or so victims, since many times the first attempts didn't give clear answers.

He noted that some of the servants seemed uneasy. *Hmm. I wonder if they are Christians. They seem to wish they could be elsewhere. I guess this seems like blasphemy to them. I hope they have the sense to stay quiet and not raise a fuss.*

The first ewe let out an agonized bleat as the priest's knife flashed, cutting the ewe's throat and then slicing its belly. His helpers held the squirming sheep tightly and pulled the body open, revealing the still squirming organs. The priest reached into the gap, pushed aside the intestines to reveal the liver, and examined it carefully. He shook his head. No revelation.

Afranius almost smiled as the helpers dragged the still dying ewe away. *I wonder why the first animal almost never gives them an answer. Does it have anything to do with the fact that they charge by the animal?* He shook his head, driving the dangerous thought away. He didn't have much faith in the process, but it was safer not to take any chances of irritating some god who might be paying attention at the moment.

Swish. The knife flashed again. This ewe was stronger and harder to hold down. Again the revelation failed.

Another swish. A third ewe died. To no avail. As did a fourth.

Afranius glanced at Diocletian, whose unease was becoming more evident. Galerius said something to Diocletian and Diocletian nodded.

The fifth sheep was a large ram and protested vigorously. It almost got away from the four helpers holding it down. But despite its heroic efforts, it too died. And died in vain.

The priest stood and glared around the gathered crowd. "The oracles are not working," he said. "There are profane people here who are obstructing the rites."[4]

For a moment there was deathly silence. Then Diocletian stepped to the center of the circle.

"I have now had enough." His voice sliced through the silence. "I order every man here, from the greatest to the least, to prove his allegiance by sacrificing to the gods." He looked around the circle, meeting the eyes of any who dared to look at him. His eyes paused at several servants who looked uneasy. But his eyes kept moving until he got to Hiram. "This includes the army as well. This order is for every commander and every soldier all across the empire. You will write the letters to make sure it happens."

He squared his shoulders, reminding Afranius of the younger Diocletian who had executed the praetorian prefect at his coronation. Diocletian looked every inch an emperor, and Afranius noted a trace of a smile on Galerius' face. *Almost as if he got his*

---

[4] Lactantius wrote that some Christians in the crowd made the sign of the cross, and this interfered with the process. Christians were considered profane people.

way about something. Is this some kind of a charade? Maybe
Galerius and the priest got their heads together . . .

But Diocletian wasn't finished. "Any commander who refuses will be demoted to the ordinary ranks. Anyone else who disobeys will be scourged and dismissed from the army."[5]

MARK

It didn't take long for word of the standoff in Antioch to reach Nicomedia. Many Christians had friends or acquaintances either in the army or in the palace there in the city. The news was shocking. The Christians had been left in peace ever since the Emperor Gallienus had voided his father Valerian's edicts against Christianity forty years before.

Lydia had just sent her students home when Irene tapped on the door on her way home from the market. "It's good to see you," Lydia greeted her with a smile. "You should stop by more often."

Irene smiled as she stepped in and closed the door. But Lydia noticed an undertone of uneasiness about her. "Is something wrong?" she asked.

"I hope not," Irene answered. "But I just heard that Diocletian issued some kind of edict against the Christians working at the palace and in the army."

A short stab of fear penetrated Lydia's heart. Ever since Mark had been appointed a presbyter, she had secretly worried

---

[5] Lactantius seems to assume that this was aimed at the Christians in the palace and in the army and was the opening shot of the persecution. Lactantius (and Eusebius) also felt that Galerius was the push behind the action and benefited from it more than Diocletian did.

about something like this. Presbyters were often in the front line of attack when persecution came. She wasn't so concerned about herself, but she couldn't bear the idea of Mark facing torture or execution.

Irene wasn't finished. "Apparently the emperor was having a divination ceremony in Antioch about a course of action he and Galerius were considering. People claim that someone saw several Christians making the sign of the cross[6] on their foreheads during the ceremony, and then it failed."

Lydia gasped and covered her mouth with her hand. "But why would he strike out against all the Christians for the actions of a few?"

"I'm not sure," Irene said. "And these stories grow very quickly as they fly from place to place. Apparently Diocletian was upset and took it as sign of disloyalty. He wants only loyal people under his command. I'm guessing it will pass and life will soon be back to normal."

Lydia nodded. "I hope so, but it does show how fragile our security is if it can happen this quickly."

Irene gave her a quick squeeze and prepared to leave. "That's true. I think we should be careful not to stir up animosity, but if worse comes to worst, God is still with us. Many of God's children made the ultimate sacrifice in the past and remained faithful."

She opened the door to leave. "I didn't want to disturb your peace of mind, but I did think you should hear what is happening. The soldiers especially will face a difficult decision.

---

[6] Lactantius called this "the immortal sign."

To remain faithful, they will need to give up their livelihood and their pension. It will be very hard for those who have a wife and a family."

Lydia watched Irene walk down the street. *At least the soldiers' lives aren't being threatened,* she thought. *Not like ours might be.* She shuddered as she thought of what the edict might mean.

Mark came home for supper several hours later, and Lactantius dropped in shortly after that. "So, I suppose you've heard the news?" Lactantius said.

Mark nodded. "Anthimus received a note this morning from a bishop in Antioch. Apparently Diocletian was upset not so much because the people who caused the oracles to fail were Christians, but because of their lack of loyalty to him."

"I think you're right," Lactantius agreed. "I received a note from Hiram as well. I have thought for quite a while that he might step out and declare his faith in Christos, but so far he hasn't. However, he does keep me updated on what goes on in the palace. He would agree with you. Diocletian isn't necessarily against Christianity, but he takes any perceived lack of loyalty very seriously. He is afraid that having people in his household who refuse to worship the Roman gods will be a threat to the empire."

"In a sense he could be right," Mark said. "The empire *is* doomed unless its people repent. That includes Diocletian and Galerius."

"That's right," Lactantius replied. "The Revelation scroll clearly states that Babylon will be destroyed. In my opinion, Babylon is referring to the Roman Empire, and it will be destroyed at the end of time. Things will get much worse for Christians rather than better."

This didn't make Lydia feel any better. "Do you think we are getting to that point? Somehow I always hoped God would put the end off for a while yet."

"There is a difference of opinion on that," Mark responded. "My mother would agree with Lactantius that it will likely happen soon. That has been the prevailing opinion over the years. In fact, the apostles expected it to happen in their lifetime. I think some of them still hoped Christos would restore the kingdom to the Jews. That idea has faded, but many still look for Christos to come back within their lifetime."

Lactantius took up the thread. "We might be facing hard times, but it will not last forever. And once it is over, we will reign with Christos."

"It sure hasn't taken you long to form your opinion on the Revelation," Mark replied. "But not everyone agrees with your view. I think the consensus is swinging over to the opinion that Anthimus holds—that the end will be the end, rather than followed by a millennium of rule over this world."

"I've heard both sides," Lactantius said with a smile. "But I rather expect this world to self-destruct, and then God will take over."

Mark shook his head and chuckled. "Maybe I should never have given you that Revelation scroll to read. But it probably wouldn't have made any difference in the long run. You would have found it sooner or later."

Lydia still looked troubled. "I don't really follow what you're saying. But I think you mean that terrible things will happen to Christians before Christos returns, don't you?

"You almost make it sound as if this will be an exciting time. But I've heard some . . . some terrible things about persecution. Some Christians were burned alive, and others were dropped over cliffs onto spears that pierced them. I even heard of some Christians who were staked out in a swamp in the hot sun. Their eyelids were cut off and their mouths tied open. Then their tormentors smeared honey all over them and left them to die with the insects crawling all over them. It must have taken them days to die."

Lactantius looked at her compassionately. "You're right. It could be very difficult."

Mark had the last word. "In the Holy Writings we find that Christos promises to be with us to the end of the world. We can trust Him to be with us, even in the hard times."

DIOCLETIAN

Galerius wasn't totally satisfied with how Diocletian had handled the situation at the divination ceremony. He was hungry for blood.

"We need to put more teeth into this edict," he said several weeks later. "A few people have taken their whippings and left for home. Most of the others have sacrificed, apparently expecting Christos to forgive them after it has all passed over. If that's all that happens, everything will be the same as before."

Diocletian frowned. "Exactly what do you mean when you say that we should put teeth into this? These people need to make a choice between giving up their faith or losing their livelihood. Either way, the problem has been solved."

Galerius shook his head. "No, it has NOT been solved! Either way, they will keep on serving Christos. The only way to solve this problem is to get rid of all the Christians in the empire."

Diocletian's frown deepened. "What does it matter if there are a few Christians around? They can't do any real damage. At least they normally aren't robbers and murders, like many other Romans these days."

"You don't understand!" Galerius protested. "Our gods are the backbone of our empire. My mother said her income as a priestess has been cut nearly in half because of these people. We will lose our strength as an empire if we allow these dogs to destroy our old religions."

Now Diocletian understood. "I forgot that your mother was a priestess. Now I know why you feel so strongly about this." He hesitated. "What is your suggestion for dealing with them?"

"Burn them," Galerius snapped. "They're just scum anyway."

"That still wouldn't solve the problem of Christians recanting and then later repenting," Diocletian said. "Or would you burn anyone who was once a Christian?" He shook his head. "No, I won't go there. We'll leave it as it is and see how it works out."

Galerius didn't reply, but Afranius could see that he still disagreed. He didn't intend to give up until he figured out how to get his way. Afranius wasn't sure what would happen, but one thing was clear—there was trouble ahead.

March 302

The uproar created by the edict soon died down. A few palace servants were whipped and dismissed, a few soldiers were drummed out of their ranks, and a few officers were demoted, but that was the extent of it.[1] Galerius left to spend the winter in his new palace farther west in Sirmium to lick his wounds, while Diocletian traveled to Egypt. What happened there surprised everyone—even Galerius.

About a month after Galerius left Antioch for Sirmium, Diocletian announced that he was planning a trip to Egypt. "Afranius and Hiram, I need you to go with me. I have to set up a new grain distribution system in Alexandria before half the city starves. Also, most of my army is down there trying

---

[1] Either the purge of the army was only haphazard or quite a few Christians caved in to the demands. Several years later, when the big persecution came along, many of them were still in the army.

to keep order, and I need to see how things are going."

Afranius blinked. "It's wintertime. That means we can't travel by sea. Going by land will take twice as long."

"We'll head south along the coast through Tyre and Caesarea. From there we can follow the trade route to Egypt," Diocletian replied. "We can take a group of cavalry along for security. With everyone on horseback, we can travel quickly. The trade route along the coast should be reasonably safe and easy to travel, even in the wintertime."

"I suppose so," said Afranius. "Though wintertime travel can be dangerous."

"So can summertime travel," Diocletian snapped. "I don't want to wait until then. Alexandria might revolt before summer. Starving people do desperate things." He got to his feet abruptly and turned to Hiram. "Start arranging for logistics. But remember, we're going to travel light.

"Afranius, get your men together—several dozen should suffice—and have them prepare for a three-week journey. We won't take a baggage train, so they'll have to carry their own food and bedrolls. We'll plan to leave as soon as we can get ready."

He caught the look on Hiram's face and relented somewhat. "Arrange for a carriage or a litter for Hiram and me. But no tents. We can sleep in the carriage."

Afranius followed Diocletian to the door and watched him stride across the parade ground to the governor's quarters. "Well, that's that, I guess," he said to Hiram, his voice flat. "And here I was looking forward to an uneventful winter in Antioch."

Several weeks later they were on their way. They were usually on the road before daybreak, rode twelve or fourteen hours, and then made camp when it became too dark to travel safely. Diocletian, nearing sixty, traveled well for his age, but he was as glad as anyone to see the walls of Alexandria on the horizon. He had traveled part of the way with Hiram in a horse-drawn litter, but he wanted to enter the city on horseback.

Even Afranius had to admit that Diocletian handsomely portrayed his standing as a powerful emperor. Most people only knew him by his appearance, and Diocletian had long ago learned the blend of haughtiness and self-assurance that kept most troublemakers at bay.

But Diocletian wasn't the only part of the procession that looked good. The soldiers had taken time to shine up their armor and weapons, and even the horses seemed to perk up as they came closer to the city. Afranius grinned as he noticed the stir on the city walls as the guards recognized the group. For reasons known only to himself, Diocletian hadn't bothered to let Alexandria know he was coming. Everyone, from the least to the most important, was caught by surprise at his arrival.

"I wanted to see what the situation was like when I wasn't around," he told Afranius and Hiram once they were settled in the hastily emptied apartments normally reserved for visiting dignitaries. His grim look indicated that he wasn't entirely pleased with what he had seen. "The proconsul and our Roman commanders seem a bit put out at me. We need to find out why."

Diocletian walked to the window overlooking a wide

courtyard bustling with activity. His guards and the accompanying band of soldiers were busy setting up a defensive berm around the building.

He nodded his satisfaction as he watched. He had won many an argument and battle by putting on a bold front. "There's nothing like looking confident," he remarked. "I've never marched with this detachment of soldiers before, but they seem to be worthy of my trust. It would be interesting to see how they react to a threat."

He swung away from the window, ready for business. "The proconsul has invited us to dinner tonight. In the meantime, we need to put together an agenda. Afranius, tell your men that we are not to be disturbed until this evening."

They sat around the table drinking Egypt's famous wine. "We need to set up a grain distribution system for Alexandria similar to the one in Rome," Diocletian said. "Africa is shipping so much of its grain to Rome that the local people are almost starving. Our local army units have had a hard time suppressing rebellion this past year. If we don't do something soon, all of North Africa will rise up against us."

Hiram was busy taking notes as they talked over the logistics of diverting some of the grain that was being shipped to Italy. But gradually it became evident that Diocletian had something else in mind as well.

"I'm tired of dealing with rebellious Africans," he said. "I've got better uses for my soldiers than having them sitting here policing Egypt. I might need to replace some of the commanders and give them orders to start cracking the whip. And maybe I'll need to find a better proconsul if this one can't keep order."

Afranius leaned back on his stool. "Maybe that's why the proconsul was irked at you for showing up unexpectedly. He probably suspects that you're checking up on him."

Diocletian got to his feet and walked over to the window. "I wanted to try out his responses. After all, we could have been a hostile force. We could have created quite an uproar if we had wanted to."

The proconsul and his guards were coming across the courtyard. "It's suppertime," Diocletian said shortly. "We'll discuss this more later. We'll be here for a month or two anyway. Hopefully we can catch a ship back to Antioch in early spring."

Diocletian threw his weight around a little and barked at a few people in higher places, but the proconsul and Roman commanders managed to calm him down. He arranged for half of the soldiers to start back to Nicomedia and placed the rest on permanent assignment to Egypt. Grain ships soon started coming to Alexandria, to the relief of the beleaguered population. Things were looking up until a messenger from the province just west of Egypt showed up for a private consultation with the emperor.

Afranius and Hiram were relaxing around a small pool in the ornate courtyard of the visitors' quarters when Diocletian returned. A fountain bubbled up through a hollow in a rock in the center of the pool, and they were trying to decide what made the water flow. Hiram thought there must be a water tower somewhere in the building, but Afranius pointed out that this just made it more difficult, because the water tower would need to be filled from somewhere.

Diocletian had bigger problems to discuss, so the source of the mysterious water pressure had to take second place.

"Do you know anything about the Manichaeans?" he asked Hiram, breaking into the discussion. He sat down on a bench by the pool.

Hiram nodded. "They are a semi-Christian sect started by a man named Mani about sixty or seventy years ago. I don't know a lot about them, except that Christians and pagans both denounce them as false teachers. Mani's teachings seem to be a mixture of paganism and Christianity." He leaned back against the stone seat and eyed the emperor curiously. "Why?"

Diocletian got to his feet and walked over to the fountain, idly watching the water gurgle from the hollow rock. "That water comes from a creek that flows down the hill behind the palace," he informed them, ignoring Hiram's question. "I asked them the last time I was here because I thought it would be an innovative idea for my palace." He shrugged. "But we don't have a creek nearby."

He turned back to Hiram. "It seems as if half-cracked religions follow me everywhere. I'm getting tired of it."

After a pause he continued. "The proconsul from the province just west of here is having problems with the Manichaeans. They interfere with local religious ceremonies and try to stop the sacrifices. They stop people from visiting the temples to worship and tell them that the old Roman gods are just demons that are leading them astray. The priests are upset because of their loss of income and prestige.

"I'm half tempted to try Galerius' plan with the Manichaeans and see how it works. I hate the idea of killing people just for sake of their religion, but they are destroying the spiritual status quo that has worked for Rome for a millennium."

He got to his feet. "Think it over and we'll talk again. I want to discuss it with the local proconsul tomorrow. Maybe we can issue an edict before we sail for Antioch."

Neither Hiram nor Afranius liked the idea of using torture or death to stop a religion. But the Manichaean situation was getting out of control, and people couldn't be allowed to interrupt public ceremonies just because they didn't agree with them. For this reason, Afranius and Hiram didn't say too much when the emperor and the proconsul decided to go ahead.

Hiram drew up the final edict for publication across the empire. This was the first time that an edict by a Roman emperor called for the burning of holy books.

We order that the authors and leaders of these sects be subjected to severe punishment, and, together with their abominable writings, burnt in the flames. We direct that their followers, if they continue recalcitrant, shall suffer capital punishment, and their goods be forfeited to the imperial treasury.

And if those who have gone over to that hitherto unheard-of, scandalous all wholly infamous creed, or to that of the

Persians, are persons who hold public office, or are of
any rank or of superior social status, you will see to it that
their estates are confiscated and the offenders sent to the
(quarry) at Phaeno or the mines at Proconnesus.

And in order that this plague of iniquity shall be completely
extirpated from this our most happy age, let your devotion
hasten to carry out our orders and commands.

In their eagerness to reform the Roman Empire, the Manichaeans had made many enemies. The first executions took place even before Afranius and Hiram left Egypt with Diocletian.

Afranius and Hiram were Romans and children of their times. Executions were common, and they had seen many of them. But they felt troubled by what was happening.

They stood at the rail looking back over Alexandria as the ship left the harbor. "Well, that's that, I guess," Afranius said. "I don't mind executing murderers and pirates, but it seems harsh to be executed because of your religion. I can't think of a god I'd be willing to die for."

Hiram was slower than usual to respond. "I feel the same way," he finally admitted. "But there was nothing we could do about it."

They stood there a moment longer, then Afranius changed the subject. "By the way, whatever became of Lactantius? Did he get tired of working for nothing?"

Hiram looked over his shoulder before replying. "He joined the Christians," he said quietly. "The last I heard, he was baptized and trying to make a living doing copying and other clerical things."

"Why did he leave?" Afranius asked, puzzled. "There are other Christians on the palace staff. He might have gotten in trouble a few years ago over that fiasco with the priests in Antioch, but he could probably have talked his way out of that."

Hiram shrugged. "I never got to talk to him about it, so I'm not sure. But knowing Lactantius, I suspect he's really put himself into this, heart and soul. He probably didn't feel free to do that while being on the palace staff."

They had left the safety of the harbor and hit the first large waves rolling in from the Mediterranean. Afranius balanced himself carefully and clutched the railing. "It's too bad; I liked the fellow. I wouldn't mind meeting him again."

"Unless you want to lose your job, you might want to steer clear of him," Hiram replied. "He might talk you into becoming a Christian too. And you and I both know that Diocletian would get pretty huffy about that."

MARK

Mark and Lydia enjoyed spring. Winters in Nicomedia were chilly and damp, and summers hot and humid. But spring was just right—the perfect time to get out of the house and take a walk.

Mark's work as a presbyter tended to bog him down. But this evening as they walked together to the new temple site, he caught the magic of the moment, though possibly more from Lydia's exuberance than from the balmy breeze.

Lydia was recovering from a sprained knee and still struggled with pain at times. The dampness in their apartment didn't help matters. The small charcoal stove simply didn't put out enough heat to banish the cold or the dampness. Today, however, she felt good as she drank in the balmy air and warm sunshine.

Mark smiled at her as she hopped over a little puddle. "You're almost like old times again," he teased. "Think you could still beat me in a race to the market?"

Lydia's eyes flashed. "Of course I could!" But then she deflated a little. "I'd better not try it though. Even though my knee feels better today, I don't want to take a chance of wrenching it again."

"Yes, you've had a pretty tough winter," Mark said. "Hopefully you'll keep feeling better now that spring has come."

"I hope so," she replied with a smile. "I wish we had time to walk out to the old coronation site and climb the hill to watch the sun set over the city."

Mark chuckled. "That might be overdoing it. It's quite a ways out there, and it would be dark before we got back."

"I know," Lydia said, "but we really should go out there for a picnic sometime. It's been a long time since we went outside the city. I wish we could have a little farm out in the country."

"That would be nice," Mark replied. "But it isn't safe to live outside the city unless you are rich enough to have your own private bodyguards. I'm not sure, though, that the city is much better anymore."

"Several women in our prayer group have been molested on the street in recent months," Lydia said. "It's barely safe to go to the marketplace by yourself anymore."

The streets were full of people, some going home from work

and others enjoying the warm weather. Here and there they recognized fellow Christians who greeted them with a smile. Neither Mark nor Lydia remembered the times when Christians were in daily danger, but they were still cautious about being identified as Christians in public. Diocletian's clampdown on Christians after the sheep sacrifice a few years ago had caused some of the old fears to spring to life again.

But tonight such fears seemed far away and unlikely. In the distance they could see the turrets of the temple of Roma, built after the city was ransacked by the Greeks over five hundred years before. Down the street from the temple was the large palace Diocletian had built after being crowned emperor. And across the large open space in front of the palace, on a hillside overlooking the palace and the city walls, stood the new church.

Mark and Lydia stopped a short distance away. "Is it open?" Lydia asked. "May we see the inside?"

"Not yet," Mark replied. "We are planning a dedication service at Easter time, and no one is allowed inside before it is hallowed by the bishops. Bishop Anthimus has been placed in charge of the ceremonies."

"Will he also be in charge of the congregation here?" Lydia asked.

Mark nodded. "I think so. There was some opposition from a few of the younger bishops, but most of the presbytery favored him."

Lydia scrutinized the building as they moved closer. "Where is the entrance?" she asked. "Do we really have to promenade in front of Diocletian's palace every time there is a service here?"

Mark chuckled. "No, the main entrance is on the other side, where we can come and go without being seen. Bishop

Anthimus really put his foot down on that issue. Several bishops wanted the entrance to be here. They felt that we should not be ashamed to show the emperor how many Christians are in the city. But Anthimus said it would be like poking the emperor in the eye and taunting him every time we had services here. He flatly refused to allow it. I've never seen him take such a firm position before."

They had walked only a few minutes when they saw a crowd of people gathering around a news board at the edge of the open area. Mark frowned. "I wonder what's going on. There must be a new announcement. Maybe I should go and see what it says."

Lydia waited at the side of the street as he found his way through the growing crowd. About fifteen minutes later he was back, accompanied by Lactantius.

"What does it say?" she asked. "Is it something serious?"

"It will be for some people," Lactantius replied. "It's an edict against the Manichaeans. I knew some of them back in Numidia."

"What do they believe?" Lydia asked. "Why are they being targeted?"

Mark and Lactantius looked at each other. "I'm not sure," Lactantius replied hesitantly. "They are a mixture of Christianity and paganism, and they tend to be rather aggressive with their beliefs. So maybe they've pushed the Roman government too far."

"It looks serious," Mark added. "The government is burning all their Holy Writings—and their leaders with them. Any other Manichaeans who refuse to give up their beliefs are to be killed as well."

Lactantius nodded and then added, "For those who are too important to be executed like that, the government will take all their goods and send them to the mines or the quarries for life. Maybe the government needs the money, and this was an easy way to get it."

Mark frowned and shook his head. "Galerius might do something like this, just out of spite. But Diocletian has always been fairer than Galerius, even if he favors the old pagan religions."

"Diocletian did pass that edict a few years ago removing Christians from the army," Lydia pointed out. "Maybe he is changing."

"I don't think so," Lactantius replied. "But he sometimes makes rash decisions when he loses his temper. I think that's what happened at the sacrifice in Antioch. I heard that Galerius wanted to start executing people and Diocletian flatly refused. He's tough—but in the long run he doesn't care for unnecessary bloodshed."

"But I don't like this." Lactantius rubbed his chin thoughtfully. "This is a major shift. Hundreds of people will die if this is enforced."

Mark nodded soberly. "I'm afraid so. And the Manichaean beliefs aren't that different from ours. This could easily spill over into more persecution for us Christians. I have a feeling we had better prepare for a change."

The presbytery and bishops met several weeks later to discuss the implications of the edict. Grim stories of gory executions had started to filter back from Africa and other places. The Christian gatherings were subdued, and Christians everywhere could see the dark shadows of their fears reflected in the eyes of other Christians. Was history going to repeat itself? It was never far from their minds, though some of the younger leaders tried to shrug it off.

"This is God punishing the Manichaeans for contaminating the Gospel message," proclaimed one bishop over the pulpit. "We have nothing to fear. God is on our side."

People looked at each other. *Whose side was God on when Emperor Decius had our forefathers slaughtered for refusing to offer sacrifices to the pagan gods?* No one said it aloud, at least not when the bishop was around. But the question was like a nagging sore—it wouldn't go away, no matter how optimistic they tried to be.

The meeting of the presbytery didn't do anything to settle people's minds. Mark and Lydia ate supper with Mark's parents a few days after the meeting. "You didn't have much to say about the Manichaean situation at the meeting," Andrew said to Mark. "How do you feel about it?"

Mark chose his words carefully. "No one knows what the future holds, but I am disappointed that some of the bishops aren't taking it more seriously."

"Well, I can't see it having much effect on us," Andrew said. "We've had freedom to worship God for a long time. A lot of people have become Christians across the empire." He repeated himself, emphasizing his words. "A LOT of people. And some of them are quite important people."

"So are a lot of Manichaeans," Mark pointed out. "Diocletian doesn't have any Christian officers or friends who might mediate for us."

There was an uneasy silence before Mark spoke again. "I wish the presbytery would take this more seriously. We could be making some preparations. I think Bishop Anthimus should consider leaving the city for a while. I know he doesn't want to, though he agrees that this could turn nasty.

"I suggested to him that he needs a break anyway," Mark continued. "I'm not sure what he'll do. He thinks he should be here for his people. But some of the congregation would feel better if he were somewhere safer in case things deteriorated."

Andrew shrugged. "Well, he can do as he pleases, but I think it's all for nothing. I'm sure this will all go away in a few months, and the Manichaeans will continue happily on their way."

It was evident that Andrew didn't want to hear anything to discount his views, so Mark dropped the subject. But Irene had dark shadows around her eyes, and she looked troubled as she listened to her husband's positive statements. She didn't speak up, however, and the conversation turned to other things.

——— GALERIUS ———

Galerius had not known anything about the Manichaean edict until he received copies by Roman post. He read it twice. Where had this come from? He hadn't thought Diocletian would ever approve such an action. What had happened to change his mind this drastically? Galerius pondered the edict, then jumped to his feet.

He strode to the door of the meeting room where he worked when he was at home. "Priscus, where are you?"

The young praetorian guard came running. "Right here, sir."

Galerius handed him some copies of the edict. "Get these hung up in public places across the city. Today." His grin was humorless. "Then go looking for some Manichaeans to practice on."

The guard looked both startled and puzzled. "Yes, sir. Right away, sir." He spun on his heels to leave, but Galerius stopped him.

"Priscus, this is a day to remember. I think it will go down in history as an important day in the history of Christianity."

Galerius' grin reminded the young guard of a vampire eager for a taste of new blood. He shuddered.

——— MARK ———

Mark took part in the dedication ceremonies for the new church, and Bishop Anthimus gave one of the main addresses. The Eucharist had been served, the Scripture readings were finished, and the vast congregation was waiting to be dismissed.

Then Anthimus stood up behind the ornate pulpit reserved for ordained leaders. Despite his age, he had a regal bearing. Silence fell over the audience as the elderly bishop spoke slowly and distinctly. "I will not keep you much longer. It has been a long service. But I have a few things I would like to say.

"This beautiful building has been likened to Solomon's temple. It is beautiful, and I trust it may long be used to glorify God. But as I sat here, I remembered what happened to Solomon's temple, and why.

"Solomon's temple was destroyed by the enemies of God's people. We have been told today by several speakers that God will protect this beautiful building because it is His and is dedicated as a place to worship Him. I would like to remind you that this was true of Solomon's temple as well. But the time came when it was destroyed.

"Solomon's temple was destroyed because God's people went astray. God pleaded with them and tried to help them. He sent prophets to warn them. Finally, when nothing else worked, God allowed His enemies to destroy that beautiful temple—the same temple Solomon had dedicated and where the glory of God had appeared so vividly that the priests had to flee.

"This beautiful church where we have gathered this morning to worship could suffer the same fate. Already the storm clouds are gathering. We do not know what the future holds, or if this building will withstand the onslaughts of the enemies of the faith. But even if it doesn't—you can.

"Let us pray . . ."

14

Autumn 302

With the two emperors hundreds of miles apart, it seemed like an opportunity for things to quiet down a bit. And they might have—had it not been for a Christian who acted without thinking . . .

Diocletian had been moody all day. In fact, he had been moody all summer, though he wouldn't have admitted it. But the people who knew him best and worked with him could have told anyone, had they dared. At such times even the emperor's best friends walked carefully. In secret, though, they sometimes talked to each other about it.

"If I had known when we left for Antioch that we wouldn't come home for three years, I would have found a way to bring my wife along," Afranius commented, looking as unhappy as he sounded. He shared a small apartment with Hiram, and it was about the only place where it was safe to share their thoughts.

Hiram was a bachelor and had never had a family to go home to. But he was still sympathetic. "I think we'll head back to Nicomedia this fall yet," he told Afranius. "I sent a letter to Galerius the other day. Diocletian wants him to come to Nicomedia for the winter."

He rolled up a scroll he had been working on. "Is it just my imagination, or has Diocletian been miserable ever since we returned from Egypt?"

Afranius finished unfastening his sandals before replying. "It isn't your imagination. I've thought the same thing. Today he was a real bear."

Hiram capped the ink pot and carefully cleaned his quill pen. "Something is troubling him. I wonder if it bothers him that he passed that edict about executing the Manichaeans. Many people have died because of it."

Afranius sat down on a leather-padded couch and carefully placed his sandals under it. "Maybe. He did get a letter by yesterday's post reporting how successful the purge has been in Africa. And Galerius wrote him last week, congratulating him. Apparently he's also been finding Manichaeans to execute in his area."

"I pity anyone Galerius gets his hands on," Hiram replied shortly. "Diocletian would have been better off finding someone less ruthless to help rule Rome. How long will it be before Galerius targets Diocletian?"

Afranius leaned back against the wall. "Diocletian has lasted longer than any emperor in the last hundred years," he replied. "Statistics will surely catch up with him sooner or later."

"He's pretty smart," Hiram said. "He knows all this just as well as we do. Sooner or later, he'll cave in and let Galerius have his way about persecuting Christianity. He'll have to in order to keep Galerius from turning on him."

"Galerius will turn on him anyway," Afranius said. "He's almost as smart as Diocletian—and he's also getting older. He's too ambitious to die as a Caesar. He wants to be an Augustus."

Hiram nodded. "That much is pretty clear. Have you put any thought into what might happen to you if Diocletian were suddenly gone?"

"I've got a bit of money stashed away," Afranius said. "Not much, but hopefully I can still draw my pension. The big thing will be staying out of sight. Galerius might ignore us if we become invisible. I don't intend to switch sides in the hopes of surviving. People who do that usually don't end up well. If Diocletian goes down, I'll go down with him."

"Those are my feelings too," Hiram said. "He's been good to us, and I'm not going to turn against him when the going gets tough."

Diocletian was having a hard time making up his mind. He wanted to spend the winter at home in Nicomedia with his wife and daughter, but he dreaded the pressure Galerius would put on him to take more action against the Christians. When he had approved the Manichaean edict, he had thought of it as an experiment to help him decide whether it was a viable solution. But all it had done was trigger bloodshed.

He had thought people would be smart enough to know they couldn't defy the Roman Empire just to worship a different god. They were just creating their own problems by being obstinate. All they needed to do was go back to the old gods and everything would be fine.

But even Diocletian could see it wasn't working that way. His men kept finding more Manichaeans. It seemed that for every one they executed, two more pagans converted. He shook his head. The same thing would happen if they started to execute Christians, no matter what Galerius thought. Anyway, he was tired of all this bloodshed. He knew he would die sometime in the next decade or so. And what if he discovered after he died that he was wrong and had been serving the wrong gods?

He threw the thought from him. What if Jupiter would catch him with it? He was too old to change gods now. He would have to take his chances—that was all anyone could do. Surely even the Christian god wouldn't be too hard on him if he was wrong.

Diocetian was relieved when Afranius and Hiram came in the door and he could start the morning meeting. "I need to decide whether I'm going to spend the winter in Nicomedia or here in Antioch."

Hiram looked up, puzzled. "You just wrote Galerius last week that you wanted him to meet you in Nicomedia for the winter. He'll be expecting you there."

Diocletian's eyebrows pulled together. "He can always come here instead," he retorted. "I don't set my plans by his wishes or notions."

"It doesn't matter that much to me," Hiram replied,

shrugging. "But Nicomedia is your capital, and it would make sense to return for a while."

Diocletian glanced at the ceiling, but the ceiling wasn't feeling cooperative this morning. "Maybe we should call for a sacrifice and see what the entrails show." He didn't sound very sure of this sudden idea. "If the gods want me to stay here, then even Galerius can't say anything about it."

Diocletian took their silence as acquiescence and nodded at Hiram. "Get things arranged. I want to get the sacrifice done within the next few days. And spread the word that it would not be a good idea for any profane people to disrupt the sacrifice this time."

——— MARK ———

Mark was reading one of the Holy Writings when Lactantius stopped by. "I've been thinking," Lactantius began.

"That's normal for you," Mark said, grinning. "You're the most 'thinking' person I know."

Lactantius smiled as well but sobered quickly. "I wonder if I should leave Nicomedia. I have a bad feeling about being here—as if something is going to happen soon."

Mark put down the manuscript he had been reading. "You aren't the only person. I've felt the same way, and different people have stopped in to talk to me about similar feelings. Bishop Anthimus is thinking about leaving Nicomedia for a while. Apparently Galerius is coming back for the winter, and I don't trust him."

Mark's face brightened as an idea hit him. "Maybe you could

travel with Anthimus. We don't want him to travel by himself anyway."

"That's an idea!" Lactantius exclaimed. "I'd be happy to travel with him. Let me know when he's ready to leave. I'll store my manuscripts with you so I can travel light. Hopefully I can return for them sometime."

Mark nodded soberly. "It'll be a few weeks yet, I think. It's hard for Anthimus to leave at a time of danger. But most of his friends want him to go."

——— DIOCLETIAN ———

In Antioch it was one of those beautiful fall days that put a bounce in the steps of most people. But Diocletian didn't seem to notice. His pessimism seemed to spread to the crowd gathered around the priests as they readied the sacrificial victims for slaughter. Afranius noticed that they had brought only three rams.

They must be feeling more optimistic of getting results this time, he thought. *Hopefully we don't need to go through another episode like the last time. These sacrifices seem to cause more trouble than they are worth.*

The priest had raised his gleaming knife over the first ram in preparation for the fatal stroke when he was interrupted by a shriek from the sidelines.

Everyone froze. A wild-looking man with a long straggly beard sprang into the circle and snatched the knife from the priest. He pointed the knife at the sky and shrieked again.

"WOE TO THE REBELLIOUS CHILDREN, SAITH THE

LORD, THAT TAKE COUNSEL, BUT NOT OF ME; AND THAT COVER WITH A COVERING, BUT NOT OF MY SPIRIT, THAT THEY MAY ADD SIN TO SIN!"[1]

Diocletian jumped to his feet. "Who is this maniac? How does he dare interrupt a holy sacrifice like this?"

Afranius had jumped to his feet as well, but several of the guards were ahead of him. They grabbed the shouting man and knocked the knife from his hand. Quickly they dragged him from the circle, twisting his arms behind his back. He continued to shriek as they pulled him away.

"WOE TO THE REBELLIOUS CHILDREN . . . WOE TO THE REBELLIOUS CHILDREN. WOE—" His voice stopped abruptly as someone slapped him across the mouth.

Diocletian was beside himself. "Get rid of him! How dare he? How did he get in here? Where were the guards anyway?"

Afranius nodded at Hiram to take charge and followed the soldiers who had taken the madman away. He caught up with them as they were trying to decide what to do with him.

Afranius pushed through the group and faced the man. "Who are you, and under what authority do you interrupt the holy rites being undertaken at the emperor's command?"

The man faced him fearlessly. "I come with the authority of the King of Kings—Yahweh Himself bade me give the emperor His message."

So the man was a Christian. Afranius's heart sank. Did not this man realize that his actions had probably just condemned thousands of people to death?

---

[1] Isaiah 30:1

"What is your name?" Afranius's voice was calm but deliberate.

The self-proclaimed prophet sagged a little. "Romanus," he said. "I'm a deacon in the Christian church."

Afranius looked the man in the eyes. "What you have done today was not wise," he said. "I doubt that your God condones mad acts like this. Not only will you probably die for your foolishness, but many others may die because of it."

Romanus wilted a little and didn't reply.

Several days later Afranius came through the public square and noticed a crowd gathered there. Evidently Romanus had been condemned to be burned. He pushed his way through the crowd, stopping to speak with the centurion in charge. The man looked relieved to see him.

"Sir, the magistrate has condemned him to be burned," the centurion said to Afranius. "But the emperor has never approved capital punishment for the Christians. What should I do?"

Afranius watched as the soldiers tied Romanus to the stake and started piling wood around his feet. Romanus was quiet, his eyes turned heavenward.

Afranius walked up to him. "What has your God been telling you today?" he asked pointedly. "Have you had any second thoughts about your actions?"

"I did what I felt God wanted me to do," Romanus replied calmly. "If I was wrong, I beg Him to forgive me. I do not ask for your mercy either way."

Afranius shook his head. "You are a brave man, though I think what you did was foolish." He turned to the centurion.

"I will verify the sentence with the emperor. Don't light the fire until I return."

Afranius was soon in the emperor's presence. "I come from the centurion in charge of the execution," he told him. "The prisoner has been condemned to be burned, and the centurion wanted me to verify with you that this was your desire."

Diocletian frowned. "Does he question the magistrate's authority?"

"No, I don't think so," Afranius replied, shaking his head. "But he knows you have never knowingly condemned a Christian to death. Since you were in the city, he felt it wise to verify the sentence with you rather than going ahead."

Diocletian relaxed. "Wise man," he said approvingly. "He should go far in his career."

He pursed his lips. "However, the man does need a lesson in good manners if nothing else. Suppose you tell them to cut out his tongue and cast him into a dungeon for a year. We'll see if that teaches him a lesson. We can always execute him later if necessary."[2]

The crowd around Romanus had grown larger by the time Afranius returned. People were jeering at him and mocking him. Some tried to break through and set fire to the wood stacked around his legs. The prisoner's eyes were shut as he tried to ignore the crowd and steel himself for what was to come. The soldiers formed a solid line around the prisoner, guarding him from the angry crowd with leveled spears.

Only the authority of Afranius' uniform got him through the

---

[2] Various sources verify this happening. Romanus was executed on November 18, 303, nearly a year later.

crowd to speak with the centurion. The centurion acknowl-edged his message but looked a little anxious. "How are we going to explain this to the crowd? They will tear him apart if they can get at him."

Afranius considered a little. "Give me a hand up onto this rock," he said, indicating a large rock nearby.

The crowd quieted as he raised his hand for silence. Many of the people knew him, and the rest recognized his uniform. "The emperor has ordered this man's execution to be deferred," he announced. "He will be returned to the dungeon for further torture."

The crowd groaned, but Afranius wasn't finished. "I want this crowd to disperse immediately. There will be nothing to see here today."

The people wavered, and there were a few catcalls, but authority gradually prevailed and the crowd started to melt away. The prisoner looked at Afranius gratefully.

Afranius addressed the centurion. "Have his tongue cut out when you get to the prison. However, don't let him bleed to death."

The prisoner's face blanched, but he didn't speak. Afranius turned to him. "I'm not sure we are doing you a favor, but that was the emperor's decision."

MARK

Galerius arrived in Nicomedia several weeks later and imme-diately started throwing his weight around. Mark urged Bishop Anthimus to leave immediately. "Brother, it is time for you to go," he told the bishop. The informal form of address showed much about the relationship they shared.

"Lactantius will be ready to leave in the morning," Mark continued. "He will take you to Omana, where you should be safe."

Anthimus bowed his head. "I will do as you advise," he finally agreed. "But I wish I could stay and suffer with my people."

"Yes, we all know that," Mark replied respectfully. "However, all of us would feel better if we knew you were safe. I trust we will meet again, but if God wills otherwise, may we meet before His throne."

Only a few people were on hand to see Lactantius and the bishop off. A large crowd would have drawn too much attention. Besides, people were already worried about the possibility of spies.

Several days' travel took Lactantius and Anthimus to Omana. Anthimus was to stay in a small house in the little village where he would hopefully be safe. Lactantius left the next day to travel farther.

Anthimus soon made friends in the village. As he had been instructed, he did not tell anyone who he was or why he was there. But the villagers soon became his steadfast friends. He was always ready to give a helping hand or lend a listening ear. He also wrote letters of encouragement to his people back in Nicomedia.

DIOCLETIAN

With the Persians seemingly staying in their place, Diocletian was finally ready to leave Antioch. He decided to return to Nicomedia before winter. A month later, everyone was back home.

Galerius had heard about the episode with Romanus. "So, did

you have the charlatan burned to ashes?" he asked Diocletian.

Diocletian shrugged him off without an answer. Galerius stared at him. "You surely didn't let him get away with such nonsense, did you? What did you do with him?"

Diocletian glared at him. "It's none of your business," he growled. "But if you really want to know, I had them cut out his tongue to teach him a lesson."

Galerius' jaw sagged. "Are you serious? Is that all you did?"

"He'll be locked in a dungeon for a year," Diocletian replied. "We can decide what to do with him then."

Galerius looked him in the eye. "You are way too soft. I don't see how you ever managed to remain a Roman emperor for almost twenty years."

Diocletian's eyes narrowed dangerously. "You might find it safer not to do your thinking out loud," he replied testily. "I have no problem executing someone for insubordination. I just happen to prefer not to execute people because they worship a different god than I do."

Galerius saw that he had pushed Diocletian too far, so he dropped the subject. However, it increased his determination to find a way to force Diocletian to destroy Christianity. He spoke about it to Valeria that night in a rare moment of openness, brought on by drinking too much wine. "I owe it to my mother to destroy those Christians." He spat out the words like a curse. "They ruined her life as a priestess. If your father won't cooperate, I'll do it on my own. At the rate their movement is growing, in fifty years it will be too late to stop them."

Valeria just listened. It would be best to keep her thoughts to herself.

PART VII

A.D. 303

The Volcano Erupts

The old man [Diocletian] long opposed the fury of Galerius and showed how pernicious it would be to raise disturbances throughout the world and to shed so much blood; that the Christians were wont with eagerness to meet death; and that it would be enough for him to exclude persons of that religion from the court and the army. Yet he could not restrain the madness of that obstinate man. . . . He determined above all to consult his gods; and to that end he despatched a soothsayer to inquire of Apollo at Miletus, whose answer was such as might be expected from an enemy of the divine religion. So Diocletian was drawn over from his purpose. But although he could struggle no longer against his friends, and against Cæsar and Apollo, yet still he attempted to observe such moderation as to command the business to be carried through without bloodshed; whereas Galerius would have had all persons burnt alive who refused to sacrifice.

—Lactantius, *Of the Manner in Which the Persecutors Died,* Chap. 11

January 303

The fury of Galerius knew no bounds. As conditions deteriorated, a frenzied priestess gave advice. As did a hooded man . . .

Galerius was relentless in his pressure on Diocletian. This morning was no exception.

Galerius waited until the morning agenda was finished and Hiram was gathering up his writing materials. "I hear that the Christians held a large celebration across from your palace this past Sunday." He glanced at Afranius. "Do you have any idea what this was all about?"

Afranius stiffened. "I'm not aware of any seditious behavior or teaching in their services."

Galerius softened his voice. "You do have spies in their midst to keep you up to date, don't you?"

Afranius met his gaze deliberately. "My men are keeping track of what is happening."

"Did you have spies at the meeting to hear what was going on?" Galerius had no intention of being sidetracked. He didn't like the influence that Afranius and Hiram had over Diocletian.

Afranius knew this, but he was not going to allow Galerius to push him around. "I don't think any of my men were at the meeting, but they have contacts who would let them know if something serious was afoot. I don't consider them to be of any particular danger at present."

Galerius frowned. "These people are always dangerous. They are silently ignoring the gods of our empire and worshipping a dead Jewish criminal who was condemned in a Roman court. And you have the audacity to say they aren't a danger?"

Afranius knew he was treading on dangerous ground. But Diocletian spoke up. "I'm sure Afranius has everything under control. He has managed to keep me alive and in power for almost twenty years."

Galerius' eyes glittered. "The Christians are the greatest danger Rome faces. We have our other enemies under control, but we are ignoring these infidels. If we did it now, we could easily move against them and eliminate them without endangering our borders."

Diocletian lifted his chin. "We have moved against them. They have been removed from the army and from most positions of political influence. I fail to see what danger they could be to us. Surely the Roman gods are not so weak that they need our help to keep from being pushed aside."

Galerius shook his head. "I fear we are going to be sorry

some day. The gods have placed us here for a reason, and they expect us to deal with their enemies. We are treading on dangerous ground."

Afranius wasn't convinced that the Christians were a danger to the empire. "Galerius is our greatest danger right now," he told Hiram later. "He is using the Christian issue as a smoke screen. I think he is working himself up to a move against Diocletian."

Hiram nodded. "But I'm afraid he wants to get rid of you first. He knows that you and the praetorians are totally loyal to Diocletian. If he can persuade Diocletian that you are shoddy in doing your duty, he might be able to move against you."

Afranius raised his eyebrows. "I'm not afraid of Galerius. My men would take him out in an instant, if necessary."

Hiram cocked his head. "Even if Diocletian took his side and ordered them to disobey you? That is what Galerius is moving toward."

Afranius shrugged. "I'll face that when it happens. I don't intend to maneuver my men against Diocletian, though I'd turn them on Galerius in a heartbeat. If it comes down to Diocletian siding with Galerius against me, then I will resign my post."

"What about your family?" persisted Hiram. "How would you protect them?"

"I have vowed to protect Diocletian," Afranius replied. "That has to come first. If I'm no longer needed or wanted, I'll face that when it comes. But I won't take up arms against Diocletian."

"Would you turn your men against the Christians if

Diocletian demanded it?" Hiram asked. "It may come to that if Galerius gets his way."

Afranius pursed his lips. "I've thought of that," he admitted. "I would certainly prefer not to be faced with that decision. However, I would have no choice but to follow orders."

Hiram paused before continuing slowly. "And if I decided to become a Christian, would you arrest me and have me executed as a traitor?"

Afranius stiffened. "Are you considering that?"

Hiram looked away. "I'm not sure. Lactantius had some strong arguments when he got converted. The older I get the more I see all the wrong in this world of ours. A god who actually *loves* humans rather than ignoring them or mocking them would have a lot to offer. I have no faith in the goodness of any Roman god, as you know."

Afranius nodded reluctantly. "I know. And I wouldn't hold it against you. But I am an honorable man and I must do my duty. If the emperor dismisses me or has me arrested, I would consider myself free to explore other options. But not until then."

Hiram's eyes held his. "So that is my answer? You would arrest me and execute me for being a Christian if you were ordered to do so?"

It was a question Afranius didn't want to answer, but he was honest. "I would die to defend you if you were attacked by an enemy. And I would never betray you, even if I knew you had converted to Christianity. But if it came down to doing my duty, I would have to follow orders."

Afranius rose. "I trust it never comes to that, but I won't stand in your way. I am beginning to understand why so many Christians do not feel it is right to serve in the army or in a political position. It brings with it an insurmountable battle of deciding who to serve. A Christian is honor bound to serve his God and to support his fellow Christians, but a soldier is bound by honor to serve the empire. And if one master demands one thing and the other master demands another, what is a man to do?"

Hiram looked up. "In a case like that, you need to choose who your real master is. But I agree, it is probably better to avoid the conflict in the first place."

Only a week later the argument between Diocletian and Galerius came to a head.

"Diocletian," Galerius snapped, "who are you protecting? Is your wife a Christian that you insist on defending them?"

Diocletian half rose from his chair, and for a moment Afranius thought it might come to physical violence between them. But then Diocletian resumed his seat.

"Galerius, you have gone too far," he said. "I wash my hands of this decision."

He turned to the men across the table. "Hiram! Send a messenger to Delphi to ask the oracle of Apollo what we should do."

He turned back to Galerius. "You want to protect the gods. Let the gods decide whether they want or need your protection."

Afranius caught the fleeting expression of triumph that crossed Galerius' face. *He has been expecting this. He knows what the oracle will say—or has a way of making sure.* He shuddered, feeling that his worst nightmare had been transported from his dreams to real life. *Here it comes, what we've all feared.*

MARK

Mark didn't know the man who slipped into his office just before he left for home. The man kept his hood pulled over his forehead during the whole discussion, and Mark would not have recognized him even if he had met him on the street the next day.

It didn't matter who he was. It was his story that kept Mark awake that night.

"Diocletian has sent a messenger to the oracle of Apollo," the man said. "The question is, 'Shall we persecute the Christians?' The messenger is expected back in a week or so.

"The man who told me this was in the meeting. He is sure the answer has been predetermined by Galerius. A time of great testing is upon us. You need to warn your people and prepare them for the worst."

The man vanished out the door before Mark could ask any questions.

DIOCLETIAN

The messenger and his guards made good time despite it being wintertime. They arrived at the temple in Delphi on the evening of the sixth day. They stayed at a guesthouse where many a king had waited his turn to share his questions with the oracle of the shrine.

Early the next morning, the messenger explained the

situation to the attendants and then waited while the priestess was prepared.

Finally, about midafternoon, the messenger was ushered into the presence of the priestess in the inner temple. She was seated on a wooden throne and dressed in an ornate brown gown with an embroidered border at her feet. Her arms, feet, and one shoulder were bare, and she wore a rich scarlet cloak draped over her head, covering her hair and forehead and shading her eyes. She had flung the cloak around her, covering one shoulder and her back, then draped it carelessly over her lap, dangling to the floor. Her eyes burned, and she had the wild-eyed appearance of being possessed by strange powers or hallucinations.[1]

The messenger bowed to her. "My master, the emperor of Rome, desires Apollo to give him direction in how to deal with the Christians in our empire." The question seemed to throw the priestess into an agonizing frenzy, as if she were having a spell. The messenger considered running from the temple but took a deep breath and stayed kneeling before her.

The woman tore at her hair and shrieked. To the messenger it seemed like gibberish, but the priestess's attendants seemed to understand what she was saying. She continued for what seemed to the messenger to be hours, but was probably about ten minutes, before she ended with a scream and then fainted. She fell off her throne into the arms of several attendants who carried her to a couch close by and tried to revive her. The other attendant ushered the messenger out the door.

---

[1] The priestess is thought to have been drugged or overcome by gases seeping from a crack in the mountainside over which the temple had been built. The life expectancy of the priestess was fairly short.

"What did she say?" the messenger asked. "Did she answer my question?"

The attendant hesitated. "Apollo was unable to answer your request. He told the priestess that the impious[2] on earth hindered him from speaking." The attendant wouldn't say more, and the messenger had to be satisfied with this. But he pondered the question and its answer for most of the trip home.[3]

The travelers returned to Nicomedia late at night, but the messenger was called into the early morning council. Everyone was eager to know what the oracle had revealed.

"So what did she tell you," Diocletian asked. "Was it some cryptic reply that we will need to try to decipher?"

The messenger looked relieved. "She said that Apollo was unable to answer your question because the impious on earth hindered him from speaking."

Diocletian looked baffled, but Galerius jumped to his feet triumphantly. "The impious on earth!" he shouted. "The Christians have interfered with the message of the gods once again."

Diocletian's eyes widened. "How can you be so sure? It could mean many things. Surely the Christians wouldn't have power over the oracle of Apollo, would they?"

Galerius shook his head, impatient at his fellow emperor's slowness to catch on. "Of course not," he sputtered. "The oracle is just saying that Apollo will not answer us because we have allowed the Christians to live. Apollo is telling us we need to destroy Christianity if we want his continued favor.

---

[2] Eusebius gives this as "the just on earth," but other sources say *impious*, which makes more sense.

[3] This was nothing unusual. The oracle often gave cryptic answers that could have various interpretations, one of which would probably come true.

We must get to work immediately on an edict like you sent out for the Manichaeans."

Diocletian was having a hard time grasping what he had just heard. But his fear and respect of the gods was such that he didn't dare take a chance of being wrong. He had held out as long as he could. "You're right," he said with determination. "We must not delay."

He turned to Hiram. "Prepare a draft edict for me to look at as soon as possible. Make it similar to the one we drafted against the Manichaeans. We need to aim at their leaders, their meeting places, and their Holy Writings."

Hiram seemed baffled by the swift course the events had taken. He started to gather his writing materials but was interrupted by Galerius.

"We need to make sure we include punishments in the edict," he said. "Judges and officers need to know what to do with the Christians."

Diocletian frowned. "We are burning the books and the buildings and arresting the leaders," he protested. "Isn't that enough?"

"No!" Galerius exclaimed, shaking his head. "We must be a lot stronger than that! We need to burn the leaders. We must give the officers permission to torture people to learn where the books are and who the leaders are. We must drown the servants and burn their masters if they do not cooperate."

Diocletian put his foot down. "No," he said firmly. "It may come to that, but for now we will leave out the instructions for capital punishment. It will be left to the discretion of the judges to use if all else fails."

The Volcano Erupts: January 303

Galerius looked as if he were ready to tear out his hair. "Don't just go halfway!" he shouted. "If we don't do this right, we'll never get it done."

"No," said Diocletian. He looked at Hiram. "Go and follow my instructions. Bring me a draft copy this afternoon. We will go over it together and decide what corrections and changes to make."

"It was the nineteenth year of Diocletian's reign . . . when an imperial decree was published everywhere, ordering the churches to be razed to the ground and the Scriptures destroyed by fire, and giving notice that those in places of honour would lose their places, and domestic staff, if they continued to profess Christianity, would be deprived of their liberty. Such was the first edict against us. Soon afterwards other decrees arrived in rapid succession, ordering that the presidents of the churches in every place should all be first committed to prison and then coerced by every possible means into offering sacrifice."

Eusebius,
History of the Church (VIII.2)

——— **MARK** ———

The hooded man showed up at Mark's office again that afternoon. Again Mark was unable to identify him.

"It has begun," the messenger said. "The question was answered affirmatively, and the persecution is to begin. The emperor has ordered his secretary to prepare an edict."

Mark looked troubled. "I have been afraid of this for several months," he replied. "I am glad Anthimus is in safety. We will need his prayers."

Mark paused before asking, "Do you know any details of the edict?"

"It is still being finalized," the man replied. "But it is to include the destruction of church buildings and Holy Writings and the arrest of leaders. Galerius is pushing for further details such as burning leaders and others who will not cooperate."

The man bowed and again slipped out the door, his mission accomplished.

Mark fell to his knees, praying for wisdom and strength. Then he called for several messengers. "Find all the presbyters and deacons," he told them. "Tell them we need to hold an emergency meeting here in the new church tonight. Tell them they have to be here—that it is very important."

The young men looked at him wide-eyed, startled by the unusual request. They left immediately, some of them running.

Mark watched them go, torn with what to do in the next several hours. He needed to warn Lydia. The guards would come to their apartment looking for the Holy Writings. Everyone in the church knew he had them. And he should warn his mother as well. She would want to know.

Mark decided he owed it to Lydia to let her know first. Maybe she could tell his mother or they could go together. His father would receive a message along with the rest of the deacons. He was a little worried about his father. Andrew had always resisted the possibility of something like this happening. What would he do if he faced the supreme test?

Lydia met him at the door, a question on her face. Mark glanced over her shoulder at the students doing lessons in the living area. "Send the children home," he told her quietly. "We need to talk."

None of the men present ever forgot the meeting at the church that night. They were the leading target of the edict, and within the next few weeks they might face the ultimate test of their faith. Most were married, and many had families. All had responsibilities in the church, and people were looking to them for direction. They carried heavy burdens—burdens that had suddenly grown much heavier.

Everyone present looked to Mark for leadership. He was one of the younger leaders, but he was Anthimus' assistant and suddenly that seemed very important. Even the radical bishops who had pushed for the new church building were suddenly glad for someone else to take charge. They had come, one by one, entering the new church through the back alleys leading to the back doors of the building. The palace across the wide street in front of the church seemed especially ominous tonight. Within its walls men were probably planning their demise.

Mark opened the meeting when most of them were there. He noticed that his father was one of the few who were missing, and his heart sank. Maybe he hadn't heard about the meeting. But his mother knew . . . Mark would need to stop in to see his parents if his father didn't come.

Mark's opening was simple and contained none of the

flowery liturgy to which they were accustomed. Somehow liturgy seemed out of place at a time like this. Instead, he found a passage in the Holy Writings that spoke to their need. "No weapon that is formed against thee shall prosper; and every tongue that shall rise against thee in judgment thou shalt condemn. This is the heritage of the servants of the Lord, and their righteousness is of me, saith the Lord."[4]

He rolled up the scroll before adding, "We need to pray before we do anything else. We need to be sure we have God's blessing on us at this time."

Everyone knelt.

——— DIOCLETIAN ———

The meeting in the palace across the street was of a different nature. The edict had been corrected and approved, and Hiram was making copies to hang in the city and to post to the other parts of the empire. Galerius noticed lights in the church across the way.

"They are having a meeting over there," he said. "Maybe we should send some soldiers over to join them. It might be a good way to get the ball rolling."

Diocletian shook his head impatiently. "We will start with the church in the morning," he stated. "Then hang up the edicts the following morning." He glanced at Afranius. "Have your men over there first thing. Search the building and destroy any writings. Strip it of valuables. If you find that ass's head they

---

[4] Isaiah 54:17

are said to worship, confiscate it. I want to see it."

Galerius rubbed his hands together. "Tomorrow is the day I have long waited for."

The group dispersed.

Late February 303

A day that strikes fear in one person's heart may bring evil rejoicing in someone else's. February 23, 303, was such a day. For the Christians, it was a day of horror, of reckoning. Would they be able to stand the test?

February 23, 303, dawned damp and chilly. The skies were overcast and threatening rain. To a casual observer it seemed like a normal February morning in Nicomedia. But it was not.

Diocletian was up early, as usual. He was glad yesterday's decisions were finally behind him, but doubts still harassed him. He shrugged and tried to throw off his misgivings. *We're going through with this. It's my duty to the gods of Rome. But Galerius isn't going to take control of things. He'd burn every Christian he got his hands on if he could.*

It never crossed his mind that his wife might have any concerns about what was happening.

In another part of the palace, Galerius jumped out of bed, telling Valeria, "This day is going to make history!"

Valeria opened one eye to acknowledge that she had heard him. But she didn't share his exuberance. Innocent people were going to die because of her husband. Maybe not today, but in the days and weeks to come. She steeled herself until he had left the room—then she started to cry.

Afranius didn't expect this day to be a good one. It was going to be a balancing act between doing his duty and keeping his men from getting out of hand and carrying things too far. *I hope Galerius stays out of the way. I can handle Diocletian, but Galerius is a different story. People are going to die because of this, and I may as well accept the fact.*

Hiram got up at his usual time. This day didn't involve him, aside from needing to supervise the copyists who were already busy with the edicts that would be hung in public places across the city tomorrow. But his grim expression did little to hide the turmoil in his heart. *I'm glad Lactantius is out of this. Hopefully he is well hidden in some secure place. Though, knowing him, he will be out trying to help others instead of worrying about himself.*

He found himself whispering a prayer for the people facing this trial in the coming days and weeks. Then he realized what he was doing. *Who am I praying to? Jupiter? He couldn't care less how many people are slaughtered. Hercules? He'll be cheering for Galerius if he notices what it is going on. The Christian God? What right do I have to ask anything of Him?*

But he knew, deep down, that only the Christian God would care about what was going on today. Diocletian and Galerius could say what they wanted, but their gods didn't care when people suffered—or what they did, whether good or bad. If they even existed, they didn't have time to worry about humans.

——— MARK ———

Mark and Lydia had spent most of the night praying. The presbyters and deacons had decided that each congregation's leaders would be responsible to nurture their own little group through the coming events. Since Anthimus was gone, Mark was in charge of the local church, along with another presbyter and several deacons.

The Christians would try to lie low. In the past, well-meaning Christians had brought extra animosity against the church by speaking publicly against their persecutors. People had smashed idols and dared soldiers to arrest them. Mark felt strongly that following the example of Jesus and His meekness in the face of persecution would leave the best testimony. Most of the elders agreed with him.

After the meeting, Mark had gone straight to his parents' dwelling. It was late, but as he expected, Andrew and Irene were still up. His father let him in.

"Well, I hope you are planning to take a more reasonable position than your mother wants to take," his father said before Mark could say anything. "I have no intention to offer myself as a useless sacrifice. If they come here for the Holy Writings, I'll give them up."

Tears ran down Irene's face. "Andrew, how can you say that? The writings are the lifeblood of the church."

Andrew set his face stubbornly. "What about my own lifeblood? Have I been such a bad husband that you want to get rid of me? My life is worth more to me than some old scrolls."

Irene choked back her tears, but Mark could see that they had gone through the whole argument before his arrival. "I can take all the writings over to our home," he offered. "Then you can honestly say you don't have any."

He hesitated. "Lydia and I are committed to accepting whatever this trial brings. I will not betray my brothers and sisters or the Holy Writings, nor will Lydia. We will die rather than do that."

His father turned away and started to pull scrolls from the cupboard. Irene came over to Mark and wept on his shoulder. "God give you strength," she whispered. "I have committed myself to the same. But your father . . ." She broke down again.

Andrew shoved the precious scrolls into a bag and brought them to Mark. "Here," he said roughly. "Take them and be gone."

Andrew looked at his wife. "Stop your whimpering!" he ordered. "Do you want to go with him as well? Then you could die for your precious writings along with him."

Mark took the bag from him, ignoring his cruel words. He knew his father well enough to know that he been suffering mental anguish in the last hours. He could see it in his eyes.

Andrew dropped his eyes, unable to face his son. He turned and shuffled into their sleeping area. "I need to work tomorrow," he said, his voice muffled. "I'm going to bed."

Mark looked at Irene, but she shook her head at his unspoken question. "No, I will remain at his side. He is not himself and will someday be sorry for his actions . . ." Her voice caught. "I—I may not be here for him then, but I will not leave him now."

Mark gathered his mother in his arms and held her. Together they wept. They both knew it could be the last time they saw each other. He pondered this on his way home. *It's strange how unimportant things can become when you face death. A short time ago, life was going on as usual, and it seemed it would do so forever. But now* . . . Mark's thoughts churned on. His heart bled for his parents. He knew his mother would die rather than betray Christos or His church. His father, on the other hand, was so blinded by fear that it seemed he would do anything to avoid torture and death.

But he will die anyway. He probably doesn't have more than a decade left. Then he'll face God and give account for his actions. Surely it would be better to accept torture and execution now than face condemnation in the Judgment. Another ten years of life are so short compared to eternity.

He stopped in the street and prayed for his parents. Especially he prayed for his father. Should he go back and talk to him again? *No, not now*, he decided. His father was so distraught that he wouldn't be able to reason with him. He would have to leave him with God. Maybe later he could reason with him.

The next morning Mark and Lydia prayed together. He had told Lydia about his parents' reactions, but his burden was much heavier than just his parents. Dozens of Christians across the city were just waking to this day of horror. Many had no idea what was ahead. He pulled Lydia close and they clung to each other for a moment.

"God go with you, my husband," Lydia whispered. "I'll visit your mother this morning. If you don't return, I will meet you at Christos' throne."

As he walked up the street toward the church, Mark marveled again at the strength and understanding of his wife. What a wonderful woman God had blessed him with. She wasn't even thinking about her own danger; she was worried about his mother's struggles. And she had confidence in him. He vowed again, as he had on their wedding day, not to let her down.

He heard the shouting and turmoil before he saw the church. Several Christians slipped out of dark alleys to lay restraining hands on him. "Stay away, brother. We still need you."

He immediately recognized them. "What are they doing at the church?" he asked.

"They broke into the entrances on both sides. They are stripping the church of valuables and smashing furniture. They are looking for a statue of Christos, I heard. They can't envision worshipping a god you can't see."

"What about the Holy Writings?" Mark asked. "Have they found any?"

"Only a few," the man replied. "We removed most of them last night after we heard what was happening. But we didn't take all of them, because if they didn't find anything, they would go looking further. It won't take them long to learn who probably has them."

DIOCLETIAN

Most of Afranius' men looked at the episode as a lark—a welcome break from the monotony of camp life in the wintertime. Afranius could hear them calling to each other about certain treasures they had found. They threw most of the valuables on a heap behind the church and appointed several soldiers to guard it against looting.

Afranius didn't help with the destruction but kept an eye on the process. He noticed several men coming out the front door with a wooden chest and walked over to them.

The first man answered his question before he could ask it. "A chest of Holy Writings, sir. What should we do with them?"

Afranius opened the chest and looked inside. It was lined with a soft, dark red cloth and contained a half dozen scrolls. He lifted one, noticing its age. It was labeled—something about the writings of Paul to the Romans. He dropped it back into the chest and closed it, running his fingers over the exquisite carving on the lid. "Beautiful chest," he commented. Then he frowned. "They must surely have more Holy Writings than this. I wonder where the rest are."

The two soldiers looked at each other. "They probably found out somehow that we were coming and took the rest away. They're smart enough to leave a few so we wouldn't think of looking for the others," the one soldier replied.

"Have you found any people?" asked Afranius.

The soldier shook his head. "I think they had a warning from someone. There are Christians working inside the emperor's palace—everyone knows that. They probably found a way to get the word out."

When that day dawned, in the eighth consulship of Diocletian and seventh of Maximian, suddenly, while it was yet hardly light, the prefect, together with chief commanders, tribunes, and officers of the treasury, came to the church in Nicomedia, and the gates having been forced open, they searched everywhere for an image of the Divinity. The books of the Holy Scriptures were found, and they were committed to the flames; the utensils and furniture of the church were abandoned to pillage: all was rapine, confusion, tumult. That church, situated on rising ground, was within view of the palace; and Diocletian and Galerius stood, as if on a watchtower, disputing long whether it ought to be set on fire. The sentiment of Diocletian prevailed, who dreaded lest, so great a fire being once kindled, some part of the city might he burnt; for there were many and large buildings that surrounded the church. Then the Pretorian Guards came in battle array, with axes and other iron instruments, and having been let loose everywhere, they in a few hours levelled that very lofty edifice with the ground.

Lactantius, *Of the Manner in Which the Persecutors Died,* Chap. 12

Afranius thought of Hiram, then dismissed the thought. Surely it wasn't him. He probably just made sure someone else passed the word. Anyway, it was of no concern right now.

"Take the chest to a safe place and burn it," he said. "Our orders are to burn any writings that we find. If you find more, add them to the fire as well."

He glanced across the street and noticed Diocletian and

Galerius watching the destruction from just outside the palace walls. He walked over to them. "We're almost finished going through the church. Do you want us to set it on fire?"

"Sure, burn it down!" Galerius said. "It'll make a sight to behold. Christians all over the city will see the fire and smoke."

Afranius looked at Diocletian, who shook his head in disagreement. "No, it isn't safe. I won't go down in history as the emperor who burned down Nicomedia, as Nero did Rome."

Galerius snorted. "As damp as everything is, there isn't much chance of that."

But Diocletian didn't budge. "It isn't safe," he repeated.

Then, turning to Afranius, he commanded, "Have your men tear it down. They can haul the debris outside the city wall, and we can have a big fire out there."

Afranius had turned to go when Diocletian called him back. "Have they found the ass's head? Or a statue of Christos?"

Afranius shook his head. "No, sir, they haven't. I think those are just fables that people have passed around to belittle the Christians. We did find a chest with some of their Holy Writings and burned it as we were instructed."

"How many writings were there?" Diocletian asked. "A big church like this should have a library as large as mine."

Afranius shook his head again. "Maybe five or six old scrolls," he said. "The chest was almost empty."

Diocletian and Galerius looked at each other. "They must store the bulk of them elsewhere," Galerius said. "Maybe they aren't as stupid as we thought."

Diocletian nodded. "Probably not." He looked at Afranius again. "Was anyone in the building? Any leaders or other workers?"

Afranius shook his head. "No, sir, it was completely deserted."

Galerius made a face. "I told you we should have jumped on them last night. One of the guards told me there were at least twenty-five men at that meeting last night. He counted them when they left."

Diocletian shrugged. "They won't get far. We'll pick them up after we publish the edict tomorrow."

Galerius snorted. "It sounds to me as though they were prepared for this. Maybe they are smart enough to have spies in the palace to forewarn them. I still think your men should have planted spies in their groups long ago. Then we'd have a list of people to go after."

Afranius ignored the discussion and headed back across the street to where the praetorians were gathering, waiting for further instructions. His second-in-command stepped out to meet him. "We've gone through the whole building, sir. Now what?"

"Tear it down," Afranius replied, "and carry everything outside the city wall. Make sure it's far enough away from the city so we can burn it later."

The commander blinked. "It would be a lot less work to just burn it where it stands," he suggested. "It'll probably take us all day to tear it down."

Afranius shrugged. "Diocletian's orders. He's afraid the fire will get out of control and set the city on fire. We have time."

The commander nodded. "Fair enough. We'll get right at it."

He turned to the praetorians. "We need axes, shovels, picks, and anything else useful," he instructed. "Maybe a beam to use for a battering ram. We're going to take the building down—level it to the ground. We'll carry the debris outside the city walls to burn."

Afranius nodded his approval. "Get everyone available to help," he ordered. "Then it shouldn't take long."

————— MARK —————

Half hidden in an alleyway behind the church, Mark and several other members of the congregation joined a crowd watching the proceedings. "Well, there goes a lot of work down the drain," said one man. "And we barely used it."

Mark didn't reply. He felt the same, but he wasn't attached to the building. He had never pushed for a fancy church. Like his mother, he would have been happy worshipping in a warehouse or even a field. But many of his fellow Christians had thrown themselves heart and soul into building this church, and its destruction would be heartbreaking for them.

The soldiers cheered as the front of the church caved in with a crash. They let the dust settle, then attacked the remaining part of the building even more vigorously.

Mark shook his head and turned away from the sight. "I need to look after some things," he quietly told the man beside him. "You know where to find me if you need me. Spread the word that we will have a prayer vigil in the old warehouse tonight for those who can get away."

The men watched him go. "He's so young for such a responsibility," one of them said.

"But well suited," another replied. "Anthimus knew what

he was doing when he left him in charge."

The men nodded. "Did you hear that his father intends to cooperate with the government?" another man asked. "Mark told me this morning."

The others looked crestfallen. "Surely not," one of them said. "How can we stand as a church if our leaders give up so easily?"

The first man looked down the alley in the direction Mark had gone. "Well, Mark is made of better stuff. He'll stand to the end if he has to."

"That's right," another agreed. "And his wife with him. She's been a good wife for him."

"I wonder about Irene," a third man said. "She doesn't strike me as one who will give up easily. It's too bad Andrew isn't more like her. She could help him through this if he would let her."

DIOCLETIAN

Hiram had a group of soldiers spread throughout the city to hang up the handwritten copies of the edict soon after dawn the next morning. Crowds soon gathered to read them. "Look, it's an edict against the Christians!" someone cried. "Maybe they're going to do more than just tear down the church."

"About time," someone else growled. "They've been getting away with too much."

"Come on," said a third voice. "They're good people. And they buy and sell a lot of goods."

"Hey," said the first voice. "Let's find some Christians and read this to them. I wonder what they'll say."

A chorus of approval rose from the growing crowd. Afranius, standing in the open gateway of the palace grounds, made no move to get involved. He knew getting the population riled up was part of the reason for posting edicts. Jealous people would betray their neighbors, hoping to loot their belongings.

He looked up as a man, probably in his mid-thirties, strode toward the group.

"Hey, Eutius," called a voice from the crowd. "Did you read this poster? It's about you." Laughter rippled throughout the crowd.

"This will set you Christians straight," chortled another voice. "You'll be grinning through a dungeon window before you know it."

The sturdy Eutius ignored the comments, strode up the poster, and read it aloud. "This is the work of Satan and his demons," he snorted.

He reached up and tore the poster from the wall. He started ripping it to shreds. "Christos will triumph over all this!" he shouted.

The crowd was stunned into momentary silence, then the uproar began. Afranius turned to the guards beside him. "Better arrest him and get him inside before they tear him to pieces," he ordered. "Though the magistrates may not treat him much better."[1]

---

[1] The account of Eutius' impulsive actions and subsequent martyrdom can be found in history.

Afranius was right. Several days later Eutius was sentenced to be burned. The area in front of the newly razed church was changed to an execution ground so Eutius could die within eyesight of the place of his indiscretion.

Eutius tried to ignore the crowd that had gathered to watch him die. But Afranius could see that reality had sunk in. He didn't answer the jeers from the crowd, and he kept his eyes closed except to glance beseechingly toward the sky. Someone noticed this. "Hey, Eutius! Are you expecting an angel to rescue you? Is your God going to come and get you?"

The crowd became noisier and louder. The common people had few amusements, and executions provided a welcome diversion from the tedium of daily life.

Afranius had no desire to oversee the execution, so he placed his second-in-command in charge of it. But he was curious about the Christians and stayed to watch. He wondered if Eutius would break before the end. Even hardened criminals did—many screamed and begged for mercy, though to no avail.

But Eutius was made of sterner material. As the soldiers piled the wood around him, he seemed to regain his strength. He began to pray aloud, asking God to forgive his persecutors and to enlighten the emperor's eyes. The commander in charge of the execution gave him time to finish his prayer, then nodded to the soldiers to light the wood with a torch.

The fire caught quickly, and the flames shot upward. As Eutius' clothing started to burn, the smoke rose around him. Then, wonder of wonders, he began to sing. The noise of the crowd died away, and the execution square became deathly quiet.

The triumphs of the martyred saints
The joyous lay demand,
The heart delights in song to dwell
On that victorious band:
Those whom the senseless world abhorred,
Who cast the world aside,
Deemed fruitless, worthless, for the sake
Of Christ, their Lord and Guide.

For thee they braved the tyrant's rage,
The scourge's cruel smart;
The wild beast's claw their bodies tore,
But vanquished not the heart:
Like lambs before the sword they fell,
Nor cry nor plaint expressed;
For patience kept the conscious mind,
And armed the fearless breast.

What tongue can tell thy crown prepared
To wreathe the martyr's head?
What voice thy robe of white to clothe
His limbs of torture red?
Vouchsafe us, Lord, if such thy will,
Clear skies and seasons calm:
If not, the martyr's cross to bear,
And win the martyr's palm.

Eutius had a good voice, but it started to falter as the flames reached his beard. He choked from the smoke and started to cough, but then forced his way to the end. With a note of triumph he sang the final words—"and win the martyr's palm."[2]

All eyes were glued on Eutius as he finished singing and then bowed his head. Suddenly he cried out a final time, "Jesu, Jesu!"

The crowd remained silent, then started to melt away. Afranius's second-in-command shook his head in wonder. "Now that was a man," he murmured to himself. "Never saw the likes."

"Strange . . . strange," Afranius muttered to himself as he walked back to the palace. "Who would have thought it?"

---

[2] *Ancient Hymns,* from the Roman Breviary: No. 61, "Hymn on the Holy Martyrs."

March 303

As the edict spread across the empire, many people gave up their lives. Others recanted. Some tried to flee, but there were few places of safety. It was a time of immense turmoil and uncertainty. Who would be next? [1]

The Christian leaders kept a low profile, but they also felt the burden to strengthen their people and support them as they struggled with fear and doubt. Mark was often gone, and Lydia often visited others to offer encouragement, especially those who were left destitute as the arrests continued. Not only the men were in danger, as Galerius realized that arresting the women would likely demoralize the men.

Since Andrew was well known as a deacon and had overseen

[1] Some historians feel Lactantius and Eusebius were biased and seriously exaggerated the situation. Yet Lactantius is the closest to an eyewitness that we have, and Eusebius wrote within 25 years of the facts.

the building of the new church, he was one of the first people the authorities sought. Early one morning soon after Eutius' death, the soldiers kicked in the door where Irene and Andrew lived.

The soldiers were in a hurry. "Where are your Holy Writings?" the soldier in charge demanded. He didn't like what he was doing, and this made him harsher than normal. "Don't try to pretend you don't have them. We know you keep them here."

"We don't have much," Andrew said, his voice shaking. "Just a few manuscripts my wife used in teaching. They are over in the cupboard."

One of soldiers yanked open the door Andrew indicated. He seized the scrolls he found and brought them to his commander. The commander gave them a quick glance and tossed them to the floor. "These aren't Holy Writings," he said, his face grim. "Don't think we're that stupid. These are just some old writings of Roman and Greek poets."

He turned to Irene, who had been watching. "Where are they? Don't expect us to have mercy on you just because you're a woman."

Irene answered quietly. "I don't expect mercy—or justice."

The commander flinched. "Other people will decide what constitutes justice. I'm just doing my job, and that is to find any Christian writings."

Irene didn't reply, but Andrew broke in. "We don't have them anymore. I got rid of them. We are willing to cooperate."

The commander looked at him contemptuously. "Really? Well, I guess we'll find out. You're known quite well in this city for your Christian activities. It'll take more than just words to get you off the hook."

He turned to Irene. "What did your husband do with the writings?

Who has them? I'm assuming he didn't actually destroy them."

Irene met his eyes without blinking. "I have nothing to say," she replied quietly.

The captain noted her calm demeanor. "So you're the strong one here. I hope you realize that women aren't exempt from the flames. Your husband might enjoy watching your execution."

He glanced at Andrew, then back again. "Unless, of course, he decided to cooperate and tell us where he stashed the writings. Then we might let him off the hook. That might not help your situation though."

Irene paled, but she held firm. "I will not betray my God or His people. Nor His message. If I need to die, I will die, and I pray that my husband will be willing to do the same."

"Don't be too sure," the captain replied with a smirk. "We have ways of helping people change their minds. But maybe we'll start with your husband here."

He turned back to Andrew. "Your wife seems a bit stubborn. How about you? Are you going to tell us what we want to know, or do I let my men work her over a bit? Or maybe we should start with you?"

Andrew's teeth practically chattered. "No! No!" he cried. "Leave us alone. I—I—" He gulped and took a deep breath. "I gave them to my son Mark, a presbyter. He took them home as far as I know. He and his wife could tell you—"

Irene gasped in horror. "Andrew! How could you?"

The captain grinned at her. "Not much of a man. You deserve someone better."

He turned to his men. "Several of you take her to prison. We'll work on her later."

"And you, my friend," the captain said, turning to Andrew, "are going to guide us to your son's house. That way he and his wife can see who betrayed them. When we are done there, we'll take you along to the palace and give you a chance to offer a sacrifice to clear your name."

Andrew seemed to hear only the last part of the sentence and looked relieved. The soldiers bound Irene's hands. She looked at Andrew as they pulled her toward the door. Her lips moved, but she did not speak. He avoided her eyes—but he would never forget the look of compassion she gave him.

Mark had already left by the time the soldiers reached his home, but Lydia was still there. She opened the door when Andrew knocked. After one glance at the soldiers outside the door and the desperation on Andrew's face, she understood immediately.

"They want the scrolls I gave to Mark," he stammered. "Are they here?"

One of the soldiers yanked him aside, and the group pushed their way into the house. Lydia had expected to face this sooner or later, but now that it was happening, it disturbed her more than she had anticipated. But not enough to shake her resolve.

"We only have some scrolls of Plato and Homer," she said calmly. "You are welcome to them."

The captain saw immediately that she was unlikely to cooperate. "Turn the place upside down and see what you can find," he ordered his men. "They've probably taken them elsewhere, but we'll see."

He turned back to Lydia. "Where is your husband? His father says he is a presbyter and would be able to help us."

Lydia didn't drop her eyes. "My husband has gone to his work. He will not help you either."

The captain raised his chin. "Don't be so sure. We have ways of loosening people's tongues. His father was certainly glad to tell us everything he knew, including his son's whereabouts."

Lydia looked at Andrew with compassion, but he refused to acknowledge her. "You will not find Mark ready to betray our God or our brothers and sisters."

Andrew flinched at her words but didn't respond.

The captain's eyes narrowed. "Well, for your sake, I hope your husband is more of a man than his father. But I warn you, the emperors are not ready to fool around. Be prepared to face the consequences of your words."

"We are ready," Lydia replied. "With God's help."

As expected, the soldiers found nothing. After finishing their search, they bound Lydia and marched her up the main street of town. Up ahead she could see the ruins of the beautiful temple that the Christians had spent so much time and money on. What would become of the brothers and sisters she knew so well? She thought of Mark and wondered how he would feel when he learned of her fate. Would she ever see him again? Would he be able to escape the net being drawn around them?

She shuddered at the thought.

So far she had not thought much about her own future. But as she saw the prison walls looming in the distance, it all started to sink in. Would she leave its doors alive? Or would she have to face the flames as Eutius did? She glanced at Andrew, who was walking beside her, and wondered what he was thinking. Was he having second thoughts? Surely he must be aware that his wife was inside these very walls somewhere.

Andrew had been suffering the torments of the damned. The soldiers had laughed at him and asked him if he wanted to accompany his daughter-in-law on her last walk. He knew the captain despised him and considered him a coward for not holding to his faith. He wondered if Lydia felt the same way. He wondered if Irene would ever forgive him. Would they all die? He couldn't stand the thought of Irene and Lydia suffering in the flames because of him. But even worse was the thought of being executed himself.

He clenched his teeth. He wouldn't go back now. He had to find a way out. It filled his mind. So what if he had to sacrifice to a demon? It was the only way out. Surely God would understand why he had to do this.

Lydia saw the mob outside the prison and realized that they were there to watch the Christians being taken into custody. For the first time she was glad for the soldiers surrounding her. A mob would show no mercy.

A few people threw rocks at them as they passed. Others shouted obscenities. A clod of ground caught Andrew in the side of the face, and he cowered closer to Lydia. A rock bounced off the helmet of one of the soldiers, and he shook his sword at the offender who threw it. Another rock caught Lydia on the shoulder, but then they were through the crowd and entered the prison doors.

The captain handed Lydia over to the prison guards, who took her to the same cell Irene was in. The door clanged shut behind her.

Irene greeted her with a hug, and the two clung to each

other, tears running down their faces. "Did they get Mark?" Irene whispered.

Lydia shook her head wordlessly. "He was already gone when they came."

Irene stepped back before asking the question on her mind. "And Andrew?"

Lydia's eyes dropped. "He led them to us. They're taking him to the shrine so he can sacrifice and be certified."

"No!" Irene exclaimed. "Oh, Christos, speak to his heart."

Outside, the soldiers marched Andrew to the shrine set up beside the prison.

"Here's a deacon who is anxious to prove his allegiance to the pagan gods," the captain told the priests. "Let him make his offering so we can continue with our work."

DIOCLETIAN

Afranius hated this kind of work, but he did his duty. As Hiram saw him come and go, he wondered what Afranius was thinking and how long it would be before he broke. He knew his friend well enough. Sooner or later something would happen. Already, Afranius tried to avoid him whenever possible.

But Afranius couldn't avoid the emperor. "Are we to be arresting every Christian, or concentrating on their leaders right now?" he asked.

Diocletian turned to face him. "Concentrate on the leaders. And on their writings and meeting places. The whole system will collapse if we take care of that."

MARK

It was midafternoon before Mark heard the news. "Your mother and your wife have been arrested," the messenger said. "The soldiers were looking for the Holy Writings, but Irene and Lydia refused to give them any information."

Mark stopped abruptly and pulled the messenger to the side of the street out of the crowd. "What about my father?" he asked anxiously. "Did they arrest him too?"

The messenger's face fell. "No, they didn't." He paused before continuing. "He betrayed you. He took the soldiers right to your door. Both Irene and Lydia are in prison, but they say your father has sacrificed to the gods, and they've let him go."

Mark's shoulders sagged. "How could he do it? He has betrayed his own wife and his daughter-in-law. How will he live with himself?"

He shook his head to clear it. "I have to find him. Surely he can see how wrong this is."

The messenger took him by the arm and stopped him from walking away. "The bishops told me not to let you go home or try to see your father," he told him soberly. "It isn't safe. They said they want to talk to you. I can lead you to them. They want you to come as soon as you can."

Mark hesitated. "There is so much to do, and I was on my way to visit some people. But I'll come and see what they want."

Another man slipped out of a dark alley close by. "Soldiers coming," he muttered. "Follow me."

They slipped back into the alley. The first messenger stopped at a stand selling fruit, as if that were his only purpose. Mark followed his guide through a labyrinth of alleys until they reached a small hut in the center of the city. His guide quickly looked both ways, then indicated a door to Mark. He kept going while Mark slipped quickly through the doorway.

Inside, a few men were sitting around a small table. He saw at a glance that several of them were bishops, along with a few deacons.

"Sit down," one of the bishops said. "I'm glad to see you. You got the news about your wife?"

Mark nodded.

"I'm sorry she was taken," the bishop said. "I'm not surprised that she refused to betray you, but I'm sorry your father led the soldiers to her. I'm afraid this is only the beginning. Too many of us are not ready for a test like this."

—————— DIOCLETIAN ——————

Afranius was sitting at his desk thinking over the day's events. It had been a full day, with lots of arrests, but Afranius realized this was only the beginning. His thoughts went back to all the people they had arrested. Some had broken down almost immediately and eagerly sacrificed so they could go home. But more had been stubborn and ended up in the dungeons.

He looked up as Hiram entered the room and sat down across from him. "So how's it going?" Hiram asked.

Afranius shook his head. "This is going to take a long time. I can't believe how many people are refusing to give up. That man Eutius was a lot more typical than I expected. I thought people would be glad for a way to escape, but a lot are holding out."

He shook his head, then continued, "We'll see how long this

lasts once the executions start." He was going to say more, but someone tapped at the door and one of the guards entered.

"Sir, one of the Christians has told us where the main bishop is," he said. "He's several days from here in a small village. Should we send some soldiers to find him and bring him in?"

Afranius sat back and looked at the guard keenly. "Who is this bishop? Do you have a name?"

"They called him Anthimus, sir. He must be an important leader, because they sent him away a few months ago already."

Afranius pinched his lips together. "We don't have many people to spare, but we'd better follow up on this. Take five or six soldiers and leave first thing in the morning."

The guard nodded and saluted before he left.

Afranius glanced at Hiram. "So the Christians have been expecting this for a while, according to that," he observed. "They are sharper than Galerius thinks they are."

Hiram nodded and opened his mouth to reply, but he never got the words out. Someone down the hallway screamed. Then there was a loud cry, "The palace is on fire! Call the guards!"

Afranius jumped to his feet and ran. People were swarming into the courtyard from all parts of the palace. Already the guards were running for shovels and buckets of water. They had trained for a fire, but this was the first one any of them had ever seen in the palace.

Fortunately, someone had seen the fire in its early stages, but it still took several hours to put it out. It was well after dark, and Hiram had already gone home when Afranius finally dragged himself back to his office. Almost immediately a messenger from the emperor arrived, asking Afranius to come at once.

Diocletian and Galerius and a few other officials were gathered in the meeting room. Diocletian looked pale. He jumped up as Afranius came in the door. "Do you have any idea what happened?" he asked.

Afranius took his place at the table. "It started at the far wing of the palace," he informed them. "It looks like someone set it. Some wood was piled against the wall."

Galerius nodded. "Makes sense. The Christians are fighting back."

Afranius eyed him carefully. *Now why would he look so smug? I wonder if he knows something about it.* But Afranius had no time to pursue the thought.

Diocletian jumped to his feet. "Is that true?" he demanded.

Afranius shrugged. "I have no way of knowing. We'll need to investigate to find out." He glanced at Galerius. "Since you seem to know so much about it, maybe you could tell us more."

Galerius glared at him, but he was the first to look away. "Well, who else would it have been? We've started to arrest their leaders and burn their Scriptures. We've executed one person and destroyed their main temple. It only makes sense, doesn't it?"

Afranius's eyes held a tinge of steel. "Maybe," he said evenly. "Or maybe someone thought this was a good time to do something that could be blamed on the Christians."

Galerius started up with an exclamation, but Afranius waved him back. "As I said, we'll investigate. But not until tomorrow. I'll set some guards both inside and around the palace to keep everything under control."

Galerius subsided, but Diocletian looked agitated. "Do we have any Christians inside the palace? Is it safe?"

The Volcano Erupts: March 303

Afranius nodded. "I'm sure we have some on the palace staff. We'll fish them out tomorrow first thing."

MARK

Mark had hardly slept since Lydia's arrest. Whenever he lay down to rest, he couldn't help thinking about her. The nights were cold, and he knew the dungeons were damp and overrun with rats. She would just have some old, dusty, filthy straw to sleep on. How could he sleep in comfort while she suffered such conditions? More often than not, he spent much of the night in prayer.

At least Anthimus is safe, he thought.

DIOCLETIAN

But Anthimus' fate was marching to meet him. The following day the soldiers arrived in Omana, looking for him. He met them at the door of his cottage and invited them in for a meal he had prepared.

"You must be hungry and thirsty," he told them. "Here are some refreshments for you."

The leader of the soldiers blinked in surprise. Most of the townspeople had been hostile and refused to cooperate. At least this old man was friendly. Maybe he could help them.

The soldiers crowded into the little hut eagerly. It had been a long, chilly day, and they were glad for the heat from the little fireplace.

"Do you know of a Christian bishop named Anthimus?" the captain asked. "I've been sent to bring him back to Nicomedia."

The old man looked at him searchingly. "Yes, I know of him," he replied. "Here, have some more porridge. I'm sorry I don't have anything better to offer you."

He filled the captain's bowl again and those of the other soldiers. "Eat up—it'll warm your innards."

It was a cheerful meal and the men cleaned up the entire kettle of porridge. When they were finished, the captain looked at their host again. "Can you tell us where to find Anthimus? We need to get back to Nicomedia with him as soon as possible."

The old man smiled. "Just let me put some clean clothes in a bag, and I'll be ready to go. It'll only take me a minute."

The captain looked up sharply, and the conversation around the table ground to a halt. "What did you say?" the captain asked.

Anthimus smiled. "I said I'd be ready to go shortly. You are looking for Anthimus, aren't you?"

He looked around the table at the men staring at him. "Well, I'm Anthimus."

The soldiers looked at each other blankly. Then they all started talking at once.

"Look, sir," the captain said. "We'll just go back and tell the prefect we couldn't find you. They'll burn you if we take you back."

Anthimus had been hearing stories of what was happening in Nicomedia. He nodded as he replied quietly, "Yes, they might do that. But I wouldn't want you to tell a lie for me. They'd punish you severely if they found out what you did."

The men started getting up from the table. "Let's just go back without him," one of them said. "No one will ever know as long as none of us tells."

The captain nodded, but Anthimus shook his head. "No, these

The Volcano Erupts: March 303

things always slip out," he replied firmly. "Secrets are like birds with wings, and they are always getting away from us. Leave it in God's hands. He'll make a way for me if it is His will. My people are dying, and I should be with them anyway."

The captain argued and so did his men, but in the end they bowed to the inevitable and took him along. The people in the village crowded the roadway, shaking their fists at the soldiers and threatening them. But Anthimus stopped them. "Don't harass them," he said. "They are only doing their duty. God must be in this or it wouldn't have happened."[2]

Back in Nicomedia, the Christians working in the palace had been arrested. None admitted to being involved in the fire, but Galerius was still certain they were. Diocletian slowly came around to his way of thinking.

"Afranius, I want to make an example of these people," he ordered. "I will not have people working for me who have an allegiance to any god except Roman gods."

Afranius was reluctant, but he agreed. One of the servants named Peter had been particularly stubborn, and Diocletian pointed him out. "Make an example of him," he ordered. "They are all to die, but make his death a slow, lingering one. Do it out in the city square in front of the palace so everyone can watch."

Hiram later described the scene in a letter to Lactantius.

---

[2] According to legend this is a true story. Anthimus is said to have led all the soldiers to Christ on his way back to Nicomedia.

COUNTDOWN

The soldiers took Peter and stripped him. Then they scourged him with a multiple-stranded whip that had sharp pieces of metal tied every handbreadth or two. It literally stripped the flesh from him.

But that wasn't all. Then they took salt and vinegar and poured them all over his wounds. Never have I heard a man scream like poor Peter screamed. He tried to be brave, but there is a limit to what a man can take, whether he is a Christian or not. He passed out several times from the pain, and the brutes waited until he came to again, then continued his torture.

Then they lit a large fire and fastened him above it. They hung him over the fire as if he were a piece of beef being broiled over a fire. They kept turning him, letting the blood and vinegar drip from his body into the fire. If they saw him passing out, they would lift him further from the fire until he came to again, then continued the treatment.

Lactantius, my friend, it was the most horrible thing I have ever seen in a lifetime of horrible things. I do not see how your God could watch that from heaven without striking the brutes who did it to the ground.[3]

There were Christians in the crowd, and the word swept through the city. A few Christians decided then and there to give up. Several deacons went into their repositories of Holy Writings and voluntarily gave them up. Others, however,

---

[3] This persecution is known as the Great Persecution or, in the Martyrs' Mirror, the Tenth Persecution. Although the gruesome torture and death of Peter is taken from other sources, the accounts of this persecution in the Martyrs' Mirror are just as horrible. The tortures used against the Christians at this time were beyond human comprehension.

resolved anew to be firm to the end. After all, even though the soldiers had dragged out the execution, it had only lasted about half a day. That was still very short compared to suffering hell fire for eternity.

But there was another reaction, one the emperors hadn't reckoned on. For the general population, Peter's execution was too much. No man, no matter how evil, deserved to suffer like that. And many in secret vowed to do what they could to help the Christians.

——— MARK ———

Mark wept when he heard the story. The remaining leaders gathered and fell on their knees begging God to stop the persecution. Or, as one of them prayed, "At the very least, O Christos, make us strong to bear the pain, should we be called on to suffer. And forgive those weaker brothers and sisters who cannot bear the pressure anymore. We are weak and very human. Help us, O Christos!"

In the dungeon the prisoners heard the story and quaked in whatever shoes they had left. They, too, prayed for grace.

Lydia and Irene were still in the same dungeon. They had given up any hope of surviving the ordeal. They only prayed that the end would be soon and quick. And they prayed for Mark. They knew how hard it would be for him when they died.

They also prayed for Andrew. Irene loved him deeply, and she knew that Andrew had loved her as well. But she also understood his nature and the fear that had driven him to do what he had done. Both she and Lydia prayed that Christos would forgive him and draw him back.

And they prayed for the survival of the church. Christos had promised that the gates of hell would not prevail against it. They claimed that promise.

Several weeks' journey distant, Lactantius read Hiram's letter and dug out his copy of the Revelation and reread it. *I think it is happening*, he told himself. *It can't get any worse than this. Our Lord will return soon.*

———— DIOCLETIAN ————

A week later, the palace caught fire again. This time the fire was massive, and much of the once imposing building was destroyed.

Diocletian exploded in frustration. "Every person in the palace and the army must offer a sacrifice. We will get to the bottom of this anarchy!"

No one was exempt. Diocletian sent Afranius to get his wife and daughter to join in the sacrifice. All his servants sacrificed. All of Prisca's and Valeria's servants sacrificed. Galerius and his servants sacrificed. Any visitors present sacrificed. This included Constantine, who was visiting in Nicomedia at the time and later became emperor of Rome.

And now Diocletian raged, not only against his own domestics, but indiscriminately against all; and he began by forcing his daughter Valeria and his wife Prisca to be polluted by sacrificing. Eunuchs, once the most powerful, and who had chief authority at court and with the emperor, were slain.

Lactantius, *Of the Manner in Which the Persecutors Died*, Chap. 12

The pagans blamed the Christians for setting the fire. The Christians blamed the pagans, especially Galerius, for setting it. Constantine, in writing about the incident later, diplomatically blamed it on "lightning from heaven."

When the whole episode was over, Galerius packed his bags. "I'm leaving this cursed place before the Christians kill me," he declared. He looked at Diocletian across the table. "If you know what's good for you, you'll do the same. This is utter anarchy."

Afranius pursed his lips and clenched his fists under the table where no one could see them. *Hypocrite! It's anarchy all right, but who is at fault?* He didn't say anything, however. For the first time in Diocletian's reign, he knew that Diocletian did not trust him. He, Afranius, was responsible for the emperor's safety, and he had failed. How long would it be until the emperor lashed out at *him*? He knew Galerius would be glad to see him go.

Diocletian dictated another decree to Hiram. This was for an internal memo and not necessarily to be posted in public. But Diocletian was clear: he wanted this fiasco ended, and he wanted it ended NOW.

* *Arrest any clergy or lay Christians.*

* *If they refuse to sacrifice, execute them.*

* *Destroy any of their Holy Writings.*

* *Destroy their meeting places.*

* *Christians are to have NO legal rights to defend themselves, whether in court or out.*

18

April 303

With the devil in control of his mind, the emperor's rage knew no limits.
It was a time of great evil and darkness for God's people.

Afranius hoped the intensity of the executions would die down with Galerius out of town, but it didn't. Diocletian seemed to have lost part of his mind. The morning agenda meetings became frenzied sessions of calling down curses from the gods on the Christians and on anyone else who dared to cross his path.

Even his wife and daughter felt the rough edge of his tongue. After one particularly bad session, Valeria sought out her mother. "I never thought I'd say it, but I wish Galerius had taken me along with him. Something is wrong with my father."

Prisca shook her head. "He's been obsessed with trying to

please the gods for so long that he's becoming paranoid. He's getting older and he's worried about dying, I think. He's afraid the gods will hold him accountable for allowing Christianity to become so prominent."

Valeria rubbed her neck. "Has he ever considered that the Christos could be the true God and that Christos will hold him accountable for what he's done to His people?"

Prisca looked up quickly. "Don't say that too loudly. We can't even trust our servants since the last holocaust your father brought on our household. But I suspect that what you just said is at the root of his problem. What if he's wrong and he dies only to discover it's too late? It plagues him night and day."

Valeria looked at her questioningly. "What about you, Mother? Are you a Christian or a pagan?"

Prisca looked at the floor. "I'm not sure. If I weren't the emperor's wife, I'd probably be a Christian. It makes the most sense to me. But when it came down to sacrificing, I wasn't quite ready to die for how I felt."

Valeria smiled slightly. "That would have made Nicomedia tremble. Imagine the emperor burning his own wife because she was a Christian. But," she sighed, "that is about where I am. I wish we could be ordinary people. Then we could go to a presbyter and get some guidance. It's horrible to be bound by our position."

——— MARK ———

Mark had slipped out to visit some of his people and was on his way back to his hiding place. The leaders had decided it wasn't safe for all of them to stay in the same place, no matter how well hidden it was. There was too much possibility of betrayal.

But careful as he was, he was taken off guard when a hooded man slipped out of a side alley and took him by the arm. "Don't be afraid," the man whispered. "I have a message for you."

He slipped between two nondescript buildings and Mark followed him cautiously. He could feel his heart beating faster.

The man had been waiting for him in the shadows. Mark was almost certain it was the same man who had warned him about the edict in the first place, but he didn't ask. The less he knew, the safer it would be for all of them.

The messenger spoke quietly, even though they were in the relative safety of the alleyway. "The dungeons are full and overflowing. So the emperor has ordered a mass execution of prisoners to make room for more people."

Mark looked up quickly. Even looking directly into the man's face, he couldn't tell who he was, though he seemed familiar.

"Your wife and mother are among the prisoners who will be executed tomorrow in the main public square in front of the palace," the messenger said. "About twenty of them will be burned together in the first batch. Later in the day some others will be beheaded. Your bishop Anthimus will be among those."

Mark stepped back in consternation. "Anthimus? How did they find him?"

"He was betrayed," the messenger said. "The soldiers who arrested him offered to let him escape—but he refused. He was afraid they would get into trouble."

The messenger tugged at his hood to make sure his face was well covered. "It will probably be safe for you to be in the crowd, but be very careful. Do not let anyone see your face. And don't talk to anyone or show any emotion. God still has a work for you after these trials are over."

The messenger slipped away so quickly that Mark wondered for a moment if an angel had been sent to warn him. The writings did speak of angels talking to people, so it could be. But it was probably a friend who had connections in the palace.

He heard footsteps coming and quickly walked to the back of the building and around the corner into the darkness. A moment later a man carrying a sword ran past, followed by two more. *That was close. I need to be more careful.*

——— DIOCLETIAN ———

Afranius had been looking for Hiram—but he was nowhere to be found. Where could the man be? He needed to talk to him about tomorrow's execution in the square. This was strange. He was always at his desk or around somewhere.

The working areas of the palace were still intact, and they continued to use them despite the smell of smoke that hung everywhere. Afranius stepped out into the parade ground to get a breath of fresh air and saw Hiram crossing from the main palace gates.

"Where have you been?" he asked. "I've been looking everywhere for you."

"I didn't like the smoke and went for a walk," Hiram replied. "What do you want?"

Afranius looked at him strangely. Hiram on a walk? In the middle of working hours?

"I need some details about that execution tomorrow morning," he replied. "How many people will there be and who are they? We also need to get more firewood."

Hiram glanced at the sky, as if in deep thought. He hardly seemed to notice Afranius.

"Oh yes, the execution," he said. "Yes, I heard about it. I have a list on my desk, I think."

"You think?" Afranius asked sharply. "You'd better have it. What's wrong with you?"

Hiram shrugged. He looked around to see if anyone was within hearing distance before replying. "Afranius, I am about at the end of my rope. I cannot put up with this much longer."

Afranius frowned. "What do you mean? What are you planning to do?"

Hiram looked him in the eyes for a moment. "You are changing too, my friend," he said quietly. "You are growing harder as the days go by. I'm no longer sure I can trust you with my thoughts as I once did."

Afranius stepped back. "Have I changed that much? I wouldn't do anything to you."

"Are you sure?" Hiram asked, an odd smile playing around his lips. "Has your answer to my question changed since that discussion we had last winter?"

Afranius wrinkled his forehead, perplexed. "Are you going daft? What question?"

He turned abruptly and entered the smoky hallway. "I need that list. I don't have time to play games."

Hiram watched him go with a curious look on his face. "Neither do I, Afranius," he whispered. "Neither do I." Instead

The Volcano Erupts: April 303

of following Afranius, he turned and disappeared around the corner of the palace.

He had barely turned the corner when Afranius came out the door again. "Hiram," he shouted, "where are you?" He looked around, bewildered, and swore under his breath. "Where did the man get to now?"

He spun around and headed for Hiram's office. Sure enough, there was the list he was looking for. He started reading down the list.

- *Irene, deacon's wife. Husband sacrificed and was released.*
- *Lydia, a chief presbyter's wife. Her husband has not been found.*
- . . . . . .

He laid down the list, thinking. *I wonder if the husband or wives of the prisoners will show up for the execution tomorrow. Maybe I should have some of my men mingle in the crowd to see if we can flush out a few of them.*

He spun around as Hiram came walking in the door as if nothing had happened. "Where were you this time?" His irritation betrayed itself in his tone.

Hiram eyed him oddly. "Did you know that the Hebrew word for messenger also means angel?" he asked.

Afranius stared at him. "Are you losing your mind? I don't know what you're talking about."

Hiram sat down behind his table. "Sometimes I feel as if losing my mind would be a good idea. It might even save my life." He picked up a scroll he had been working on earlier.

Afranius shook his head and left. *Hiram sure is odd today.*

He has something on his mind. He stopped outside the door to his own working area. *Surely . . .* The thought struck him to the core. *Surely he isn't still thinking about converting to Christianity. He must be going crazy if he's considering that.* Then he thought of something else—and his blood ran cold. Someone had been passing information to the Christians, and Hiram knew more about things around here than anyone else. He needed to watch him a little more closely . . .

Afranius turned and looked down the hallway toward Hiram's workspace.

——— MARK ———

Mark decided to go to the execution. It would be his last chance to see Lydia and his mother. He would do as the messenger suggested and wear a hooded cloak. It would be chilly in the morning anyway. If he got caught, then he'd just get caught. If only he could talk to Lydia just one more time. A tear slipped down his cheek.

He was in the crowd when the prisoners were brought into the square. Mark strained to get a glimpse of his beloved wife and his mother, but he couldn't see them yet. A few men jeered at the women and made lewd remarks, but mostly the crowd was somber. The spirit of entertainment was gone, and reality was setting in. These people being executed were their former neighbors. Some were even family members.

Mark looked around cautiously and noticed a few other Christians—some from his own congregation. He caught his breath as he noticed his father. Stony-faced and cold-looking, he looked as if he could strangle someone. Mark pulled his hood farther down over his eyes.

He noticed another person nearby wearing a hood and took a closer look. It was his friend, the "angel." So he was here too. Was he watching out for him?

The guards had piled firewood and dry branches in a large circle, leaving room for the prisoners inside its perimeter. They marched the prisoners inside, pushing the crowd back a little. Even the soldiers looked grim. They sensed the mood of the crowd and weren't taking any chances.

Then Mark saw them. Lydia and his mother were holding hands and their eyes were sweeping the crowd. Lydia's eyes paused for a moment as they came to Mark, and he barely restrained himself. Then they passed on. *Did she see me? She would know I'd probably be here if I haven't been caught.* He wished he could run up to the group and join her. He shifted uneasily and noticed that the man with the hood slipped a little closer, as if ready to restrain him from any foolish move.

Then his attention was wrenched back to the prisoners. The soldiers were lighting the fire, and the prisoners started to sing. He saw Lydia helping, her eyes turned toward heaven. He wasn't sure how much longer he could take this, but he wanted to stay with her until the end. Surely he could do that much for her. He couldn't be at her side, but he could stand in the crowd and pray that her pain would be bearable.

And pray he did. Many others in the crowd prayed as well. He bowed his head as the smoke and the smell of burning clothing and flesh rose toward heaven as a sweet incense—an offering of love for the Savior who had died for them. Now they were dying for Him . . .

He felt a hand on his arm and looked up into the eyes of the hooded man. "You should leave before the crowd thins out too much." He barely heard the whisper, but he realized the wisdom of the advice.

As he slipped away, he noticed his father once more. He was stalking through the crowd to get away from the scene, roughly shoving aside anyone in his path. His heart ached for his father, but now wasn't the time to talk to him. *He betrayed Lydia, and yet he always loved her. He must be suffering terribly. More than I am. He doesn't even have Christos to give him peace.*

His heart ached and he glanced over his shoulder. If only he could have Lydia's body and give her a decent burial. But he knew that the rage of Rome didn't stop when people died. Even after death, they desecrated the bodies and destroyed them. He would never see Lydia again on earth. But she had remained faithful to the end. He remembered the glow on her face as she had helped to sing the songs of victory.

Victory. Strange to think of death as a victory, but that's what it was. She was at peace now. No more pain, no more fear, no more temptation. For a moment he almost envied her.

—— DIOCLETIAN ——

The guards disposed of the ashes and any partly burned remains from the prisoners. Even the guards were strangely sober. Hardened as they were, seeing the way these Christians

The Volcano Erupts: April 303

died unnerved them. But right now they had a job to do. This mess had to be cleaned up because they were going to execute a second batch of prisoners that afternoon.

One of the prisoners was a bishop named Anthimus.[1]

———— LACTANTIUS ————

In his temporary refuge, Lactantius heard the stories from Nicomedia. The executions continued for several years in the west, and about eight years in the east. At first hundreds, then thousands, of people died.[2]

He wrote the following in his book about persecutors and persecution . . .

> Presbyters and other officers of the Church were seized, without evidence by witnesses or confession, condemned, and together with their families led to execution. In burning alive, no distinction of sex or age was regarded; and because of their great multitude, they were not burnt one after another, but a herd of them were encircled with the same fire; and servants, having millstones tied about their necks, were cast into the sea. Nor was the persecution less grievous on the rest of the people of God; for the judges, dispersed through all the temples, sought to compel everyone to sacrifice. The prisons were crowded; tortures, hitherto unheard of, were invented; and lest justice should be inadvertently administered to a Christian,

---

[1] According to the Martyrs' Mirror, Anthimus was horribly tortured and then beheaded.

[2] Estimates go as high as 20,000 people, but most historians estimate that 3,000 to 3,500 people died during this persecution.

altars were placed in the courts of justice, hard by the tribunal, that every litigant might offer incense before his cause could be heard.

A.D. 311

Wickedness always has consequences. No one, not even the emperor of Rome, is exempt. "Be not deceived; God is not mocked: for whatsoever a man soweth, that shall he also reap" (Galatians 6:7).

Galerius had reached the top of the Roman ladder. Diocletian was gone, having retired to his fancy palace by the Adriatic almost six years ago. This left Galerius a free man. Free to slaughter Christians as he pleased. Free to live it up without Diocletian peering over his shoulders.

But things were not as he had expected. The Christians refused to roll over and die. In fact, if he didn't know better, he'd think there were more of them now than when the persecution started.

What good did it do to rule the most important empire in

the world if people would not listen to you? And now, after eight years of persecuting the people who had destroyed his mother, things were no better.

And to top it off, he was sick. Not just sick as in having the flu, but deathly sick. Sick in his inward parts, which seemed to be rotting away. At least it smelled that way.

Was this how it would end? After all his efforts, he had accomplished nothing. Maybe the Christian God *was* the only God, as He claimed to be. Maybe God was punishing him for trying to destroy His people.

Maybe if he could get the Christians to pray for him, he would get better. It was his last hope.

He called for his secretary. "I want to post a new edict," he said. "I am going to reverse the edict that Diocletian passed against the Christians."

His secretary stared at him, no doubt wondering if he had left his senses.

Galerius started to dictate. He had it all figured out. But it was the ending that really flummoxed the secretary. "Wherefore, for this our indulgence, [Christians] ought to pray to their God for our safety, for that of the republic, and for their own, that the republic may continue uninjured on every side, and that they may be able to live securely in their homes."

The secretary looked at him once again, then vanished to his own office to prepare the posts that would go forth.

Six days later, on May 5, 311, Galerius was dead.

DIOCLETIAN

Diocletian was a lonely man. Though he had told people he wanted to live quietly and find meaning in life by tending to his cabbage patch, it hadn't turned out that way. Nor had he found joy in the huge palace he had specifically designed to symbolize his life and his destiny—as one of the gods.

He sat on a bench in the central courtyard of his seven-acre palace in Dalmatia, the land of his childhood. He had designed it with the palace in Alexandria in mind. The pool in the center was even bigger than the one in Alexandria, and the fountain had more pressure. People were amazed when they saw the water dashing and gurgling down over the rocks. Large green plants were placed throughout the courtyard, and the sun shone through specially colored portals.

When Diocletian had laid down his position as emperor and retired to this palace, he came alone. Prisca had refused to come with him. Instead, she had decided to stay with Valeria, a decision that would someday cost her life.[1]

It left Diocletian alone. And his cabbages just didn't make up for it.

Prisca. She had been the most beautiful woman he had ever seen when he first met her. That she was a commoner hadn't bothered him, because he was too. Even after he was emperor, he had never seriously considered replacing her with someone else.

---

[1] When Galerius died in 311, Licinius, the new emperor, was entrusted with the care of Prisca and Valeria. After Valeria refused Licinius' marriage proposal, the two women fled to Emperor Maximinus for protection. He also tried to get Valeria to marry him, and when she refused, he banished her and her mother to a small village in Syria. At the death of Maximinus, the women fled. After being on the run for about a year, Licinius' soldiers captured them and beheaded them.

I wonder what changed? I am sure she loved me too, but in the end she refused to come with me. She always had a hard time accepting the persecution of the Christians. Galerius asked me once if she was a Christian. I now see that everything changed around that time. Maybe I went too far when I forced her to sacrifice. I'll probably never know. She doesn't answer my letters. I wonder where she is.

And what became of Afranius and Hiram? I thought I could leave them in Nicomedia to look after my interests, but they both resigned and vanished.

He paced back and forth beside the pool. *Did I do the right thing with the Christians? But I was the emperor! It was my duty to suppress Christos. Why do I feel guilty for doing my duty?*

He glanced around the courtyard. Three temples faced the open area, with the biggest one dedicated to Jupiter. Since Diocletian had retired earlier than he expected, this temple had never been completed, but it was still one of the most beautiful temples known. He smiled joylessly as he looked at the twelve stone sphinxes he had stolen from Egypt and placed here to guard this temple. *Surely Jupiter will honor me in the afterlife for this temple. No one else has built one like it.* But the doubts kept surfacing. Did Jupiter even care? Or notice?

Across the courtyard was a temple honoring a Roman god of health. A lot of good that had done him. He could hardly get out of bed in the morning or walk around his own palace. At this rate, he'd soon be dead.

He thought again of Prisca. Would she miss him once he was gone? Or even remember him? And Valeria? In retrospect, appointing Galerius hadn't been a very good idea. In the end Galerius had just pushed him aside and taken over.

Diocletian was becoming more agitated by the minute. The new emperors had torn apart his greatest innovation, the tetrarchy. Sure, they had asked him to come to a coronation a few years ago and help. Some people had even suggested that he should come out of retirement himself. But he knew better than that. Galerius had tolerated him while he stayed out of the way, but he knew what would happen if he got involved again. Now Galerius was dead, but it was too late.

I'm a failure. He had long suspected it, but this was the first time he allowed himself to think that it might be true.

All his good ideas. All his reforms. All his attempts to restore the old religions that had made Rome great. None of it had worked. There were more Christians now than ever, and very few people cared. There was even talk about legalizing Christianity in the western parts of Rome—though he was sure that would never happen.

Still, he was a failure.

And he was lonely. Very lonely.

Diocletian died in December 311, perhaps from suicide, and was buried in his palace in Dalmatia. Three or four centuries later, the palace was renovated to be used as a church honoring several martyrs who had died during the persecution. It appears that during the renovations, workers found Diocletian's body and threw it into the Adriatic Sea.

It was a sad ending for a man who once had such lofty dreams.

MARK

It was a beautiful spring day and Mark decided to go for a walk outside the city. So many things had changed. Galerius had died a year ago, soon after releasing an astonishing edict freeing the Christians from persecution. Diocletian was gone too. He had died from suicide about five months ago, if the rumors were true.

Mark had never returned to his home after Lydia was arrested. He had walked past a few times, and recently he had noticed that it had been rented to someone else. That hurt, since he had spent the happiest years of his life there. But every day he gave his hurts to Christos. Even though he would never forget Lydia, he was glad she had escaped the troubles facing the Christians.

Lydia always wanted to walk out to the coronation hill and have a picnic. Today would be a good day for that. He had packed a bit of a lunch and left the city soon after the gates were opened in the morning. It still felt strange not to worry that someone might be trailing him or getting ready to betray him.

He took his time, because he had given himself all day. He took a deep breath of fresh air, tinged with the subtle fragrance of spring flowers. *What a beautiful day. Lydia would have enjoyed this.* He brushed a tear from his cheek as he glanced back at the city. *I've never known any other home than Nicomedia, but it'll never be quite the same again.*

He thought back over the years as he wandered on down the roadway, paved with stone blocks. He had seen Diocletian's army take this road when they set out that first spring after the coronation. *Life was good back then. It's good I couldn't look ahead twenty-five years and see what all would happen.*

Much had changed in the past eight years. Diocletian had taken sick and abdicated his throne. Some said that Galerius had forced him to abdicate, but no one knew for sure. Word was that Diocletian had built a new palace in his homeland and retired completely from public life. Galerius had taken his own course in persecuting the Christians after that, doing his best to destroy Christianity. But the emperors in the west mostly ignored his raging edicts and even in the east people did as little as possible without getting in trouble. Thankfully it was over, at least for now.

It was almost lunchtime when Mark reached the hill where Diocletian had been crowned emperor. He walked up the rocky hillside until he reached the place where Diocletian had executed the praetorian prefect when he became emperor.

A lot of history had been made right here. Little had anyone suspected that Diocletian would turn on the church so viciously. Yet if Lactantius was to be believed, Galerius was really the force behind all that. Diocletian had only done what he thought was his duty. He had never been as vindictive as Galerius.

Mark sat on a rock overlooking the plateau where Diocletian's soldiers had stood for the coronation ceremony. In the distance he could see the city. Several years ago he had been consecrated as a bishop to take Anthimus' place. Although this had made him more of target than ever, the Christians had rallied around him to protect him, and the soldiers had never found him.

His mind wandered back to Lydia. *I wonder if she can see me, or thinks of me?* He remembered the Revelation and the passage about the souls of the martyrs under the altar. *Lydia is part of that group. And my mother.* He wiped another tear, but the pain had lessened somewhat over the years. *Their troubles are over. They are at peace, and I'm sure they would never want to come back.*

He bowed his head. *Thank you, Christos, for taking them home where they are safe and at rest.*

His thoughts drifted to his father. He had met him only a few times after Lydia and Irene were executed. His father had turned into a bitter old man and had no interest in talking to his son. Mark had tried to help him lay down his bitterness and accept the love and forgiveness of Christos, but it was as if his father didn't even hear him. For his own sake and the sake of the church, Mark had stopped trying to meet up with him. Now his father was dead too.

Mark watched as the sun sank lower in the west. *I need to start for home. I don't want to spend the night out here; they lock the city gates at dusk.* He glanced at the fleecy clouds drifting across the sky. Almost he could imagine the great cloud of witnesses the writer to the Hebrews spoke of. Maybe Lydia was up there in the clouds watching him.

He shook his head. *No one knows, really. Maybe she's still sleeping. But in the Revelation, John saw the souls of those who were slain for the Word of God under the altar in heaven.* Mark liked to think of Lydia as one of them. She was waiting. Waiting for God to restore all things. Waiting for him.

Epilogue

Word started drifting from the west around this time about strange things happening in the life of Constantine, the newest of the emperors. They said he'd had a vision of Christ and had painted Christian emblems on his soldiers' shields. Then he had fought a battle against tremendous odds and won.

Christians everywhere were wondering what this might mean. Something new was in the air. Was it possible that Rome could eventually have a Christian emperor? What would that mean for them and for the church?

The younger leaders were enthused at the possibilities. But the older ones looked at each other soberly and shook their heads. How could someone follow the teachings of the Savior and be an emperor?

Something didn't ring right.

Where now are the surnames of the Jovii and the Herculii, once so glorious and renowned amongst the nations; surnames insolently assumed at first by Diocletian and Maximian, and afterwards transferred to their successors? The Lord has blotted them out and erased them from the earth. Let us therefore with exultation celebrate the triumphs of God, and oftentimes with praises make mention of His victory; let us in our prayers, by night and by day, beseech Him to confirm for ever that peace which, after a warfare of ten years, He has bestowed on His own.

—Lactantius, *Of the Manner in Which the Persecutors Died,* Chap. 52

Bibliography

"Addressing the Emperor," *Roman Army Talk,* May 21, 2010. Retrieved from <https://www.romanarmytalk.com/rat/thread-16877.html>.

Barnes, Timothy David. *Constantine and Eusebius,* Google Books, Harvard University Press, Cambridge, MA, 1981.

Bowman, Alan, Averil Cameron, and Peter Garnsey, eds. *The Crisis of Empire, A.D. 193-337,* Vol. 12 of The Cabridge Ancient History, pp. 170-183, 589-671, Cambridge University Press, 2005. Retrieved from <https://doi.org/10.1017/CHOL9780521301992>.

Bužančić, Dr. Radoslav. "Diocletian's Palace: So Much More Than an Emperor's Vegetable Patch," *Current World Archaeology,* No. 71, May 2015. Retrieved from <https://www.world-archaeology.com/issues/cwa-71/> and <https://www.min-kulture.hr/userdoc-simages/TISAK%20NOVO%202/028-034_CWA071_Diocletian_MECMcCSC.pdf>.

Ferguson, Everett. *Baptism in the Early Church: History, Theology, and Liturgy in the First Five Centuries.* William B. Eerdmans Publishing Company, Grand Rapids, 1961.

———. "Ordination in the Ancient Church (III)," *Restoration Quarterly,* 5(2), 1961. Retrieved from <https://digitalcommons.acu.edu/restorationquarterly/vol5/iss2/1>.

Florus. Loeb Classical Library, 1934. Retrieved from <http://penelope.uchicago.edu/Thayer/E/Roman/Texts/Florus/poems/omnia*.html>.

Gardner, Iain and Samuel N. C. Lieu, eds. *Manichaean Texts from the Roman Empire,* Cambridge University Press, 2004, p. 118. Retrieved from <https://doi.org/10.1017/CBO9780511616891>.

Lactantius. *Of the Manner in Which the Persecutors Died,* in *Ante-Nicene Fathers*, Vol. 7, by Philip Schaff. Retrieved from <https://www.ccel.org/ccel/schaff/anf07>.

Mattingly, Harold. "Jovius and Hercules." *Harvard Theological Review,* 45 (2), 1952, pp. 131-134, published online by Cambridge University Press, 2011. Retrieved from <https://doi.org/10.1017/S0017816000020770>.

Pizon, Capt. F.X. "The Turkish Straits Vessel Traffic Service," Turkish Marine Research Foundation publication 25, n.d. Retrieved from <https://www.afcan.org/dossiers_techniques/tsvts_gb.html>.

Rice, Carl Ross. *Diocletian's "Great Persecutions": Minority Religions and the Roman Tetrarchy,* History Thesis, North Carolina State University, Raleigh, 2016. Retrieved from <https://repository.lib.ncsu.edu/bitstream/handle/1840.16/11014/etd.pdf?sequence=2&isAllowed=y>.

Scheidel, Walter, and Elijah Meeks. *Orbis: The Stanford Geospatial Network Model of the Roman World,* n.d. Retrieved from <http://orbis.stanford.edu/>.

Southern, Pat. *The Roman Empire from Severus to Constantine,* Routledge, New York, 2001.

Stark, Rodney. *The Rise of Christianity: How the Obscure, Marginal Jesus Movement Became the Dominant Religious Force in the Western World in a Few Centuries,* HarperCollins, San Fransisco, 1997.

Wace, Henry and William Coleman Piercy, eds. "Diocletian, Emperor," *Dictionary of Christian Biography and Literature to the End of the Sixth Century,* Wikisource. Retrieved from <https://en.wikisource.org/wiki/Dictionary_of_Christian_Biography_and_Literature_to_the_End_of_the_Sixth_Century/Diocletian,_emperor>.

Wayman, Ben David. "Lactantius's Power Struggle," *Political Theology,* 14 (3), 2013, pp. 304-324. Retrieved from <http://tandfonline.com/doi/10.1179/1462317x13z.0000000005>.

Wikimedia Foundation, Inc. "Diocletian," n.d. Retrieved from <https://en.wikipedia.org/wiki/Diocletian>.

———. "Diocletianic Persecution," n.d. Retrieved from <https://en.wikipedia.org/wiki/Diocletianic_Persecution>.

———. "Lactantius," n.d. Retrieved from <https://en.wikipedia.org/wiki/Lactantius>.

———. "Pythia," n.d. Retrieved from <https://en.wikipedia.org/wiki/Pythia>.

————. "Feeding the Military," n.d. Retrieved from <https://en.wikipedia.org/wiki/Food_and_dining_in_the_Roman_Empire#Feeding_the_military>.

About the Author

Lester Bauman was born into an Old Order Mennonite home close to Kitchener, Ontario. Later his family joined a local conservative Mennonite church. As a young-married man, he taught for five years in several Christian schools. Later he worked for thirteen years out of a home office for Rod and Staff Publishers, Inc. as a writer and editor. During this time, he and his wife Marlene moved with their family from Ontario to Alberta, where they live presently. They have six children and eleven grandchildren, and are members of a local Western Fellowship Mennonite Church.

During his time with Rod and Staff, Lester wrote ten books, including *The True Christian* and *God and Uncle Dale,* both available from Christian Aid Ministries. He spent a number of years in Alberta working as an HR manager in a corporate setting. He now works for the Christian Aid Ministries billboard evangelism ministry out of a home office, doing content writing for their website, answering correspondence, and writing resource materials.

Lester has written several other books published by Christian Aid Ministries: *Sylvester's Journal, What Is the Bible?, The Matthew Challenge,* and *Searching for Meaning.* He is working on additional books as time allows.

You can contact Lester through his personal website at www.lbauman.ca or by email at lester.bauman@gmail.com. You may also write to him in care of Christian Aid Ministries, P.O. Box 360, Berlin, Ohio 44610.

About Christian
Aid Ministries

C hristian Aid Ministries was founded in 1981 as a non-profit, tax-exempt 501(c)(3) organization. Its primary purpose is to provide a trustworthy and efficient channel for Amish, Mennonite, and other conservative Anabaptist groups and individuals to minister to physical and spiritual needs around the world. This is in response to the command to "... do good unto all men, especially unto them who are of the household of faith" (Galatians 6:10).

Each year, CAM supporters provide 15–20 million pounds of food, clothing, medicines, seeds, Bibles, Bible story books, and other Christian literature for needy people. Most of the aid goes to orphans and Christian families. Supporters' funds also help to clean up and rebuild for natural disaster victims, put up Gospel billboards in the U.S., support several church-planting efforts, operate two medical clinics, and provide resources for needy families to make their own living. CAM's main purposes for providing aid are to help and encourage God's people and bring the Gospel to a lost and dying world.

CAM has staff, warehouses, and distribution networks in Romania, Moldova, Ukraine, Haiti, Nicaragua, Liberia, Israel, and Kenya. Aside from management, supervisory personnel, and bookkeeping operations, volunteers do most of the work at CAM locations. Each year, volunteers at our warehouses, field bases, Disaster Response Services projects, and other locations donate over 200,000 hours of work.

CAM's ultimate purpose is to glorify God and help enlarge His kingdom. ". . . whatsoever ye do, do all to the glory of God" (1 Corinthians 10:31).

The Way to God and Peace

We live in a world contaminated by sin. Sin is anything that goes against God's holy standards. When we do not follow the guidelines that God our Creator gave us, we are guilty of sin. Sin separates us from God, the source of life.

Since the time when the first man and woman, Adam and Eve, sinned in the Garden of Eden, sin has been universal. The Bible says that we all have "sinned and come short of the glory of God" (Romans 3:23). It also says that the natural consequence for that sin is eternal death, or punishment in an eternal hell: "Then when lust hath conceived, it bringeth forth sin: and sin, when it is finished, bringeth forth death" (James 1:15).

But we do not have to suffer eternal death in hell. God provided forgiveness for our sins through the death of His only Son, Jesus Christ. Because Jesus was perfect and without sin, He could die in our place. "For God so loved the world that he gave his only begotten Son, that whosoever believeth in him should not perish, but have everlasting life" (John 3:16).

A sacrifice is something given to benefit someone else. It costs the giver greatly. Jesus was God's sacrifice. Jesus' death takes away the penalty of sin for all those who accept this sacrifice and truly repent of their sins. To repent of sins means to be truly sorry for and turn away from the things we have done that have violated God's standards (Acts 2:38; 3:19).

Jesus died, but He did not remain dead. After three days, God's Spirit miraculously raised Him to life again. God's Spirit does something similar in us. When we receive Jesus as our sacrifice and repent of our sins, our hearts are changed. We become spiritually alive! We develop new desires and attitudes (2 Corinthians 5:17). We begin to make choices that please God (1 John 3:9). If we do fail and commit sins, we can ask God for forgiveness. "If we confess our sins, he is faithful and just to forgive us our sins, and to cleanse us from all unrighteousness" (1 John 1:9).

Once our hearts have been changed, we want to continue growing spiritually. We will be happy to let Jesus be the Master of our lives and will want to become more like Him. To do this, we must meditate on God's Word and commune with God in prayer. We will testify to others of this change by being baptized and sharing the good news of God's victory over sin and death. Fellowship with a faithful group of believers will strengthen our walk with God (1 John 1:7).